Praise for

LAVINIA WREN AND THE SAILMAKERS

Irene Drago's remarkable new novel *Lavinia Wren and the Sailmakers* is an uncommonly deft love story woven into the very fabric of Maine's rich shipbuilding history. The tale unfolds during the heyday of sailmakers and shipyards and schooners and Navy ships. Drago is so good at capturing our most elemental human bonds, and all the while we are riveted by the cinematic backdrop she paints of war and toil and loss and hope. Find a good chair and settle in for a most wonderful read.

—Susan Conley, award-winning author of five books, including *Landslide, Elsey Come Home,* and *Paris Was the Place*

Irene M. Drago has written a wonderful book, so finely crafted and a tribute to the seafaring folks of this town!

—Renny A. Stackpole, author of *The Gillchrest Papers,* director emeritus of the Penobscot Marine Museum, and a past president of the Thomaston Historical Society

Drago did her homework. Through research, interviews, and family records, she literally became her main character and experienced the tastes and smells of an early coastal New England shipbuilding town in the late nineteenth century.

She provides an accurate and delicious slice of Thomaston's rich maritime history initiated by a chance meeting with a generous, history-loving descendant of the prosperous Dunn and Elliot dynasty. Access to years of letters, diaries, and photos from several generations were made available through which she brought the family back to life.

If you are from a seafaring town, you'll recognize the characters. If not, you will know them when you finish the book.

—Margaret McCrea, author of *Maine Sail,* watercolor artist, and a past president of the Thomaston Historical Society

Don't miss Irene M. Drago's other novels:

DAUGHTERS OF LONG REACH

2018 Next Generation Indie Book Award Winner

American poet Walt Whitman (1819–1892) once wrote: "As soon as histories are properly told there is no need of romances." But Bath author Irene M. Drago might prove him wrong. This is a shipbuilding, seafaring family love story, folding in real history and real people, with thoughtful fiction to fill out this clever tale.

—Bill Bushnell, literary critic/columnist: Bushnell on Books

I actually read the novel in one day, unable to stop reading. Irene writes great dialogue, which is something I always admire, because it is not easy to do.

—George Smith, columnist, author, and
Maine outdoorsman (1948–2021)

Drago delivers a beautifully written debut novel set in Bath, nestled along the coast of Maine. The story, steeped in local maritime history, deftly weaves past and present, honoring core New England values—love of family, love of history, and the importance of fighting for what you believe. Readers will be well pleased!

—Julie Shea, founder of The Mustard
Seed Bookstore in Bath, Maine

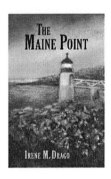

THE MAINE POINT

Irene Drago effectively blends past and present in her novel *The Maine Point*, and she does it with style.

> —Bruce Robert Coffin, award-winning author
> of the Detective Byron Mysteries

Three of the Maine families featured in the first book— Daughters of Long Reach—reappear here in two separate year groups: 1936–1943 and 2018–2020. Drago's careful plotting allows the three family connections to slowly emerge...a tender story of fiction and love. Perhaps Anna said it best: "History is a myth shaped by the storytellers."

> —Bill Bushnell, literary critic/columnist: Bushnell on Books

I loved Irene's description of places, ships, architecture, and different cities. She captured the spirit of all locations like an artist paints a picture. I liked the whole book very much, with every other chapter a different love story united by friends and family over decades. The characters came out of the book and into my home.

> —Pat Davidson Reef, literary critic/columnist, award-
> winning author of *Dahlov Ipcar / Artist, Bernard Langlais
> Revisited,* and *David C. Driskell: Artist, Educator, Author*

Lavinia Wren and the Sailmakers

IRENE M. DRAGO

Cover Art
Laurie Burhoe

*1878 Map of Thomaston, Maine, courtesy of
the Maine Historic Preservation Commission*

Designed and produced by:
Maine Authors Publishing
12 High Street, Thomaston, Maine
www.maineauthorspublishing.com

Printed in the United States of America

For Joe, my sailmaker

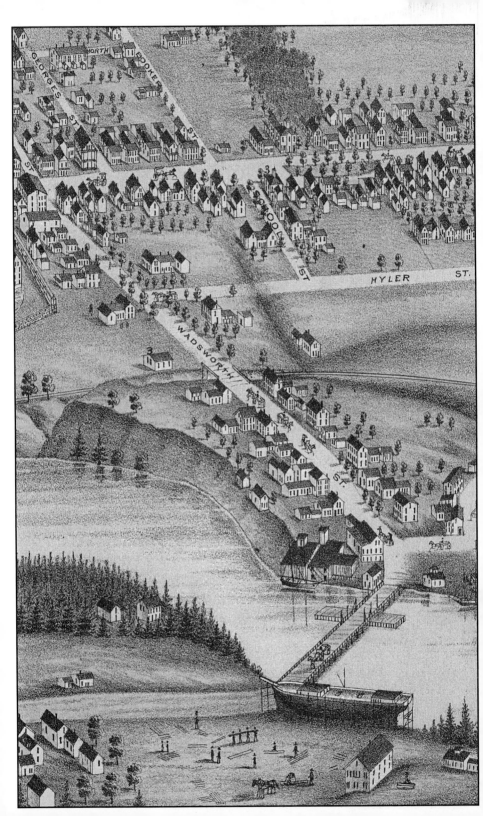

Covering many a road of ground,
Lay the timber piled around;
Timber of chestnut, and elm, and oak,
And scattered here and there, with these,
The knarred and crooked cedar knees;
Brought from regions far away,
From Pascagoula's sunny bay,
And the banks of the roaring Roanoke!
Ah! What a wondrous thing it is
To note how many wheels of toil
One thought, one word, can set in motion!
There's not a ship that sails the ocean,
But every climate, every soil,
Must bring its tribute, great or small,
And help to build the wooden wall!

"The Building of the Ship," 1849,
Henry Wadsworth Longfellow (1807–1882)

Contents

Part Four
1899–1905

Part Five
1908–1924

Lavinia Wren and the Sailmakers

Part One
1865

The *Sunbeam*

Gray Rowley was standing before the mast of the *Sunbeam* admiring the sun going down over Boston Harbor when James Sutton looped an arm around his neck and shouted, "Taste that air! 'Tis the taste of home."

"It's better than I remember," boomed Gray.

And James hollered back, "Better than rum!"

The seventeen-year-olds succumbed to laughter. But as soon as their euphoria passed, they glanced back at the quarterdeck and spotted the captain. Without saying another word, they returned to their duties. After eighteen long months, they were about to complete their first voyage without a mark against them, and they didn't want to ruin that record seven miles from shore.

Neither Gray nor James could have possibly known that the captain wasn't bothered by their hoots and hollers; rather, he understood their jubilance. On this chilly September morning, the first Thomaston-built vessel to circumnavigate the globe was arriving home, and like the young sailors, the two-year-old bark was completing her maiden voyage—an occasion to celebrate.

When the captain ordered the mate to drop anchor near Fort Warren, Gray looked toward the city of Boston and grinned like a boy feasting on candy. They had rounded the Horn—50 degrees latitude to 50 degrees latitude in March 1865, passing two fateful weeks at the mercy of sea and sky. Now they were close to home.

A few hours later, after the harbor pilot had helped them tie up at Constitution Wharf, Captain Charles Ranlett discharged the crew with wages and one by one they walked down the gangplank to enjoy the comforts of Boston—beans, molasses, whiskey, and pretty girls. Gray and James followed the second mate, Ed Dalton, because he knew his way around the waterfront.

"Eh, Mate!" called James. "Where are we headed? Is there a tavern nearby?"

Without looking back, Ed exclaimed, "More than one! Though we're headed to the Bell in Hand, and The Crier Inn is right beside it."

Flashing a smile, James replied, "That's music to my ears." Then he glanced at Gray and started to whistle.

But Gray was lost in thought. In his mind's eye, he could see the crew hoisting sails on a gusty spring day in 1864, leaving Thomaston, Maine, for St. John, New Brunswick. During that passage, he grew accustomed to the force of the sea and the bark's response—the slatting of the sails, the creaking of the masts, and the groaning of the hull. By the first of May, he was ready to cast his fate with the *Sunbeam* again, though he was worried about Confederate warships prowling the coast. Every sailor aboard knew that the American Consul in New Brunswick had advised the captain to fly the Union Jack if he wanted to evade the wrath of the *Alabama*. They also heard his response, loud and clear. Now on Yankee soil, Gray remembered Captain Charles Ranlett singing "America" when they raised the stars and stripes, and the anchor.

James gave him an elbow. "We're in Boston, Gray, where everyone drinks whiskey and ale, and people talk like us. Relax."

Gray nodded, but he didn't say a word. Still reflecting on the voyage, he recalled the crew's fear of being boarded by privateers; and their relief when they took on a pilot off the coast of Australia near Kangaroo Island and discovered that the *Alabama* had been sunk in June. From Australia, they sailed to Callao, Peru, and then on to the Chincha Islands where they remained anchored and on board until the ghostlike coolies filled the *Sunbeam*'s hold with guano.

"Gray, are you ill?" asked James as they followed Ed and the rest of their shipmates through the cobblestone streets of Boston.

Gray shook his head. "Sorry. I was just thinking of the guano. I could see those slaves shoveling that manure, carrying those seabird droppings to the top of the cliffs then sending it down those chutes to the lighters, the boats that were rowed and pulled to all the merchant ships waiting offshore."

"Why would you recall the worst memory of a long voyage? Those heaps of guano smelled worse than the muck of a thousand stables, and those coolies were being worked to death. I pray I don't have to return to the Chincha Islands anytime soon."

"Some memories stick with you," said Gray with a shrug. "Until last May, I never dreamed that tons of bird waste would be as valuable as gold, an elixir for worn-out soil in Ireland and all over Europe. We saved some farms by bringing that 'gold' to Cork."

"Well, I choose to remember the end of May, the twenty-ninth to be exact, when the *Sunbeam* met the *Sparkling Wave* in the North Atlantic. Her captain hailed us and shouted, 'The war is ended! Lee surrendered!' Remember that day?"

"Of course I remember; I also remember the bad news. Off the coast of Ireland near Cork, we heard that Lincoln had been shot and killed, and that news sank my heart."

"Edward!" called James. "Gray needs an ale, followed by a whiskey or two! How far is that tavern?"

"It's around the corner!"

"Hallelujah!" cried James. Then he placed his hand on his friend's shoulder and confessed, "I'm haunted by daydreams and nightmares, too, but the best remedy is up ahead. There's nothing a good ale can't fix."

Seated at a long table near the bar, the first mate, Mr. Cal Stimpson, stood up to propose a toast. "Here's to the Yankee sailors that brought the *Sunbeam*, her cargo, her captain, and his family home to Faneuil Hall and Quincy Market."

Twelve men raised their glasses and shouted, "To us!"

As soon as Cal sat down, the second mate popped up. "And let's raise a glass for the *Sunbeam*'s cook, Washington Peters. Though he's not with us at this table, he's a free man, and he doesn't have to fear, ever again, the noose of a Johnny Reb."

"Hear, hear!" cried the sailors and mates.

An old salt sitting in the corner took out his fiddle and played a sea shanty, and the men started singing till their noise became a roar. Gradually, the fiddler mellowed his sound and let quieter stories fill the room. At sunset, the Bell's owner, a prudent man, brought over a large bowl of pork, beans, and molasses, and set it in the middle of the crew's table. Then one of his barmaids added baskets of cornbread, a stack of plates, and a dozen spoons; another brought mugs filled with ale. The food was a saving grace, and the frothy ale was the happy ending the sailors needed to venture out and find the inn next door. In groups of two and three, they left the Bell smiling, with full bellies and sleepy eyes.

To save a few coins, the crew, except for the mates, decided to double up. Gray and James, being the youngest, were given the room in the attic, but they didn't seem to mind. Their bodies ached with fatigue, too much whiskey and ale, and too many beans with thick molasses. It was a wonder they could climb the stairs. They fell into their beds with their clothes and shoes still on and thought they would sleep for days, but then they felt the stillness of their perch and both stared at the ceiling. The room was quiet. There were no masts above them and no waves below them. Without the rocking of the ocean, they couldn't sleep.

Gray whispered into the dark, "James? Are you awake?"

"Aye."

"I can't stop thinking of the voyage."

James rolled to his side. "About the gypsies in Cádiz? Because that's what I'm thinking of…that woman with the scarves and dangling earrings who looked into the crystal ball and said we would find a pirate's treasure across the sea."

Without turning his head, Gray replied, "Not exactly, though I do remember Andalusia—the sunny beaches, the cathedral of Santa Cruz at the heart of the city, and the whitewashed buildings all around it. Most of all, I remember the dark woman who told us treasure was waiting for us on the other side of the deep blue sea. Did we circle the globe to discover there's a trove of silver and gold buried along the Georges—Pirate's Cellar and Treasure Point?"

"You're too poetic to become a second mate," said James matter-of-factly. "Maybe that's for the best. There's not a captain I know who would sign on two second mates, and I'd hate to sail without you."

"I've had the same worry, but I should tell you…"

"Tell me what?"

"I don't see my future on any bark, or schooner for that matter; I see myself on land, working, and living under a roof like the one above us now."

A ray of moonlight slipped through the window, illuminating Gray's profile, and James whispered across the room, "We've just set foot on Yankee soil. It's too soon to say that you're not going back to the sea. Tomorrow we'll look for a boat, maybe a schooner, heading north to Thomaston, and we'll be walking up Ship Street, or Wadsworth, Green, or Knox before the week is out. But Gray, if you decide to stay on land, I know a sailmaker who will gladly find you a bench in his loft if I ask."

"I might like sitting on a bench on a steady, dry floor. I'll think about it. You'll be signing on for another voyage, though, right?"

When James didn't answer, Gray closed his eyes. Minutes later, both sailors were snoring loudly, enjoying the comfort of a quiet room at last.

Prison Bell

Lavinia Wren was watering the garden in the dooryard of her uncle's cape when the sound of the prison bell sliced through the morning air and froze her feet in place. Despite the warmth of the summer sun, she shivered. Shielding her eyes, she looked up and saw a guard at the top of the stone wall. As usual, he was patrolling the perimeter of the prison, protecting the innocent from the guilty. He wore a uniform like a soldier and carried a black stick. When he spotted her, he waved as if to say good morning, though the bell cast a dark shadow. Vinnie shook her head and her honey-blond hair swept across her face. She dropped her watering can and covered her ears, but her splayed fingers didn't stop the tolling. She started to run toward the river as fast as her skinny legs would take her. When she reached the end of the wall, she turned onto the path that led over the field to the shipyard. With her eyes fixed on the ground, she ran until she stumbled and fell into the sinewy arms of a tall older boy.

Catching her, he shouted, "Whoa! What's your hurry?"

"I'm running away. Can't you see?"

"Oh, I can see just fine, especially when I'm looking up, not down." Stepping back, he studied her face. "Hmm.

Are you related to Emery Payson? You look like him around the eyes."

"What if I am?" she asked, fixing her ocean-blue eyes on his sunburned face.

"Then I'd have to ask why you're running away. Mr. Payson is a good man, one of the best shipwrights in town. He works for John McDonald at Chapman and Flint, right?"

Vinnie pursed her lips then let her words fly. "My uncle works at the shipyard. I don't know his boss's name, though. And it doesn't matter. I'm not running from my uncle; I'm running from that awful bell.

"Who are you anyway?"

"I'm Charlie Flint." He turned and pointed toward the Georges. "My dad and uncle own that shipyard over there, Chapman and *Flint*."

"I reckon that makes you important."

"Yeah, you could say that. I'm fifteen and old enough to apprentice at the yard if I want."

"Do you?"

"I'm not sure, but probably not. I'm only here in the summer and sometimes at Christmas. My family moved to New York a while ago. We live in Brooklyn Heights most of the year. My Uncle Isaac and my dad take care of our shipping business in New York, and John McDonald runs our shipyard here in Thomaston. I'll be graduating from Brooklyn Polytechnic in three years."

"And then you'll be smart, right?"

"Eh, be nice. It's my turn to ask a question. Why do you hate the bell so much?"

"The bell is tolling because someone is dying. Death is permanent—"

"*Permanent*. That's a scary word."

Vinnie didn't respond; instead, she stared at the gold flecks in Charlie's eyes and took a deep breath.

"How old are you?" asked Charlie, squinting in the sunlight.

"I'm thirteen. Almost."

"Almost? When's your birthday?"

"The third of December."

"That's not *almost*; that's months away."

"What does my birthday have to do with anything?"

"Nothing, but—"

"But what?" asked Vinnie, lifting her chin.

"You're too young to know about dying."

"I know a lot. I know the dead don't come back—not ever, not even once."

As Charlie dropped his gaze and kicked the dirt, the prison bell stopped. The execution was over. The prison guards would unlock the cell doors and let the inmates return to their assigned labor at the woodshop, the paint shop, or the cobbler's shop, knowing that one of them had been hung by his neck until dead.

"At last," said Vinnie under her breath, and Charlie met her eyes.

When she started to cry, he looked up and spied an eagle soaring above. Then he studied the field, stripped of trees but kissed with lupines, and waited for her weeping to subside.

"I saw your uncle a few minutes ago at the yard," he said in a quiet voice. "The *St. Charles* is on the ways. They laid her keel a few weeks ago. She's the sister of the *Pactolus*, the bark we'll be launching soon."

Dropping her hands, Vinnie blinked. "*St. Charles*? Did they name her after you?"

He laughed. "No, I'm Charles Ranlett Flint, but I'm not a saint."

Brushing by him, she giggled, "I can see that."

Then she flew toward the river and Charlie shouted, "Wait! What's your name?"

11

She didn't answer; instead, she kept running through the tall grass and the wild blue and white lupines until she spotted her uncle standing beside the hull of the *St. Charles*. When she called his name, he turned and shouted back.

"Hello, Sunshine!"

And Lavinia flew into his arms.

Later, when Lavinia entered the store near the Upper Corner, she saw Charlie Flint talking with the shopkeeper. Surprised, she quickly hid between the stacks of dry goods, wooden toys, boxes, stools, and other handmade gifts and necessities like brooms and harnesses. At the shipyard, her uncle had given her twenty-five cents to buy something pretty, something to remind her of the beauty in the world. As she walked back up Wadsworth Street, also known as Prison Lane, to Main Street, she decided to look for a small wooden box with a tight-fitting lid. It would be a treasure box for seashells, buttons, arrowheads, and sparkly rocks. Her favorite boxes at the store had a flower etched on top. That's what she was looking for when she was distracted by Charlie's voice.

"Hello, Mr. Pease. My father would like to know when his new carriage will be ready. He wants me to drive it to church on Sunday because my mother doesn't like to *take the board* when she's wearing a pretty dress with fancy shoes."

Peering over his spectacles, Jonathan Pease grumbled, "It's too hot and dry to worry about snow or mud, though I wouldn't want to walk in fancy shoes any time of year. Tell your father I spoke with the overseer at the prison, and he assured me the carriage would be ready by the end of the week. They don't let the prisoners dawdle. Hard labor is…hard labor. If your father is in town, he can pick up his shiny new surrey on Friday."

"Yes, sir. He's not in town, though. He's still in New York."

The shopkeeper's face softened. "Then you can pick it up for him. And for the record, I think you've grown half a foot since the last time I saw you. Don't be such a stranger. We miss the Flints around here."

"Thanks, Mr. Pease. If my mother lets me, I'll gladly pick up the surrey...but I have another question—"

"Oh, you do, and what would that be?"

Peeking through an opening between the stacks of wooden boxes and toys, Vinnie watched and listened.

"I was wondering if you knew Emery Payson's niece. I mean you know almost everybody, right?"

Jonathan looked at the boy standing at his counter and nodded. "I know her. Why do you ask?"

"Well, I just met a girl who said Emery Payson was her uncle, and I didn't even know Mr. Payson had any family in town, except for his wife."

"I see," said Jonathan, pushing his wire-rimmed glasses up on his nose. "You met Lavinia Wren, the little bird we call Vinnie. She arrived after you and your folks moved to Brooklyn... She arrived under rather sad circumstances."

"How sad?" Charlie asked.

"Her father was killed during the Peninsula Campaign. Frank Wren and Emery Payson were best friends. They grew up together in Wiscasset, and Frank married Emery's sister, Cora."

Jonathan paused. He looked at the clock over the door, pulled a handkerchief out of his pocket and wiped his brow.

"In the spring of sixty-one, Frank and Emery answered the call. They went to Augusta to muster in with the Third Maine Regiment—a bunch of us from Wiscasset and Damariscotta did the same. We served under Colonel Oliver Otis Howard. On the first of June in sixty-two, the colonel lost an arm at Fair Oaks and Frank was reported missing. I remember that day like it was yesterday. Though we claimed a victory, that was the closest we got to Richmond. At the end of June, we lost the battle at Chickahominy. We could have used the fire of the colonel in that swamp, but he was still recovering from his wounds and Frank was presumed dead. Emery and I survived unharmed...at least on the outside."

"What about Lavinia's mother?"

"Like I said, it's grim. Mrs. Wren was a casualty of the war. When Frank stopped writing, Cora got worried, and she decided to look for him. She wrote to Sarah Sampson, the nurse from Bath who was marching with the regiment, and Sarah wrote back. She told Cora how badly the campaign was going and invited her to join them in the tents as a nurse. Hoping to find answers, Cora left Vinnie with her sister-in-law, Susan Payson. Within a month, she learned that Frank had been killed in action. A few weeks later, she came down with the fever and died."

Charlie swallowed hard. "That's the saddest story I've ever heard. No wonder she was running from the bell."

"The bell?"

"Yeah, the prison bell was tolling this morning to announce a hanging. Vinnie knew that, and it bothered her a lot. She said it reminded her of death."

"That's right," said Jonathan. "This morning they hung that man who murdered a woman in Bridgton for her dead husband's pocket watch. And son, they call that justice."

Stepping out from the rows of neatly stacked shelves, Vinnie cleared her throat. Holding up a small box with a daisy carved on its lid, she asked, "Mr. Pease, how much does this cost?"

"Two bits," replied Jonathan.

Vinnie walked up to the counter, placed her shiny silver quarter on the smooth white oak, and left the shop.

Charlie followed her out the door. "Wait!"

Vinnie stopped and spun around. "You could have asked *me* for my name."

Stepping beside her, Charlie said, "I did. When you ran to the shipyard, I called to you. I asked you for your name, but you didn't answer."

With her lips pressed together, Vinnie turned to face him.

"I just...wanted to know you," he stammered. "That's all."

"And now you do. I'm Lavinia Wren, the poor little orphan girl who lives at the Upper Corner with her aunt and uncle. But you don't know me. I'm not poor, and I'm not little."

"I can see that, though you aren't big."

She scowled but said nothing.

"You know what?" asked Charlie.

"What?"

Offering his hand, he smiled. "You don't know me, either. I'm Charlie Flint, and I'm pleased to meet you."

She shook his hand and bit her lip.

"Do you like to fish?"

"I don't know," she said, raising her brows.

"Well, I'll be working with the shipwrights this week. I'm going to help them get the rosewood and mahogany ready for the cap'n's quarters on the *Pactolus*. But I'm goin' fishing on Saturday. You can come if you want."

Vinnie's eyes opened wide. "Uncle Emery gave me one of his ol' poles last summer, though I don't know how to fish, and he's too busy to teach me."

"Hmm. I can fix that. Meet me at the toll bridge on Saturday morning at ten o'clock." Then he turned and strolled down the lane.

Vinnie shouted after him, "I'll bring my pole!"

Without looking back, he lifted his hand and waved.

A Letter

Unaware that Miss Catland was standing behind her, Vinnie unfolded Charlie's letter, placed it on her lap, and started to read it for the fifth time. She had stopped paying attention to the lesson. Multiplication and division were a bore.

"What are you reading, Lavinia?" asked Miss Catland.

"It's nothing," replied Vinnie as she quickly folded the letter and slipped it into her pocket.

Determined to uphold her reputation as the strictest teacher at Bailey School, Miss Catland fired back, "Well, if it's nothing, you won't mind sharing it with the class."

"But I do."

"Well, if you can't bear to share, you can stand in the corner till the end of the day, but you'll have to give me that slip of paper, the one you find more interesting than the math problems on the blackboard."

Vinnie jumped up. "I'll stand in the corner, but I won't give you my letter."

"Oh, it's a letter. How nice," said Miss Catland, pointing toward the corner at the back of the room. "Go! I'll deal with you later."

When the school bell rang at three o'clock, a dozen children rushed out the door. Only lucky number thirteen remained. She was standing in the corner, waiting to hear the roar of the cat. Tired from a long day of trying to teach children who would rather be skipping stones or looking for frogs at the pond, the pretty twenty-year-old moved slowly toward the back of the room. She straightened the desks, picked up a pencil, a piece of chalk, and a wad of paper that Rufus had probably thrown at Georgie. When she finally reached Vinnie, she put her hands on her hips.

"What am I going to do with you?" she asked, knitting her brow. "I should take the paddle to you, though I've done that twice already, and it's only the end of September."

Vinnie pressed her lips together and placed her right hand over the pocket of her moss-colored dress, protecting her letter.

"Tell me, who sent you the letter that's so important you have to read it during class? And I presume not for the first time."

"I don't have to tell you, and I won't."

Miss Catland stepped closer and raised her hand. She paused, then shook her finger less than a foot in front of Vinnie's turned-up nose. "You listen to me, Lavinia Wren. This town has tried to make you feel at home. We know you've lost a lot and you're hurting, but the rules apply to everyone, including you."

Stepping back, she lowered her voice. "Let me guess. The letter is from Charlie Flint. Thomaston is a close-knit community. Everybody knows you and Charlie became friends over the summer. That boy has a big heart and he's a lot of fun, but he's older than you and he spends more time in New York than here. The Flints are rich—richer than most people. Mr. and Mrs. Flint have plans for their son. Maybe you should get to know your classmates and make some new friends."

Vinnie dropped her head. She pulled the letter out of her pocket and gave it to her teacher.

"He just said he missed rowin' his boat, fishin' at the Crick, and swappin' stories with me."

Hearing the quiver in Vinnie's voice, Peggy Catland, the daughter of a shipmaster, returned the paper still folded in a square.

"I don't need to read it. The words are for you, but I wish you'd talk with me or someone else the way you talked with Charlie. He isn't the only good listener in town. The fact is, he won't be back till Christmas."

Vinnie nodded, shoved the letter in her pocket, and ran out the door. She didn't stop running until she reached the Upper Corner. Outside Mr. Pease's store, she bent down to tie her shoe. When she stood up, Gray and James were standing in front of her.

"Did you lose a locket?" asked Gray, cocking his head.

Looking from one to the other, Vinnie noticed their faces were ruddy, and they both had long brown hair tied back at the collar; their dark-blue coats, too heavy for September, were unbuttoned, and they were built like sailors. Though they resembled each other, only one had light-green eyes, washed by the sun, and that's the one who took her breath away and left her speechless.

"Cat got your tongue?" asked James with a wry smile.

Vinnie's neck turned red, and she found her voice. "No, and she didn't get my letter either. Now leave me be!"

James stepped back, but Gray softly said, "I'm sorry. Sounds like you've had a hard day. We've been gone for almost two years, and it appears we've forgotten how to be nice to our neighbors."

"I'm sorry, too," said James.

Glancing sideways, Gray gave his friend a half-smile, then focused on the fiery fair-haired girl. "Like I was saying, we're from here, but we don't know you, and we shouldn't have teased you that way."

"My name is Lavinia Wren, but everybody calls me Vinnie—except my teacher, the cat."

"The cat?"

"My teacher's name is Miss Catland. She doesn't like me very much."

"Well, I'm sorry to hear that, but I'm pleased to meet you. My name is Gray Rowley."

"I'm James Sutton," said James, offering his hand. "We sailed around the world with Captain Ranlett and now we're back."

Vinnie shook his hand then offered hers to Gray.

He shook it and murmured, "Are you cold?"

"No... I'm not cold."

"Then why are you shaking?"

They all laughed—the carefree sailors and the serious girl.

Susan Payson was sweeping the kitchen floor when she heard the door creak. She looked up to see Vinnie setting her basket down on the sideboard.

"You're late and I was beginning to worry. Did Miss Catland keep you after school again?"

"Yes."

"What did you do to deserve that punishment?"

"Nothing."

"It's always something, child. Now sit down and tell me what happened."

With a heavy sigh, Vinnie plopped down on the nearest chair. Aunt Susan stood her broom in the corner, poured two glasses of water, placed them on the table, and sat across from her niece.

"I'm waiting."

"I was reading a letter during class."

Susan pursed her lips and nodded. When she spoke, her voice was low. "Who was the letter from?"

"Charlie Flint."

"I see," said her aunt, twisting her hands. "Why is a letter from Charlie so important that you have to read it in school for the second time?"

Vinnie blushed. "The third or fourth time...I can't remember."

"Answer my question, Lavinia."

Silence filled the room. Vinnie bit her lip and stared at the glass of water she hadn't touched. Aunt Susan didn't budge.

"I'm still waiting."

"I guess I miss him."

Aunt Susan placed her hands flat on the table and looked hard at her twelve-year-old niece. "Charlie is almost sixteen—he's too old for you, and he lives a world away."

Vinnie's lip began to tremble.

Susan softened her gaze. "Oh, my dear, there's a wide divide between the Flints and us. I hear that Isaac Chapman, Benjamin Flint, and Edward O'Brien, a *millionaire*—the first in Thomaston and the fourteenth in the United States—bought a whole block in Brooklyn Heights, New York. They're building a row of houses on Montague Terrace, and Charlie's father and uncle will live in identical houses on the corner lots of the same street, just like they had planned to do in Thomaston but didn't."

Vinnie's eyes filled with tears, though they refused to spill.

"I'm sorry, Vinnie. I should have introduced you properly to some good families around here who know your uncle and me. You need a friend your own age who shares your interests."

"Who…who would that be?" stammered Vinnie, choking back the tears. "The girls at school think they're better than me because I'm an orphan and I'm from away."

Aunt Susan looked directly into her niece's stormy eyes. "Listen to me, Lavinia. Before the war, your father was a ship carver in Wiscasset. He made figureheads for ships built in Bath, Wiscasset, and Damariscotta. Your Uncle Emery apprenticed in Wiscasset and now he's one of the finest shipwrights in Thomaston."

"What does that have to do with anything?" asked Vinnie, wiping her cheek with her sleeve.

"It has everything to do with who you are. You're not alone, Vinnie. You have your uncle and me, and you're a part of a proud Yankee family. I'm to blame for not introducing you properly to the folks around here. There's a ship carver in town, Harvey Counce. He has a daughter about your age. On Sunday, I'll introduce you to her."

"You don't have to do that. It's not your fault I don't have friends. Besides, I met two boys today, Gray Rowley and James Sutton."

"Oh, my Lord! Those aren't *boys*. I know Gray and James. They're sailors, and that makes them men."

Vinnie put her elbows on the table, cupped her heart-shaped face in her hands, and sighed. "I don't know, Aunt Susan. They looked like boys to me. They told jokes and laughed out loud. They acted as if they wanted to play. Men never act that way; they just work."

"Oh, my darlin', men like to play, especially with girls. I'm taking you to the Congregational Church on Sunday. We'll take the buggy. The Counce family will be sitting in the third row on the east side. We'll sit two rows behind them. After the service, I'll invite Mrs. Counce and her daughter, Amelia, to visit that afternoon for tea and ginger cookies."

"We'll need sugar to make cookies," replied Vinnie with a lilt in her voice.

"Don't worry about the sugar. I'll buy some tomorrow at Fernald's. We need flour, too. There's not much in the cupboard right now. I'm overdue for a trip to the grocery store. The war is over and we need to start living again."

Vinnie giggled. "I don't know, Aunt Susan, but maybe fair winds have followed those sailors to Thomaston."

"I doubt that," said Aunt Susan, standing up and smoothing her apron. "But right now, there's work to be done if we're going to have visitors on Sunday. This house looks as tired as I feel."

"Don't worry. I can help."

"And you will! Now go change. When you're cleaning house, you shouldn't wear your school clothes. We'll start at the back of the house and work our way forward, and since your room is at the back, you can start there."

"All right. I want to show Amelia all the things I've collected, and most of them are under my bed so I need to pull them out and dust them off."

Susan Payson, once a beauty, patted the twist of thick chestnut hair at the back of her neck and looked at her niece with tired eyes. "Most of the things you've gathered in that room can be thrown away. The true keepsakes should be placed neatly in your grandfather's chest at the foot of your bed."

Vinnie jumped up and rushed over to her room, the bedroom off the kitchen, but she stopped at the door. Glancing back at her tall, graceful aunt, she noticed the dark circles under her eyes.

"Thank you, Aunt Susan. I'm looking forward to meeting Amelia on Sunday. I need to make a friend. You and

Uncle Emery have been good to me, and I'm sorry if I cause you trouble. I just miss my parents so much."

"I know, dear, I know. No one can replace your mother and father, but you're not alone. You have us. We're you're family. Maybe Amelia will become a friend. All you need is one true friend. Remember the story of Noah and the ark?"

"Yes, I remember that Bible lesson—two by two."

"That's right," said Aunt Susan, pushing back from the table. Now it's time to make this little house shine. Today I'm glad it's not as big as those sea captains' houses along Main and Knox Streets."

Hours later, after cleaning her room, helping with dinner, and finishing her homework, Vinnie pulled down her star quilt, fluffed her pillow, and climbed into bed. Exhausted, she closed her eyes and said a prayer for her parents in heaven, her aunt and uncle, Charlie, and everyone at the prison across the street. Then she rolled over and added one more prayer.

She whispered, "Dear Lord, please keep the nightmares away." Then she opened her eyes and jumped out of bed.

She lit the lamp on her nightstand and carried it into the kitchen. When she found the basket of clothes waiting to be washed in the corner, she rummaged through it until she felt her soft cotton dress with the folded letter still in its pocket. As soon as she pulled it out, she hurried back to her room. Placing the lamp on the table, she sat on the floor, unfolded the paper, and read Charlie's words once more.

A Letter

Dear Vinnie,

It's eleven o'clock, and I can't sleep. I'm in my room on the third floor of our big house in Brooklyn Heights, and I'm missing the Georges, the shipyard, smelting on Oyster River, fishing with you at the Green, rowing my boat, and listening to your stories and your uncle's stories, too. Brooklyn Polytechnic is hard. The teachers drill us in mathematics and science all day long. I finished a set of geometry problems a half hour ago. You don't need a saw, a hammer and nails, or a needle and thread to do geometry; you need a ruler, a protractor, a pencil, and paper. It should be easy, but it's not. I'm not complaining. I prefer hard to easy, but going to a technical school is like being in a horse race every day. Everyone here wants to win, and I'm surrounded by really fast horses, but I'm determined to outrun them all.

Last July, you asked me if I wanted to apprentice with the shipwrights at Chapman & Flint, but I didn't have an answer. Now I'm sure. My answer is no. A shipwright stays in one place and builds one vessel at a time. I want to run a shipping business and connect people around the world. Of course, first I have to finish my course of studies. I'm tired tonight, but tomorrow is another day at the races and I'll be ready.

Have some fun at Bailey School. Thomaston Academy will be bigger and harder. I have no doubt you'll be ready. You're the smartest girl I've ever met, and I've met a lot of girls. I hope I get back to Thomaston before Christmas. Mother thought we might visit in October. If so, I can take a few days off from school then. If not, I'll see you at Christmas and you can tell me what's happening at the Upper Corner. I hope the bell hasn't tolled since I left. I'd rather it never tolls again, but we know that won't be the case. There's good and there's evil in this world, and that will never change. When the bell tolls, we have to be brave.

Your friend,
Charlie

Vinnie opened her grandfather's sea chest, folded Charlie's letter, and placed it in the ditty box. Then she turned off the light, climbed back in bed, and quickly fell asleep.

Friendship

Pulling back on the reins, Uncle Emery stopped his buggy near the Congregational Church. He quickly jumped down from the driver's seat and tied Spar, his handsome Morgan, to a post. Then he turned and offered Aunt Susan his hand. She was wearing a black velvet, turban-style hat with an ostrich feather set in a rosette at the side, and her cerulean blue dress had a tight bodice, puffy sleeves, and a long, full skirt. When she stepped down, she sparkled like a sapphire. He gave her a peck on the cheek, then lifted his niece, light as a feather, and set her feet in her fancy, laced-up boots on Main Street.

As soon as Vinnie's feet touched the ground, she felt an urge to spin. Wearing a rose-colored dress with a lace collar and a stylish bonnet tied with a ribbon, she looked all of sixteen. Uncle Emery, on the other hand, was dressed in his work clothes, and his mustache was sorely in need of trimming.

"I'll be waiting here at noon. I trust you both can walk the rest of the way. Be careful when you step onto those boards. You'll have to pick up your skirts, but you do look pretty."

"Thank you, Uncle Emery. Aren't you coming with us?"

He patted her shoulder and said, "Sorry; I'm not the church-going kind." He looked at his wife and grinned. "I'm counting on you to pray for me, though."

Aunt Susan tossed her head and picked up her skirt. "Oh, it's a glorious day! Maybe we're headed for an Indian summer."

"I doubt it," he chuckled. "Now, be off. You don't want to be late, and those petticoats will definitely slow you down."

"That's the plan, my dear. We want to be noticed."

"Oh, everyone will notice. You haven't been to church since last April."

"That's right," whispered Aunt Susan. "I went to church in April to thank God for the end of the war, and now I'm going to pray for healing and prosperity."

He whispered back, "I hope he's listening. If anyone wants to know, I'll be at Paul French's. He's the best cabinetmaker in town, and I'm going to ask him to make Vinnie a writing desk."

At the end of the service, Aunt Susan and Vinnie waited until Mr. and Mrs. Counce and Amelia exited their pew. Then they followed them to the back of the church. When they reached the staircase leading to the social hall, they were forced to stop, and Aunt Susan bumped into Mrs. Counce.

"Pardon me."

Glancing over her shoulder, Mrs. Counce smiled. "No need to apologize, dear. Everyone bumps elbows when they're waiting for refreshments. This entryway is too small, and with the social hall upstairs, the line for the punch always stops at the bottom of the stairs."

Vinnie giggled and Mrs. Counce gave her a wink, then touched Aunt Susan's arm and kept chatting. "If we're lucky, everyone ahead of us will be generous and leave a few of Minnie Todd's apple tarts."

"Wouldn't that be nice? Minnie's tarts are worth waiting for."

Mrs. Counce looked surprised. "How do you know Minnie?"

"Our husbands work together at the Chapman and Flint yard. My husband is Emery Payson, the shipwright."

"Of course! I know that name. My husband is a ship carver, so he's worked for most of the shipbuilders in town. I'm sure he's made more than one figurehead for Chapman and Flint. I've heard him praise John McDonald and his right-hand man, Emery Payson." She took Aunt Susan's hand and said, "I don't think we've been formally introduced. I'm Madeleine Counce, and I think we should be friends."

"My name is Susan, and I agree."

As they shook hands, Amelia chimed in, "You're both wearing identical hats."

Fixing their eyes on each other's hats, the two women laughed and kept laughing until heads up the line turned. Madeleine pulled a handkerchief from her sleeve and wiped her nose.

"This is my daughter, Amelia. She's thirteen and very observant."

Smiling, Aunt Susan replied, "This is my niece, Lavinia Wren. She'll be thirteen in December, though much to my chagrin, she acts much older."

"I'm sure they'll get along like peas in a pod."

"Would you like to come by our house this afternoon for a cup of tea?"

"Yes, that's a lovely invitation. I think we'll be ready for tea after spending the morning in line! What time should we arrive?"

"Around three o'clock. We live on the east side of Wadsworth Street, the second house from the corner. There's a flower garden in the dooryard and a big chestnut tree out back. It's easy to find."

"I know that tree and I've admired that garden. We'll be there at three. Now, let's hope we reach the punch bowl upstairs before half-past two."

By the time Vinnie and Amelia left the church, they were chatting away like old friends. In fact, they were strolling on the boards toward Knox Street when Madeleine's voice, loud and clear, interrupted their afternoon bliss.

"Amelia, why are you walking west when we live east? Your father is probably home already. We have to hurry now. You'll see Lavinia later."

Amelia called back, "Coming, Mother." But as she turned to say goodbye to Vinnie, she glimpsed two boys.

"Don't look now, but I think those boys standing on the corner are watching us."

"What boys?" asked Vinnie

"They're both tall, wearing short coats, and they have dark hair tied back at the collar. Wait—one is smiling at us."

"And the other?"

"Oh, my word, they're waving at us!"

Vinnie turned her head and her mouth dropped open. Gray Rowley and James Sutton were indeed waving at them.

"Amelia! Are you coming?"

Amelia squeezed Vinnie's hand. "I have to go home, though I'd much rather walk with you to that corner and meet those boys. They seem to know you." As she turned to head east, she glanced back, waved at the boys, and whispered, "You must tell me everything when we visit later today."

Amelia walked away with her shining black hair falling below her shoulders. At that moment, Gray and James crossed the street and headed toward Vinnie, though she could see James's eyes were following her breezy, beautiful friend.

"Ay, who was that raven-haired beauty?" asked James.

Stifling a laugh, Gray chimed in, "Hello, Vinnie. I almost didn't recognize you under that fancy bonnet. Did you go to church this morning?"

Vinnie blushed. "Yes, I went to church with my aunt." Then she turned toward James. "My friend's name is Amelia Counce. We just met, but she's already my dearest friend."

James rolled back on his heels. "I can see how dear she is; I'd like to be her friend, too."

"Of course you would," said Gray, giving his shipmate an elbow. "One can never have enough—"

"Friends, right?" asked a gravelly voice behind them.

By the look on Vinnie's face, both boys knew they were in trouble. To add to their alarm, Mrs. Payson, their mothers' friend, was approaching Vinnie from behind.

Aunt Susan placed a hand on Vinnie's shoulder and calmly intervened. "My goodness, if it isn't Gray Rowley and James Sutton. I thought you boys signed on to Captain Ranlett's crew."

Uncle Emery stepped forward. "I thought you'd both be second mates by now. Won't one of you be sailing on the *Pactolus*? She's on the ways right now. We'll be launching her next month."

Lifting his chin, James replied, "I'll be her second mate, sir."

With a furrowed brow, Uncle Emery nodded. "That's what I heard, and I'm glad. There'll be no need for you making new friends in town. You're a Cape-Horner for life and you'll be answering the call of the deep till your strength gives out." Then he turned his chiseled face toward Gray. "And what about you? Have you swallowed the anchor, or will you find another vessel and sail as an officer?"

"No, sir. I won't sail as a second mate and serve betwixt and between the quarterdeck and the fo'c's'le. And I have no desire to be a bloody—I mean *nasty*—first mate, who beats on the crew, except for the captain's steward."

"Then what will you do, lad?"

"I'm not sure, but I want to live and work by the sea, and there's no finer place than here to do that."

Rubbing his three-day beard, Uncle Emery looked hard at Gray. "I can't say I disagree. I'm a shipwright, and that's all I've ever wanted to be. Don't waste time. Decide. If you want to stay in Thomaston, you'd be wise to learn a shipbuilding trade. Why don't you stop by the joiner shop at Chapman and Flint?"

Shoving his hands in his pockets, Gray bit his lip.

"Think about it," said Uncle Emery with a slight smile. "While you do that, leave my niece and her friend alone. The two of you have sailed around the world with Captain Ranlett—you're men, not boys."

The young men nodded and walked away.

At precisely three o'clock, Madeleine Counce knocked on the Paysons' front door with Amelia at her side. Both had changed their clothes, including their hats. Madeleine was wearing a silk-plush turban with a veil, trying to make a good impression and spark a new friendship. Born into a family of blockmakers, Madeleine was fully aware that Thomaston was an aristocratic town where shipbuilders were kings. Unlike the vessels they built, vessels that "spoke" to every other vessel they encountered under sail, townsfolk didn't speak to every person they met on shore.

There was a definite social order, and most of the towns-folk were aware of it. Madeleine was prone to breaking the rules, though.

When Aunt Susan opened the door, she greeted her guests with a warm smile. "Welcome! We're so happy to see you twice in one day!"

As soon as Madeleine stepped into the Paysons' cape with its steep, gabled roof, gleaming white clapboards, and light-oak door, she took Aunt Susan's hand and gushed, "Your home sparkles just like you. I spotted your flowerbeds as soon as our carriage turned the corner. They're delightful! I adore late-blooming sunflowers and hydrangeas."

"Lavinia is our gardener. We've planted a wide variety of annuals and perennials, and she keeps them all growing and happy. Without her, I fear only the geraniums would survive."

"I doubt that," smiled Madeleine, "though you're lucky to have someone who likes to dig in the earth and plant and prune as much as you!"

Stepping from behind her mother, Amelia chimed in, "The plants under my care always wither and die."

Aunt Susan laughed out loud. "Lavinia, why don't you show Amelia your room while I put on the kettle and chat with Mrs. Counce?"

"Follow me," she said, glancing at Amelia. "My room is off the kitchen."

As soon as the door closed behind her, Amelia tossed her bonnet on the bed and spun around.

"Tell me about the boys."

"You mean the boys that were standing on the corner of Main and Knox Streets?"

"Yes, little bird! What other boys did we see today?"

Vinnie cocked her head and grinned. "Their names are Gray Rowley and James Sutton, though I don't really know them. I met them walking home from school last week. They're sailors, home from a long voyage with Captain Ranlett."

Amelia's brown eyes opened wide. "And what did they have to say?"

"Not much. Though James did say you were a raven-haired beauty."

"He did?" asked Amelia, sitting down on the rope bed and feeling the comfort of its soft quilt.

"Yes, he did, then my uncle came over and told them to leave us alone."

"Why would he say that?"

"I'm not sure, but my uncle knows Gray and James. He knows they sailed on the *Sunbeam*, and he said they were men, not boys."

"I see, and your uncle thinks we're too young. Why does age matter so much to old people?"

Vinnie sat on the edge of the bed. "I don't know, but I don't think my uncle is old, and my aunt, who's even younger than my uncle, said the same thing."

"I'm curious. What exactly did *she* say?"

"She said Gray and James had gone to sea and they were men, not boys. In fact, I think that's why we went to church this morning. She wanted me to meet you, and she knew your family attended services at the Congregational Church."

"No! I don't believe it! My mother wondered why she had never seen you there before."

"Are you angry? My aunt meant no harm. She used to go to church every Sunday — to the Baptist church around the corner, but she stopped during the war. After my parents died, she didn't think God was listening anymore."

The room fell silent.

Putting her arm around Vinnie's shoulders, Amelia replied, "I'll never be angry with you. You're my best friend from this moment on, and friends look out for each other no matter what. I just wish the *older* people around here would let the *younger* people decide who they should talk to!"

"I agree," said Vinnie looking her new best friend in the eye. "Can you believe this all started because I read Charlie's letter during Miss Catland's lesson on multiplication and division?"

Flopping on the bed, Amelia squealed, "Oh, I believe it. Now tell me, little bird, who's Charlie? You know so many boys!" She reached for the pillow and tossed it at Vinnie. "But before you tell me about Charlie, tell me about James—the one who said I was a beauty."

"James is the darker one. He's going to be the second mate on the *Pactolus*."

Closing her eyes, Amelia sighed. "Why don't you hit me with that pillow? I'm such a foolish girl."

"Maybe, maybe not," giggled Vinnie, tossing the pillow back to her friend.

The Sail Loft

As Gray passed the steam box—where long planks were made pliable to form graceful bows and broad sterns—he smelled the pine chips scattered about the yard and felt at ease. Nowhere else did the salty fragrance of the sea and the woodsy scent of the forest mix so beautifully as at the heart of a busy shipyard. Breathing deeply, he paused to admire the *Pactolus*, tied up at the wharf with riggers aboard, and the *St. Charles* on the ways with framers at work. Both looked magnificent against the backdrop of a bright azure sky and Watson's Point.

"The *Pactolus* is a beauty, wouldn't you say?" asked a deep, low voice.

"She is," replied Gray, turning to see the shipwright Emery Payson.

"Ayuh, she'll be ready for her maiden voyage soon, and your friend James will be her second mate. Where will you be?"

The riggers were singing, "John Kanaka." Gray chose to listen to their hauling shanty rather than answer.

Emery pulled his pipe out of his pocket but didn't light it. No one smoked in the yard. Instead, he tapped the bowl on his palm and started to sing along:

I thought I heard the Old Man say,
John Kanaka-naka tulai-e.
Today, today is a holiday,
John Kanaka-naka tulai-e!

Gray smiled and joined the chorus.

Tulai-e, oh tulai-e, ooh!
John Kanaka-naka tulai-e!

"I won't be hoisting sails on another bark again," said Gray, fixing his eyes on the riggers hanging from the ropes. 'John Kanaka' has a lot of verses and sailors keep adding more, but would you like to hear the one that haunts me the most?"

Sticking his pipe in his mouth, Emery nodded, and Gray sang out in a deep, rich voice:

We're bound away around Cape Horn,
John Kanaka naka, tulai-e!
We wisht ter Christ we'd niver bin born,
John Kanak-naka, tulai-e!

The last notes were swept away by a zephyr, and the old man and the young man savored the moment. When Emery pulled his pipe out of his mouth, Gray took that as a sign and explained himself.

"Sailing from the Chincha Islands to Liverpool with a hull full of guano isn't a good memory. The cargo stinks, and the voyage is longer for the odor. I'd rather go home every night to a sweet wife, a warm hearth, and a baby I can rock and sing to sleep."

Emery sat down on a slab of granite. Out of habit, he stuck his pipe back in his mouth and puffed even though there was no tobacco. Looking at the *Pactolus*, he thought about all the vessels he had helped to build and all the sailors who had hauled the ropes and hoisted the sails. The riggers kept singing and the old man motioned for the young man to sit down beside him. After a while, he put his hand on Gray's shoulder.

"Do you see the two men standing with Captain Tobey on the quarterdeck?"

"I do," said Gray.

"That's Thomas Dunn and George Elliot, the sailmakers. You should talk with them."

Gray turned to face the shipwright, the Yankee with salt-and-pepper hair, the soldier who had fought with the Third Maine under Colonel Howard at Bull Run and Fair Oaks, and stammered, "Why...why should I do that, sir?"

Emery pulled out his pipe and fixed his gaze on the young man with a boyish face.

"Listen, son, you need to learn a trade. In fifty-six, before the war, Thomas Dunn opened a sail loft with Captain William Tobey at O'Brien's Wharf. Together they built a good business. As fate would have it, though, some men will always answer the call of the sea. A few months ago, Chapman and Flint offered Captain Tobey command of the *Pactolus* and he said yes, leaving Thomas to run the business by himself. The Dunn family and the Elliot family are connected, and they've been working here since the twenties. Thomas apprenticed with his uncle, Richard Elliot, years ago. When Richard's son, George, heard that the captain was going back to sea, he saw an opportunity and decided to partner with his cousin."

"That's quite a web you're weaving, sir. I'm glad Mr. Dunn's cousin has joined him in a prosperous business, but what does that have to do with me?"

Emery tapped his pipe on the palm of his hand and paused. Then he advised the mariner in a serious tone to follow his gut and look on land to find his future.

"You should apprentice with Dunn and Elliot. They're good men and they're the best sailmakers in town. Hell, they're the best sailmakers from here to New York Harbor."

For the first time in a long time, Gray was rendered speechless. He hardly knew the old salt sitting beside him, yet he was offering him an introduction to a future he had dreamed about for almost two years, a future *by* the sea, not *on* the sea.

"Cat got your tongue, Mr. Rowley?" asked Emery, closing one eye. "Maybe you need to think about it. Maybe you haven't swallowed the anchor quite yet."

Gray shook his head. "No, no, sir. I don't need to think about it. Can you introduce me to the misters Dunn and Elliot today?"

Looking up at milky-white clouds, Emery laughed. Then wiping his cheek with the back of his hand, he said, "Yes, I can. Follow me up the gangplank. You can meet them on the deck of the *Pactolus* as the crew bends on her first suit of sail. Come on, you're about to see the pride and beauty of a sailmaker."

When Vinnie climbed the stairs to the sail loft, a sunlit space surrounded by salt-coated windows, she wasn't expecting to see Gray sitting on a bench on the west side of the room, and neither were Mrs. Counce and Amelia by the look on their faces. The girls froze as they watched Mrs. Counce walk up to the handsome young sailmaker.

"Where's my cousin?"

With yards of stiff white duck stretching across his knees and a leather palm tied around his hand, Gray looked up and smiled.

"Good afternoon, ma'am. Who might your cousin be?"

"George Elliot, the man who usually sits at this bench. What's your name?"

"My name's Gray Rowley. I'm the new apprentice."

"Do I know you?" she asked, studying his beardless face.

"We've never spoken, but I was raised on Lowell Street and went to school at Thomaston Academy until I sailed with Captain Ranlett."

"Well, I'm Madeleine Counce."

Gray took off his palm, set it on the bench, and stood up. "I think Mr. Elliot and Mr. Dunn are in their office meeting with a shipbuilder. They close the door when they meet with someone important. I can get 'im if you like. It's almost noon—my lunch break."

Touching her lips, Madeleine paused. "You're very kind," she smiled, "but that won't be necessary."

As soon as Vinnie saw Mrs. Counce smile, she nudged Amelia and the two girls stepped over to the bench just in time to hear Madeleine's parting words.

"I can knock on their door. Mr. Dunn and Mr. Elliot won't mind if I interrupt their meeting. We're family. My grandfather was John Elliot, the blockmaker who came to Thomaston in the 1820s and encouraged his family to get involved with the town's maritime affairs. By the way, I sat at a bench on this floor during the war and made tents for the Union soldiers."

Gray nodded. "It's good to be part of something big, like a family, a business, and a cause."

Madeleine smiled again. "Nice to meet you, Mr. Rowley. I hope you'll stay at Dunn and Elliot for a while."

"Oh, I plan to, Mrs. Counce. I prefer a steady floor to the rolling deck of a ship."

Turning to leave, Madeleine caught the girls grinning. At that moment, she glanced back at the handsome young man. "I like the way you think, Mr. Rowley, and you have the brightest green eyes I've ever seen."

Gray, Vinnie, and Amelia all blushed at once.

At flood time, close to noon, the Chapman & Flint yard was alive with framers, caulkers, shipwrights, riggers, sailors, investors, and spectators. Everyone was excited to see the *Pactolus*, a bark named for the Lydian river god who ruled over streams flecked with gold, slip over the ways. Only six months had passed since the end of the Civil War, and the launching of a vessel was proof that Yankee shipbuilding had survived. Ladies in fancy bonnets and men in bowlers or black mariner's caps, all flaunting their finest clothes, were dotting the hill from the prison wall to the lower end of Ship Street. Like the Greeks, Romans, and Norsemen who had sailed before them, the people of Thomaston were about to witness an ancient ritual. The bark *Pactolus*, with the fore- and mainmast rigged square, and the mizzenmast rigged fore and aft, was owned by some of Thomaston's most prominent men, including Isaac Chapman, Benjamin Flint, John McDonald, Thomas Dunn, George Elliot, and Captain William Tobey.

In 1865, when few Americans would see a baptism of the waves, the townsfolk of Thomaston, families that started a golden enterprise by building the schooner *Montpelier* for General Knox in 1803, would enjoy the view from the banks of the Georges or the deck of the bark.

Vinnie and Amelia had decided they would board the *Pactolus* with Uncle Emery and Amelia's father. As soon as the blocks were kicked out from beneath the hull, they would run from port to starboard, shouting and hollering as the bark plunged into the water and rocked from side to side. At least that was their plan. Aunt Susan had warned them to stay away from the aft because she knew the vessel would go over the ways stern first, and that would be the roughest place to be. She also told Vinnie that she and Mrs. Counce would be standing on terra firma—solid ground. A veteran of many launches, she was certain the event would be unforgettable no matter where they stood.

Hurrying toward the gangplank, Vinnie thought the day couldn't get any better, but then she heard a deep voice calling her name.

"Vinnie! Lavinia Wren, wait!"

She turned to see Charlie running toward her. Amelia saw him, too.

"Who is that darling boy?"

Vinnie didn't answer.

When Charlie reached her, he came to a halt and grinned.

"Don't look so surprised! I'm a Flint. I couldn't miss the launch of the *Pactolus*!"

Amelia smiled. "It appears my friend has lost her voice and her manners—"

"I haven't lost either, though I am surprised."

Laughing, Charlie looped his arm around Vinnie's shoulders and gave her a squeeze. "I've missed you, too, little bird."

Clearing her throat, Amelia piped up, "I'm Vinnie's friend, Amelia Counce, and that's my father and Mr. Payson waiting at the gangplank. We should join them."

"Yes," said Vinnie, taking Charlie's hand. "It's time for beauty and grace to slide over the ways!"

Vinnie felt the rising tide as she boarded the *Pactolus*; then, stepping foot on the glistening pine deck, she witnessed the wonder of Chapman & Flint. The tall masts with heavy sails waiting to be unfurled took her breath away, and the sight of her uncle chatting with John McDonald, the master builder, filled her with awe. When her gaze moved aft to the quarterdeck, she pursed her lips. Standing by the wheel, the captain was talking with George Elliot with Gray and James just a few feet away.

The picture of those four men, groomed to perfection, made her whistle.

"What are you whistling at?" asked Charlie.

Following her friend's gaze, Amelia's eyes widened.

Charlie looked up. "That's Captain Tobey with the sailmaker, but I don't know the young officers."

"Only one is an officer," said Amelia quietly. His name is James Sutton. He's the second mate."

"And the other?"

"His name is Gray Rowley," said Vinnie. "He's an apprentice at the sail loft."

Charlie cocked his head and fixed his eyes on Vinnie's face. "Why, Lavinia Wren, you're blushing. How did you meet such dashing young men?"

"I met them by accident."

"By accident?"

"Yes, I bumped into them on my way home from school one day."

"I see."

"Then Vinnie introduced me to them after a Sunday service," added Amelia. "James and Gray are best friends. They sailed around the world with Captain Ranlett."

"Whoa! Captain Charles Ranlett?"

"Yes," answered Vinnie. "Why do you look so surprised?"

"I'm his namesake. I guess my parents are fond of Captain Ranlett."

"No!" exclaimed both girls, cascading into laughter.

"Yes," replied Charlie with a hint of a smile. "My full name is Charles Ranlett Flint, and I'd like to meet those men over there."

"You will!" cried Vinnie, taking Charlie's hand.

Part Two

1874–1877

Home Again

"Lavinia!" called Aunt Susan from her sewing room upstairs. "Do you hear that knocking? Someone's at the door. Please see who it is."

Vinnie hurried to the door, humming a tune her Sigma Kappa sisters had taught her, with a carrot in her hand. Before turning the knob, she put the carrot in her mouth and wiped her hands on her apron. When she opened the door, the half-peeled carrot fell to the floor.

"Have I surprised you again?" asked Charlie, bending to pick it up.

"Always," said Vinnie, reaching for the carrot. "I was just getting supper ready and—"

"And you got hungry," said Charlie with a heart-stopping smile.

"Ayuh...guess so. Can you stay? I'm sure my uncle would love to see you."

"I wish I could, but I have a train to catch. I'm actually here to pick up a rug. All the ladies in Brooklyn Heights admire my mother's hooked rugs, and she tells them they're made by Susan Payson of Thomaston."

Vinnie nodded.

"I also have a few gifts to deliver from my mother and

Mrs. McDonald, who both appreciate your aunt's talent for turning scraps of wool into works of art."

Leaning to the right, Vinnie spied two packages waiting on the passenger's side of the buggy. "Will you need help carrying in those boxes?"

Charlie grinned like he was fifteen, not twenty-four. "No, I think I can handle it."

"Good. Since I haven't seen you since last June, and you stopped writing letters long before that, I'm not inclined to help you, but my aunt will be happy to see you."

Stunned, Charlie tipped his hat. "I guess I deserve that, but let me try to—"

"No need to explain," said Vinnie, tossing her head.

From the corner of her eye, she glimpsed a guard on the prison wall watching them, and she took a deep breath to steady her nerves.

"I think I understand. You have a train to catch, so why don't you get those gifts, come inside, and make my aunt feel better about the fact that the Chapman and Flint shipyard has moved to Bath, and the McDonald family has moved with it."

"Oh, Vinnie, I'm sorry. It wasn't my family's fault. It was a matter of eminent domain. For the greater good, the Knox and Lincoln Railroad needed our shipyard. They laid their tracks where we built slipways and launched our ships. People call that progress."

"Uncle Emery doesn't call it progress. He calls it the beginning of the end of shipbuilding in Thomaston. He won't leave, though. John McDonald asked him to move to Bath, but he refused. He's working for Walker, Dunn and Company now."

Kicking a stone with the toe of his expensive leather shoe, Charlie replied, "The winds are always changing. To survive, we have to anticipate the weather and keep adjusting our sails."

"Do I even know you?" asked Vinnie, shaking her head. "I'll be returning to Colby in the fall. My aunt and uncle will miss me terribly, but I won't be gone long. I'll come home again, and I'll work to keep Thomaston safe and prosperous. Where will you be?"

"I'll be—"

"Glory be, if it isn't Charlie Flint!" cried Aunt Susan from the foot of the stairs. "I just finished the hooked rug I promised your mother. Perfect timing," she said as she stepped toward the door. "Why are you standing outside? Come in, Charlie."

He raised his hand and flashed a smile. "Give me a minute."

Then he turned around, walked over to his buggy, and collected the gifts. When he returned, there was a glint in his eye. He looked happy to be there.

"Are you thirsty?" asked Aunt Susan as she ushered him to the kitchen.

"A little."

"Well then, let me pour you some cider."

Stepping into the sunlit kitchen, he saw a large, cast-iron pot simmering on the cookstove and took a deep breath.

"If dinner tastes as good as it smells, I wish I could stay longer."

"You're going to miss Vinnie's chicken and dumplings, and that's a shame because it's always delicious. Since Vinnie has come home, having finished her first year of college, she's been cooking every night. Her kindness is a blessing and a challenge. Emery and I are gaining weight. So much so, I may have to let out the waist in his pants and my skirts."

Placing the gifts on the long table that stretched from the south-facing window to the center of the room, Charlie sighed wistfully. "Oh, to have such a problem. If only I

49

could say my pants don't fit because I'm eating too many home-cooked meals."

Eyeing the boxes on the table, Aunt Susan tilted her head and smiled. "Are those gifts for me?"

"Yes, they are," said Charlie, sitting down at the table and fixing his eyes on the tall pine hutch next to the door. The hutch had a marble top and three shelves, each one edged with white lace and filled with pretty plates, platters, cups, and saucers.

As Aunt Susan filled three copper mugs with frothy cider, Vinnie followed Charlie's eyes. When she realized his focus had shifted, she quickly closed her bedroom door, sat down next to her aunt, and took a long sip of cider.

Charlie cleared his throat. "Yes, the gifts are for you, and I also have my mother's payment for the rug she asked you to make for her entrance hall at Montague Terrace." He pulled an envelope from his vest pocket and passed it across the table.

Opening the envelope, Aunt Susan gasped. "I wasn't expecting such a large amount. Your mother is too generous. How could a rug be so valuable?"

"Well, your rugs are priceless. All the women in Brooklyn Heights covet the rugs you've made for my mother. They can't believe you weave flowers and kittens from scraps of cloth and burlap sacks. You're a Maine treasure."

"You're incredibly kind, Charlie," blushed Aunt Susan.

Vinnie chimed in, "He has a silver tongue. I'll give him that."

Aunt Susan tilted her head and gave Vinnie a disapproving look.

"Thank you, Charlie. I have your mother's rug rolled up and ready to go. Don't forget to take it with you when you leave. Can't you stay for supper? Vinnie was just getting it ready when you arrived. She's truly a wonderful cook."

"I'm sure she is, and I wish I could stay, but I'm taking the train to Woolwich in an hour."

"Don't you know, Aunt Susan? Charlie is a merchant prince. He has lots of people to see and deals to make. Isn't that right, Charlie?"

Charlie sat up straight. "I'm not a prince, though I'm a partner with Gilchrist, Flint, and Company of New York."

A soft breeze stirred the curtains at the window and a quiet hush filled the room.

Aunt Susan broke the silence. "I haven't spoken to you or your folks in a while. What have you been up to? What's kept you away?"

Charlie looked at Aunt Susan's warm eyes, framed by dark brows and fine lines, then turned to meet Vinnie's ice-blue stare and swallowed hard. When his voice returned, he spoke to Vinnie.

"Well, after graduating from Brooklyn Polytechnic in sixty-eight, I looked for work on the waterfront. First, I worked as a dock clerk, making four dollars a week. Then I started passing out my business card at every shipping office on South Street and developed my own clients, becoming quite adept at delivering valuable cargoes such as wine. Later, I volunteered my services to William R. Grace, eventually earning a salary. While working for Mr. Grace, I met his father-in-law, Captain George Gilchrist. The captain and I got along so well we decided to form our own company, a ship chandlery. That makes me a resourceful merchant, providing sailcloth, tar, oakum, whale oil, rope, and other supplies."

Charlie lifted his copper mug and took a swig of cider, letting the froth stay on his lips until he slowly wiped it away with the tip of his tongue.

Once again, Aunt Susan broke the ice. "My goodness, you are definitely a 'Live Yankee'! I'm exhausted just hearing about your enterprise. We do need a lot of sailcloth here in Thomaston. I understand our sailmakers still provide Chapman and Flint with sturdy suits of sail that last longer than most. Though when they need replacing, Dunn and Elliot will do that, too."

With his gaze still fixed on Vinnie's pursed lips, Charlie nodded. "Yes, and I hear they're opening a new sail loft at the foot of Green Street. My family and John McDonald are indebted to their skill. Speaking of our master builder, wouldn't you like to open your presents? The larger one is from the McDonalds."

Reaching for the package, Aunt Susan laughed out loud. "Oh, Charlie, I thought you'd never ask. I can't wait another second."

When she tore off the paper, it was Vinnie who gasped. "Unless I'm mistaken that's one of Edward Frost's new stencils. We read about them in the paper. Remember?"

"Yes, Frost is a well-known salesman from Biddeford, and he's developed floral and animal patterns on zinc that can be used for making hooked rugs. I believe this pattern, the lion surrounded by shields, is the most popular. You can even see the colors of the Stars and Stripes on the shields. What a splendid gift!"

"So, you like it," grinned Charlie.

"Yes! It's exquisite. I don't deserve such a precious gift from Isabelle and John."

"I suspect they disagree. Mrs. McDonald told me you were the best rug maker in Thomaston, if not all of New England. And Mr. McDonald said he would never have been able to launch the *Pactolus* in sixty-five and the *St. Charles* in sixty-six without the help of Emery Payson. They are fond of you both and miss you more than you know."

"Do you see them often?" she asked, still holding the stencil in her hand.

"Not often, but I visited them on my way here, and I'll see them again on my return. Without a bridge, the train cars still have to be ferried over the Kennebec. I'll meet them at the dock and be sure to tell them how pleased you are with their gift."

"Please do. Tell them I'll make them a rug using E.S. Frost and Company's stencil."

Witnessing her aunt's joy, Vinnie's lips parted and silently mouthed, *Thank you.*

And Charlie mouthed back, *You're welcome.*

"Don't forget the other gift," said Vinnie pointing to a box wrapped in brown paper and tied with string.

As she untied the string, Aunt Susan looked twenty years younger. Charlie gave Vinnie a wink.

"Oh, my Lord, it's a sampler made and signed by Sarah Tobey Flint."

Vinnie echoed her aunt's amazement. "It's beautiful!"

Holding the wooden frame at arm's length, Aunt Susan read the message written in blue counted cross-stitch and surrounded by a circle of red poppies, *"Though my feet may leave, home is forever in my heart."*

Vinnie looked at Charlie and her eyes melted, though he didn't return the look. His head was bowed, and he was pinching the bridge of his nose. She noticed his shoulders were moving up and down as if it was hard to breathe. That was the first time she saw Charlie Flint cry.

Freedom

As Vinnie made her way home from the first meeting of the Thomaston Ladies Literary Association that she was able to attend since starting her second year at Colby, scores of red and gold leaves danced about her feet. The elms along Main Street were almost bare, but as she turned the corner on to the lane, she noticed the copper beech tree in her uncle's dooryard was holding on to its crown. Autumn was by far her favorite season, and she was happy to be spending a few days at home where she had a respite from her studies in Waterville. As one of the first women to attend Colby, she was beginning to feel unwelcome in the male-dominated halls. Her sorority sisters, on the other hand, were enormously supportive. In fact, one of them, Mary Low, offered her a ride to Thomaston in the Lowes' family carriage so she could celebrate her uncle's forty-fifth birthday. Feeling a chill, she wrapped her shawl tighter around her shoulders and quickened her step. Tomorrow she would cook an unforgettable dinner of French onion soup, Yankee pot roast, carrots, and light, fluffy biscuits with lots of butter. This afternoon she would bake a rum cake. Just the thought of her aunt and uncle's kitchen made her smile. In the whole wide world, it was her favorite place to be.

Once inside the cozy house on Wadsworth Street, Vinnie took off her shawl and hung it on the hall tree. Placing her books on the side table, she shouted "Hello" even though she was fairly certain no one was home. Her uncle worked at the shipyard seven days a week, and her aunt volunteered at the prison every Saturday afternoon. She was committed to teaching the female prisoners to hook rugs using red-and-black rags from old prison garb. When no one responded to her cheery greeting, she marched into the kitchen and reached for her apron. With her hands behind her, she blindly tied the apron strings into a bow, and started to sing, "Oh my darlin', oh my darlin' —"

"Oh, yes," whispered a voice behind her as her arms were gripped and squeezed against her body.

She opened her mouth, but a sweaty hand smothered her scream. Writhing, she fought to free herself until the monster spun her around. His scarred face terrified her, and his red-and-black uniform triggered a memory. He was one of the inmates at the prison, and she had seen him before. When she was visiting the women's block with her aunt, she had passed him in the yard. He was shackled and flanked by two guards. At school she had read about the prison system, and at home her aunt told her about the warden's cruel tactics. Early on, troublemakers were often placed in a hole for months at a time with only a Bible to read while they endured extreme temperatures, a diet of hardtack and water, and countless hours of solitary confinement. Now, staring at her assailant's face, she saw his empty eyes — his ghostliness.

"Don't scream. I may want you, but I won't take you. I just want some clothes, food, and money."

Vinnie nodded.

The foul-smelling man dropped his hand just as Vinnie heard the first sharp whistle. Within seconds, the prison bell rang. Soon, the guards, police, and trained dogs

would be out looking for the escaped prisoner, the man
who was standing in front of her, still gripping her arm—
so close, but out of everyone's sight except hers.

"Give me a shirt, pants, and—"

Vinnie started shaking. She was going into shock.

The man softened his grip. "Listen, I've spent more
time in the dog-hole than any man living. I've tried to
escape three times. The last time they caught me, they put
me in the dog-hole for a whole year." His grip tightened
as his anger intensified. "I won't go back!"

Trembling, Vinnie whispered, "My uncle's clothes are
in the bedroom at the front of the house. There's some
money in the top drawer of the hutch behind me. I can
give you some bread and apples. Please don't hurt me."

The escapee reached one arm around her and opened
the drawer. He took the money then grabbed a knife.

"Take me to your uncle's clothes. If you make a wrong
move, I'll take you for pleasure, then kill you. Don't think
I won't."

She led him to the front bedroom, opened her uncle's
chest of drawers, and pulled out a pair of work pants and
a wool shirt. He started to unbutton his prison garb with
one hand, holding the knife in the other. She closed her
eyes and turned around.

"You're doin' good," he whispered, holding a knife to
her back. "Now let's get that food."

She opened her eyes and started to walk. As they
approached the kitchen, she heard the front door swing
open and turned to see a man hurling himself forward,
knocking the knife out of the monster's hand. She screamed
as she watched the men wrestling on the floor, both reaching for the knife that was less than six inches from her feet.
She kicked it with her right foot, then jumped out of the
way as the escapee pinned Gray to the floor and beat him
with his fists.

"Stop! You're killing him. I'll give you—"

"Sam Harlowe!" shouted a guard, entering the house with a fierce barking dog on a short leash. "Stop or I'll let Boomer tear you to pieces. He has your scent and you've got no place to go."

Sam rolled to his back and Vinnie, standing a mere three feet away, noticed his body took the form of a cross. His fists were open, and his eyes were fixed on her face. Shaking and terrified, she blinked back tears as she watched Gray struggle to stand. He was dripping with blood from his mouth, nose, and left ear. One eye was swollen shut. Within seconds, a policeman arrived at the door. As soon as he identified the man lying on the floor as the escaped prisoner, he blew his whistle to alert the rest of the search party. Then he ordered Sam to stand up and put his hands behind his back.

Aunt Susan was at the prison teaching the female inmates when she heard the whistles, and she reacted accordingly. She told the overseer she had to leave immediately and ran to the main gate, where she ordered the guard to let her pass. Knowing she lived across the street, the guard threw open the gate. By the time Aunt Susan pushed through the crowd in the parlor, Sam Harlowe was standing at the kitchen door with his hands tied behind his back; Gray was sitting in one of the spindle-back Windsor chairs at the kitchen table, and her niece was at his side, washing his cuts and bruises.

"Lavinia! Are you all right?"

Turning to meet her aunt's eyes, Vinnie dropped the washcloth into the bowl of sudsy water and rushed to her aunt's open arms.

"Oh, Aunt Susan, I've never been so scared. He didn't hurt me. Gray stopped him. He risked his life to save me. And the guard and his dog saved us all."

The floodgates broke. Vinnie pressed her face into her aunt's full bosom and wept.

"Go ahead, my sweet bird, let those tears go. Sing your song. Let everyone know you're alive."

On Monday morning, after all the D&E sailmakers had finished their allotted work at O'Brien's Wharf, each hoisted a bench over his shoulder and walked to the new sail loft at the foot of Green Street, where Thomas Dunn and his cousin George were waiting with heavy duck already cut so they could begin seaming and roping without delay. Walking along Water Street, grateful for the ten-minute break and the salty breeze, the men talked about the escape attempt that had failed because of the courage of one of their own. As the story passed from man to man, the details changed, the level of terror was augmented, and the rescue of Lavinia Wren became a terrifying tale. This reached the ears of Gray Rowley, the sailmaker at the end of the line, who saved Thomaston's beautiful songbird from the ugly claws of Sam Harlowe.

Less than forty-eight hours ago, Gray had wrestled with a convicted killer to save Lavinia. Looking down, Gray paused to shift the weight of his bench and steady his nerves. When he looked up, he saw Otis Perry and Rufus Small walking a few feet ahead of him. They were talking up a storm. When their words hit him, Gray shouted.

"No one carved an H into Lavinia's cheek! Harlowe threatened her, but he didn't cut her."

Glancing back, Otis replied, "That's not the story I heard."

Gray rushed forward, stopping only when the end of his bench touched Otis's back. "Well, I was there."

"So tell us what you know, because I heard Sam Harlowe raped her, then swapped his prison uniform for her uncle's clothes."

"You've got the story wrong," hissed Gray. "He didn't hurt her physically."

Rufus put his bench down and Otis followed suit. They both turned around slowly, but Rufus spoke first, "Don't get so riled up, Gray. We all know you're the one who saved her. Otis didn't mean no harm."

"I stopped Harlowe. He's big, but I took him down. I have the injuries to prove it. He gave me a bad beating, but he didn't put a mark on Vinnie."

Otis cocked an eyebrow. "Vinnie? Is that what her *friends* call her? I didn't know the two of you were so close."

Gray put his bench down, stretched to his full height, and leveled his gaze at Otis. "We're not *close*. But yes, her friends call her Vinnie."

Rufus, the oldest sailmaker at D&E, placed his hand on Gray's shoulder. "Everyone knows you're the one who rescued the lovely lady. No one knows, though, why you were there at that moment. Why not put the rumors to rest?"

Gray dropped his head.

Then, lifting his gaze, he focused on the kind-hearted sailmaker. "Call it a stroke of good luck. I didn't plan to be there."

"You mean you just happened to be walking by when you saw an escaped prisoner run across the road and force his way into the Paysons' home?"

"Yes and no. I was heading home from work when I remembered my ma had asked me to pick up some milk and eggs from the store, so I was by the Paysons' front gate on my way to Fernald's when the bell started ringing."

"Lucky for Lavinia Wren," said Otis.

"I didn't know she was there. The gate was open and the front door was ajar. That didn't seem right. My ma and Mrs. Payson are good friends, and Ma always says that Susan Payson is one of the smartest women in town.

She lives across from the prison. Why would she leave her door open?"

"She wouldn't," said Rufus, rubbing his chin. "So, you went up to the door to check on Mrs. Payson?"

Gray said yes and fell silent until Otis poked him with another question. "Was Emery in the house?"

"No, only Vinnie. As soon as I stepped into the parlor, I saw Sam Harlowe, though I didn't know it was him at the time, pushing her into the kitchen with a knife at her back. I jumped him from behind. After that it's a blur. When the guard arrived with his dog, Harlowe was pounding my head against the floor. I think Boomer's growl and sharp teeth saved us."

Otis disagreed. "No, Boomer saved *you*, but you're the one who saved Lavinia."

"Don't worry," said Rufus picking up his bench. "We'll handle the nasty rumors, but first we need to set up our benches at that fine new loft up the street, or Thomas Dunn and George Elliot will fire all three of us."

On his way home, after working a ten-hour day, Gray decided to stop by the Paysons' house to see how Vinnie was faring. His head still hurt, and he was having trouble sleeping and eating. He thought of Vinnie constantly. Imagining her pain was far worse than his, he knocked on the door. Mrs. Payson answered.

"Oh, Gray, you look awful! If I didn't know you, your black eye and fat lip would frighten me."

Gray took off his cap and tried to smile. "Forgive me, Mrs. Payson. My bosses said I looked like a pirate this morning. I suppose you're not fond of pirates, and I don't want to scare you, but I've been worried about Lavinia. How's she feeling today?"

Susan Payson opened the door a little wider and waved him in. She took his cap and hung it on the hall tree then turned to face him. "Vinnie's upstairs in my sewing room. She's hardly spoken to anyone, not even to me. Emery and I can't send her back to school until we know she's all right." Looking into his eyes, she pleaded, "Please go up and talk with her. Maybe she'll listen to you. Maybe she'll open up."

"Which way do I go?"

"Turn right at the top of the stairs," said Susan with smiling eyes.

He placed his hand on the railing and climbed the narrow steps to the short hallway between the north and south gables, then turned right. As soon as he reached the softly lit room, he saw Vinnie sitting near the window. She was bending over a floral pattern, hooking a rug with deft hands. He stood in the doorway, transfixed by her beauty, the shimmer of her golden hair, the definition of her high cheekbones, and her long eyelashes. After a while, he found his voice and stepped into the room.

"Hello, Vinnie. I've been wondering how you've been faring since Saturday, so I decided to stop by. Your aunt said I could come up and see for myself."

Silence filled the room. He shifted his weight then met her eyes. "How are you feeling? We're all worried about you."

"I'm fine. How are you?"

Keeping his eyes on hers, he answered, "It hurts to smile and eat. In truth, my whole head hurts, and so do my fists. I feel horrible, and I think you do, too, though you don't show it."

She shook her head. "I'm sorry. It's my fault."

"No, it's not your fault. You have nothing to be sorry about."

"I gave him my uncle's clothes. It's all my fault. I should have fought harder, but I gave in to my fear and look what happened," she gasped, choking back tears.

"Vinnie, may I sit?"

Wiping her cheek with the back of her hand, she nodded.

He sat down on the blue-and-green rug at her feet and crossed his legs as if he was sitting by a campfire.

"We should talk about what happened. I saw him, Vinnie. You did the right thing. He was bigger and stronger than you and bigger and stronger than me."

She turned her face toward the window and he could see that her lips were trembling. Rocking back, he whispered, "Everyone in Thomaston knows you're a brave woman. You did not give in to fear; you outsmarted your attacker. You bought time—time for help to arrive."

"I almost cost you your life!" she cried. Standing up suddenly, she let her hook and the unfinished rug fall to the floor and clenched her hands.

Still sitting cross-legged by her feet, Gray looked up and softly said, "You didn't. Help arrived. Not the cavalry, but a few able-bodied men with a well-trained dog. Sometimes goodness prevails."

Gray's words had a dramatic effect. Vinnie opened her hands and invited his touch. He stood up, wrapped his arms around her, and kissed her on the forehead.

A Coastal Christmas

Whenever Vinnie was home from college, she visited the D&E Sail Loft as often as possible. It was a good place, filled with good people. She and Amelia found lots of reasons to stop by. More often than not, they delivered a message or a package, but sometimes they stopped by the office to chat with Thomas Dunn and George Elliot, the owners, because they were both Mrs. Counce's cousins, and they were kind.

Winter comes early in Maine. In the middle of November, Vinnie's trips home became less frequent and by the middle of December, she couldn't wait till Christmas to go home so she planned a surprise. On the sixteenth of December, after her last class ended, she met her sorority sister, Nellie Sprague, and they left Waterville together in a carriage driven by Nellie's father.

The next morning, Vinnie woke up in her own bed. She dressed, poured a steaming cup of tea, buttered a biscuit, and rushed out the door with a basket over her arm. As she scurried down Wadsworth Street, she practiced what she was going to say to her favorite sailmaker in case she had an opportunity to speak with him: *Merry almost Christmas, Gray. I've brought some gifts from my Aunt Susan that you may want to share.* With no one beside her to listen and respond, she giggled and swung her basket. When she arrived at the loft and stepped onto its expanse of clean floor, she was greeted with the redolence of new duck and the applause of twelve sailmakers.

"The lovely lady is back!" cried Rufus, and a dozen "good mornings" followed.

George Elliot himself rushed over and tipped his bowler.

"Wonderful to see you looking so well, Miss Wren!"

Vinnie smiled. "I'm happy to be home, Mr. Elliot. May I speak with Gray, please?"

He winked. "You'll find him sitting on his bench in the far corner."

"Thank you," said Vinnie as she turned her face toward the sunny window and spotted Gray.

She walked across the floor with the hem of her blue silk dress brushing the boards, and the eyes of every sailmaker followed her. When she reached Gray, she handed him the basket, covered with a white cloth.

"My aunt thought you might enjoy a loaf of her bread and a jar of her strawberry preserves. She also packed some molasses cookies."

Surprised to see her, Gray stood up and took the basket, his cheeks flaming red.

"I thought you were taking exams and wouldn't be—"

"A friend offered me a ride. I just got home last night, or I would've baked the cookies myself."

"Why didn't you tell me you were coming home early?"

She whispered back, "I wanted to surprise you."

"Well, you have," he said in a low voice.

Pressing her lips together, she waited.

He set the basket down on the bench and gave her a half-smile. "Please tell your aunt I appreciate her gift. I'll share it at lunch. And tell her I'll stop by the house this evening to thank her in person."

"All right; we'll be waiting."

Vinnie didn't notice the quiet until she turned to leave. Every sailmaker was busy with his hands but listening with his ears. When she reached the double doors, she touched her hat to make sure it was secure and stepped into the blustery day without looking back.

At the post office on Main Street, on the same block as the Thomaston Bank and the C.W. Stimpson Dry Goods Store, the postmaster greeted Lavinia like an old friend.

"Good morning, Vinnie. How long are you home for?"

"A whole month, and I'm not going to open a book," she said gleefully.

"Not one?" he asked, lifting his brow.

She leaned over the counter. "Well, maybe one or two, but only the ones I *want* to read, not *have* to read."

"I see," he said with a nod. "And how is your second year of college going?"

"It's going well. I'm studying world literature, philosophy, history, and French."

"Well, that sounds exhausting."

"Oh, it's not too bad. I like to read and write. In fact, I'm working on an article for the newspaper."

"You are! What's that about?"

"It's about prison reform."

The postmaster coughed, then took out his handkerchief and wiped his brow.

"Is anything wrong?"

"No, nothing's wrong. I'm just surprised. I mean, I'm glad you're able to concentrate on your work after your scare."

Vinnie focused her crystal-blue eyes on the postmaster's jowly face until he broke down and explained himself.

"I mean after your ordeal with Sam Harlowe, the—"

"Let me assure you, sir, I'm fully recovered from that unfortunate experience. Besides, the prison system is bigger than one person. It's bigger than one criminal and one vile act. It's about justice."

"I agree," said the postmaster, putting his handkerchief back in his pocket. "You are an amazing young woman, and I'm not alone in that opinion."

He handed her two cream-colored envelopes. The first was addressed to Miss Lavinia Wren, the second to Mr. and Mrs. Emery Payson. She flipped hers over to read the return address and admired the handwriting out loud.

"What exquisite penmanship and what a lovely surprise! Thank you. Have a good day, sir."

The postmaster smiled. "You, too." As she walked out the door, he called out, "Merry Christmas, Lavinia!"

Standing in front of the bank, she opened her mail and read it as if it was marked *Urgent*.

Dear Lavinia,

On behalf of Dunn & Elliot, please join us at the sail loft on Water Street at eight o'clock in the evening, the thirty-first of December, for hors d'oeuvres and libations to celebrate New Year's Eve. Music and dancing will be provided by the Burkett's Quadrille Band.

Wishing you peace and joy at Christmas and always,
Thomas and Elizabeth Dunn, and George and Mary Ella Elliot

Vinnie pressed the creamy paper to her breast and smiled. Then she slipped the coveted invitation into its envelope, tucked it in her pocket, and pulled up her collar. It was starting to snow, and a cold wind blew strands of her hair, freed from a dozen pins, around her face. Opening the heavy door of the dry goods store, she could see her uncle at the counter and decided to wait in the sleigh out front. As she climbed onto the passenger seat, she heard her name and turned to see her dearest friend walking toward her.

"Why if it isn't Amelia Counce! I was hoping to see you today!"

"And now you have, though it's a miracle we can see anything in this blowing snow."

Vinnie shouted, "I'm waiting for Uncle Emery. Wait with me. We can wrap ourselves in this blanket."

"I'd be foolish to refuse any blanket on such a frigid day. Pull me up and I'll sit beside you for a while!"

Laughing, Vinnie offered her hand, and Amelia, rather gracefully, hopped onto the sleigh. The horses tossed their heads and whinnied, but Vinnie's soft *whoa* and a slight tug on the reigns quickly steadied them.

"I didn't think you'd be home until next week," said Amelia as she pulled the woolen blanket over her lap.

"Why does everyone greet me that way?"

"And who is everyone?" asked Amelia.

"Mr. Elliot, Gray, the postmaster, and you."

"In that order?" asked Amelia.

Vinnie poked her with an elbow and changed the subject. "I received an invitation to Dunn and Elliot's New Year's Eve party."

"James and I are going, too!"

Vinnie grinned. "Oh, I see! You and James are going together."

"Well, yes, we are," blushed Amelia. "I was waiting for you to come home so I could tell you in person. Last week, on my birthday, James asked me to marry him."

"No, he didn't," said Vinnie, tugging at her friend's mitten.

"What are you doing?" Amelia said with a laugh.

"I'm checking to see... Oh my Lord! You said yes! I've never seen a pearl surrounded by so many sparkling diamonds."

At that moment, Uncle Emery approached the sleigh. "What are you two laughing about? I could hear you from inside the store."

"Amelia's getting married!" exclaimed Vinnie.

Taking the reins, his eyes filled with glee. "Who's the lucky man?"

"Captain James Sutton," replied Amelia.

"James Sutton! I thought his ship *John Bryce* just docked at South Street Seaport in New York, and he wouldn't be back for a few more weeks."

Vinnie smirked. "I guess he was in a hurry to return to Thomaston." Then she looked wide-eyed at her friend and murmured, "Did he take the train?"

Placing her boot on the snow-covered boards to climb down, Amelia smiled. "As a matter of fact, he did. And thanks to the Knox and Lincoln Railroad, he arrived home last Tuesday and asked me to marry him on Wednesday."

Uncle Emery beamed. "Captain Sutton is a lucky man! You'll have to stop by the house and show Susan your ring. She'll want to see that rosy pearl set among stars."

"I didn't know you were a poet, Mr. Payson. Thank you! May I come by tomorrow?"

Tipping his hat, he smiled. "Come around five and stay for supper. James is welcome, too."

"He's at the bank right now and he's giving me a ride home, so I'll tell him then."

Clutching the blanket with one hand, Vinnie blew a kiss with the other and shouted into the wind, "See you soon!"

At half past five that evening, Vinnie answered a knock at the door. The moment Gray stepped in, she stood on her toes and kissed him. He wrapped his arms around her and kissed her back until Aunt Susan coughed politely and called hello from the top of the stairs.

Releasing Vinnie from his embrace, Gray looked up and greeted the older woman with a cheerful "Merry Christmas!" Vinnie took his hand, knowing they had been caught in a kiss and there was no going back. Her aunt would have questions, but she would have to wait for the answers. She'd been home less than twenty-four hours and needed time to sort out her feelings and the changes that were happening all around her.

"And Merry Christmas to you, Gray."

Taking off his cap, he flashed a toothy smile. "Thank you for the basket this morning. The other sailmakers and I enjoyed your bread and jam, but I didn't share your molasses cookies. I'm not generous when it comes to cookies, especially yours."

Aunt Susan laughed, "Oh Gray, you're so charming. Let me take your coat. Why don't you and Vinnie sit by the fire, and I'll bring in a tray with some biscuits and cider. Emery won't be home for another hour, so dinner is delayed this evening. He's discussing some plans at the shipyard with Amos Walker."

"I hear they're going to start building a bark, the *Minnie M. Watts*, this spring," said Gray, handing over his coat with his cap tucked in a sleeve.

"Yes, and that's good news for everyone on the waterfront, but I'm sure you don't want to talk about work. Sit and enjoy a peaceful moment."

Easing into the Windsor chair across from Vinnie, he smiled. "I don't mind talking about work. I love what I do."

Aunt Susan paused at the doorway to the kitchen. "You do?"

"Why do you look so surprised?" he asked, shifting his focus from Vinnie to her aunt. "I'd rather work at the loft than anywhere else. The floor is dry and doesn't move, the expanse is well-lit, and the gentle noise is rhythmic. My hands are moving to make something beautiful and useful."

"Honestly, Gray," said Vinnie shaking her head, "I think you're the bard of the sail loft."

"That's all right. We admire poets in this house. Don't we, Lavinia?"

Vinnie replied, "Oh yes, Aunt Susan. Poets are magicians. They pull words out of their hat and give us wings."

"Well, I'm glad," said Gray as his neck reddened. "Perhaps I sound poetic because I'm grateful. Since Amos Walker and Thomas Dunn became partners, their shipyard on the old Knox estate has been booming. Over the last seven years, they've built almost twenty vessels, two-masters, three-masters, a barkentine, and now a bark. All that shipbuilding has sparked the sailmaking business, as well. Today, Mr. Elliot offered me a raise and made me a supervisor."

Vinnie said, "How wonderful!" and Aunt Susan echoed her excitement.

"Congratulations, Gray! Now I really should get that tray and pour some cider to celebrate."

As promised, Aunt Susan returned with her favorite black tray, stenciled with gold fleurs-de-lis, and set it on the table near the fireplace. She poured three mugs of hot mulled cider while Vinnie served Gray a small plate of nuts, raisins, and shortbread. And as soon as they all had a cup in their hand, Aunt Susan made a toast.

"May Christmas and the New Year bring many blessings."

"Especially to those we love," added Vinnie in a lilting voice.

They all reached across the table and clinked their mugs, then took a sip and leaned back to savor each other's company. Gray regaled them with stories about the sail loft, including how all the sailmakers had found Lavinia's surprise visit amusing. After she left, the men had teased him without mercy for having fallen under a pretty lady's spell. At lunch, they had emptied the gift basket and made the bread and jam disappear.

"Did they know I was the one who made the gift?" asked Aunt Susan with a smile.

Vinnie piped up. "How would they know if I failed to tell them? I'm sorry, but I wanted to make a good impression."

Aunt Susan's eyes crinkled with laughter. "Oh, sweet girl, it appears you made a very favorable impression." She took a sip of cider and shifted her gaze back to Gray.

"Have you heard from your friend James?"

"Yes, I have," he smiled. "He returned home last week after a long voyage—"

Vinnie interrupted. "I was going to tell you at dinner, Aunt Susan, but good news can't wait. James and Amelia are engaged to be married!"

"My goodness! When?"

Gray chuckled. "That's always the question when it comes to marriage. Rumor has it Captain Sutton is going to take command of a new ship. I suspect the wedding date won't be set until he knows when that ship will be ready. Foremost, he's a mariner."

Aunt Susan nodded. "I'm afraid that's true, especially in Thomaston."

"What a sobering thought," said Vinnie quietly. "But Amelia is strong and loving. She'll be a good wife."

Gray winked at Vinnie. "I'm sure she will."

"My dears, I too have some news, though I'm not sure this is the time to share it."

"Well, now you must," said Vinnie matter-of-factly.

"Yes, I'm afraid I must," sighed Aunt Susan. "Recently, I learned that Warden Rice ordered Sam Harlowe to be placed in the dog-hole for fourteen months, the longest period of time in the prison's history, for trying to escape."

As all the color drained from Vinnie's face, Gray clenched his jaw.

"Fourteen months," repeated Vinnie, shaking her head.

Gray stood up. "Men like Harlowe can do great harm. Warden Rice knows that, and so do I."

"Oh, Gray," said Aunt Susan, "I didn't mean to upset you on such a fine day."

Bowing slightly, Gray replied, "You've been nothing but kind, Mrs. Payson. Thank you for the early-morning gift and the refreshments this evening. I'd best be going now. My mother will have supper on the table at half past six, and she likes the family to sit down together for the last meal of the day."

"You're a good man, Gray, and I'm glad Dunn and Elliot appreciate you." Then turning toward her niece, she said, "Lavinia, Gray's coat and hat are on the hall tree, but why don't you show Gray that beautiful rug you're working on before he leaves."

"Of course," she said, standing and smoothing her stylish dress, the one she had bought to impress him.

In the hallway upstairs, she took his hand and said, "I'm sorry."

"For what?"

"I'm sorry Sam Harlowe's name was mentioned. I don't want to remember—"

Gray stepped closer, covered her lips with his mouth, and kissed her until she forgot everything but him. When they pulled apart to breathe, she smiled up at him and he kissed her neck until she giggled.

"We should stop."

"How I wish there was a bed up here so we could tumble into it."

Kissing his ear, she whispered, "That sounds like an indecent proposal. Besides, there isn't a bed, only a cradle."

He stepped back and echoed her last words, "Only a cradle?"

"Yes, it's in the nursery at the end of the hall, opposite the sewing room."

"But your aunt and uncle don't have any children. I mean, they don't have children of their own."

She met his gaze but didn't say a word.

"I'm confused," he added.

"My aunt suffered several miscarriages. Then when she finally managed to give birth to a healthy baby boy, he soon fell ill and died. His name was Francis. He was named after my father."

He wrapped his arms around her and held her close. "I'm so sorry."

She looked up, and he kissed her softly. "I'll wait to tumble in bed with you when I can wake up with you every morning."

The Dance

When Vinnie stepped out of the carriage, she reached for Gray, who took her gloved hand and guided her to the snow-covered street. Flashing a smile, he squared his shoulders and helped her navigate the snow until they arrived at the boards leading to the main entrance of the sail loft on Water Street. Approaching from the west, Vinnie noticed every window was glowing with candle-light, and there were sacks filled with sand and lit by candles lining the walkway from the street to the door. Guests were arriving in a steady stream, and every time the door opened Vinnie heard music—the guitar, fiddle, fife, and trumpet of Burkette's Quadrille. She squeezed Gray's hand.

"Is this real? I feel like I'm dreaming!" she exclaimed.

Gray stopped a mere ten feet from the loft and touched her cheek. He bowed his head and murmured, "It's not a dream. We're here under the stars. I love you."

Astonished, Vinnie turned her head so her lips touched his and murmured, "I would kiss you right now, except I'm certain that's the Honorable Edward O'Brien and his wife approaching us."

"No," he said glancing back. Then he stood up straight and sighed, "Of course it is."

They both turned and waved at one of the most distinguished couples in town, and Edward and Polly waved back.

Vinnie took Gray's hand, and they continued their walk toward the candlelight.

Inside, Gray helped Vinnie take off her long black coat, which opened in the back from waist to hem to allow for her bustle. As soon as her coat was off, his eyes fixed on her creamy neck and full bosom enhanced by the tight-fitting bodice of her indigo gown, and he groaned.

"Gray, behave yourself!" breathed Vinnie in a soft, mellifluous voice.

He shook his head. "How can I when you look so tempting?"

In reply, she raised her hand and touched the thick wavy hair that was falling boyishly over his brow. "You must because every shipbuilder in town is here, and they're watching."

As he hung their hats and coats on the peg, he smiled. "You're right, though resisting you tonight won't be easy."

"Nor will it be easy for me," she said, taking his arm.

"Why is that?"

She looked up and winked. "Tonight, my love, your emerald eyes are sparkling, and you've captured my heart completely."

"So, you're mine?"

"Yes," she answered. "Now would you please ask me to dance?"

His handsome face broke into a full-blown grin. Taking her hand, he led her to the middle of the floor. With all the benches pushed aside, and evergreen wreaths and swags hanging from the ship's knees and crossbeams, the sail loft had been magically transformed from a workspace to a social hall. Without missing a beat, Gray and Vinnie began to two-step about the room, smiling, laughing, and holding each other. Lost in the music and the moment, they didn't notice the other couples on the dance floor until one came up beside them.

"Look, Amelia! Is that Gray and Vinnie? Aren't they the lovebirds of Thomaston?"

Amelia laughed, Vinnie blushed, and Gray cocked an eyebrow.

"Happy New Year!" he exclaimed. Then fixing his gaze on Amelia, he added, "I hear you said yes to the dashing captain. He's a lucky man."

"Thank you, Gray, though I feel I'm the lucky one."

James shook his head and grinned. "Enough! A captain should never blush. Now, sir, may I dance with the lovely Miss Wren?"

"If she wishes," replied Gray. "And I hope Amelia will dance with me."

With an elegant curtsy, Amelia said yes. As the music slowed to a waltz, Vinnie offered her hand to James.

As they traveled around the dance floor, Vinnie started the conversation. "You must be so happy. Tomorrow we begin 1875, and before the year is out, you'll be wed and at the helm of a new ship."

"We haven't set a date yet. It's true Edward O'Brien has offered me command of his next ship, the *Belle O'Brien*, but they won't start construction on her until spring. Who knows when it will be ready to launch? Until then, I sail on whatever vessel needs me the most under the house flag of O'Brien."

"Spoken like a captain from Thomaston. You've just returned home after a year at sea. Will you take Amelia on your next voyage?"

The music stopped and James sighed. With his hand

still on her shoulder, he looked into her eyes and quietly said, "Lavinia, it's New Year's Eve. Let's celebrate tonight and worry about the waves tomorrow."

"Excuse me," said Gray in his deepest voice. "If you don't mind, I'd like to dance with my sweetheart again. After all, she arrived on my arm, and you're engaged to another."

James's dark-chocolate eyes crinkled with mischief. "You've caught us! We've been plotting to change your marital status." Taking Amelia's hand, he glanced at Vinnie and murmured, "Don't worry. He's not a horse. I'll lead him to water, and he'll drink."

She curtsied, showing off her gown's deep neckline, and murmured, "I'm counting on it."

Seizing the moment, the two couples twirled around the dance floor as if no one was watching, but they were. Lavinia Wren and Amelia Counce were two of the most beautiful young women in Thomaston, and they would influence the men they chose to marry and the places they chose to live. That night, the moon and the stars belonged to them. Anything was possible.

The war to save the Union had dramatically changed deep-sea trade, but the Yankee shipyards had survived. They were building again. On the eve of 1875, square-riggers were sailing around Cape Horn with an assortment of cargoes to and from ports on the west coast. They were carrying coal from Great Britain to the Pacific; guano from the Chincha Islands of Peru to Europe, Ireland, and England; case oil to Yokohama, Japan; wheat from San Francisco to Le Havre, France; and lumber from Puget Sound to distant ports around the world. The sailmakers of Thomaston had a reason to celebrate.

With her shoulders squared and her chin up, Vinnie danced in Gray's arms. Heeding Captain Sutton's advice, she focused on the music and the moment, not the waves of change that were forever rolling over the banks of the Georges River and her hometown.

As Gray and Vinnie prepared to leave, an hour after midnight, Vinnie noticed the warden of the prison chatting with a group of shipbuilders near the doorway, and a cold shiver traveled up her spine.

"Are you all right?" asked Gray.

"Yes," she whispered.

"I'll get our coats. I can hear the wind from here. It's going to hit us hard."

Tossing her head, she replied, "Not as hard as seeing Warden Rice over there."

Gray looked and his smile disappeared. "Don't worry. We're leaving." He quickly found their coats, and a moment later they walked out the door holding hands.

It was snowing, and even though the wind was howling, the myriad of sparkling snowflakes calmed their souls and filled them with wonder.

"I'm sorry, Gray. I shouldn't let anyone—especially Warden Rice—steal our happiness on this of all days."

"I agree," said Gray, lifting her hand to his chest. When they reached the carriage, he kissed her cheek before helping her up onto the seat. On their way up Wadsworth Street, he spoke again. "We can't right all the wrongs, but we can seek justice. I know you'll be going back to Colby in a few weeks. I'll wait for you. If you choose to work for prison reform, I'll support you."

"Oh, Gray, you are the dearest man in all the world. I love you more than I can say."

Pulling back on the reins, Gray said "Whoa" and halted his Morgan in front of her aunt and uncle's home. "Then just say yes."

"Yes?" she asked with a rising voice.

"Will you marry me, Vinnie?"

Her smiling eyes said yes, but she cupped his face in her cold hands and said the words out loud. "I will marry you, though not until I graduate."

He whispered, "I'll wait."

After sealing it with a kiss, he reached into his pocket and pulled out a ring, a sapphire set in white gold between two diamond chips. Slipping it on her finger, he said, "I should've shown you this before I popped the question. I wanted to do this right." He kissed her softly. "This ring belonged to my grandmother, Alice. She had blue eyes, too."

"It's perfect, and you did do it right."

Under the early-morning sky, they kissed again, at first gently, then passionately until Uncle Emery stepped outside.

"Lavinia! It's time to say good night or good morning. Oh, heck, it's time to come inside so I can catch some sleep."

Vinnie called back, "In a minute."

Gray jumped down and hurried to Vinnie's side of the carriage. As he helped her down, he gave her a wink. "I asked your uncle for your hand, you know."

"Did he say yes?"

"He did."

She put her arms around his neck and stood on tiptoes to peck his cheek. "I'm glad, but I would've said yes anyway, my love."

Short Days and Long Nights

The young professor, André Beaumont, a new addition to the faculty, put down his chalk and faced his class of ten students, nine male and one female. "The hourglass is empty. Read and annotate the next ten chapters for Wednesday."

Vinnie quickly put on her hat and coat, wrapped her scarf around her neck, and hurried out the door. Her four sorority sisters, the first females to enroll at Colby, wished they had registered for Professor Beaumont's Greek class, but they hadn't. Vinnie was the only female in the class, and she didn't like it. She preferred Longfellow, Whitman, and Thoreau to Socrates, Plato, and Aristotle. Furthermore, she was too in love with Gray to notice the professor's caramel eyes.

Despite the day's tedious beginning, she was determined to finish her essay on "Song of Myself," the poem by Walt Whitman that compared democracy to grass—a blade merges with many to form a resplendent field of green. With words and metaphors spinning in her head, Vinnie began to wonder what Whitman's true intent was when he published his volume *Leaves of Grass* in 1855, a mere six years before the Civil War broke out, killing thousands. Could he imagine the number of broken bodies that would cover the fields, including her father's and then her mother's?

Vinnie pulled her soft cochineal scarf over her nose and walked down the steps of Champlin Hall, one of the oldest redbrick buildings on College Street. She headed south toward her favorite place, the library nestled in the east wing of Memorial Hall—the stone building with an eighty-foot tower dedicated to the men of Colby who had given all to preserve the Union. The strong wind didn't stop her. She put her head down, cradled her books, and focused her mind on the work ahead, not the river beside her or the men behind her. Though she was usually drawn to the beauty and force of water, she rarely looked at the Kennebec because it reminded her of the Georges and home. Like the tides, she had to keep moving. If she stopped, she might fall into the abyss called *loneliness*. Though she was almost halfway through her college studies, she was undeniably homesick. She was blessed to be staying with Mrs. Knight, the kindest widow in Waterville and the owner of a grand Victorian home, but she missed her aunt and uncle and longed for Gray. Surrounded by a sea of men, she only wanted one.

"Lavinia!" shouted a voice over the roar of the wind.

Glancing over her shoulder, Vinnie saw her Sigma Kappa sister Louise Coburn rushing toward her. She stopped and called back, "Good morning!"

In a blink, Louise arrived at her side windswept and out of breath. "Why must you walk so fast?"

"Good morning, Lou. It's cold, and I want to get to my favorite seat in the library. Hurry with me!"

"I will," sighed Louise, quickening her step, "but no one would dare take your seat."

When they reached the hall, Vinnie touched the plaque beside the door as if to say *I remember you* to all the soldiers lost in war. Louise noticed and tapped it, too.

"You're a dear heart, Lavinia Wren," whispered Louise. When they stepped into the library, she gave her friend a nudge. "Look, your table and chair by the window are ready and waiting. Imagine that!"

Vinnie smiled, "Ask and you shall receive—"

"A place to work," laughed Louise.

"'Tis true, though you know the librarian will throw us out if he catches us talking. You better find your hiding spot in the stacks and avoid his wrath."

Louise shrugged her shoulders. "All right, but I'll see you tonight at the pledge ceremony. Don't forget. Come at half past seven so we can get the pins and refreshments ready. Dr. and Mrs. Hanson have been so kind to me, letting me stay in their home and letting our sorority meet in their parlor. I don't want to burden them."

"Don't worry. I'll be there. By tomorrow we'll have two more sisters. The seven women of Colby will all be members of Sigma Kappa!"

With a glint in her eye, Louise replied, "If you have your way, we'll all be working for prison reform."

Vinnie cocked her head and smiled. "Justice is a worthy cause."

"I agree. See you tonight. Wear something blue—the color of Waterville!"

At dusk, the temperature often dropped far below freezing, so Vinnie arranged to ride over to the Hanson's house with Lizzie Hoag. Lizzie's family lived in Waterville, and her father was always willing to take the ladies of Colby across town by carriage or sleigh, depending on the weather.

"Thank you, Mr. Hoag," said Vinnie, stepping out of the sleigh. "A mile isn't too far to walk, but on a night like this, your horses and sleigh saved us!"

Wilbur Hoag tipped his hat. "It's always a pleasure to help the lovely ladies of Colby. I'll be back at ten to bring you home."

"Thanks, Pa," said Lizzie with a wave as she turned toward Vinnie and grinned.

Looping arms, they walked up the granite steps to the stunning glass and mahogany door. As Vinnie knocked, she spied Louise placing evergreen branches in a white ceramic vase. A moment later, the door swung open, and the Sigma Kappa sisters rushed in shivering.

"Thank heaven, you're early," said Louise.

"Like I promised," said Vinnie with a wink. "What can we do?"

"There are two pies in the kitchen that need to be sliced. Can you get them ready, Lizzie?"

"I can do that. Where will I find the napkins, forks, and plates?"

"Next to the pies," she said, turning on her heels to face Vinnie. "Can you mix the punch?"

"Yes, but I need to know how much brandy to add."

Rubbing her chin, Louise replied, "That's a difficult question, Miss Wren, but I suggest using less than your heart desires."

"You know me too well, but I'll behave myself tonight. I want to set a good example for our little sisters."

"Please do! As soon as our *big* sister arrives, we'll set up some folding chairs in the front parlor and light the lamps."

"Aye, aye, Captain," said Vinnie snapping to attention.

Louise glanced at the grandfather clock standing like a guard in the entryway and took a deep breath. "Mary said she'd be here no later than twenty of seven. I think I'll fetch those chairs. They're in the music room."

Turning on her heels to head toward the kitchen, Vinnie replied, "Don't worry. We'll be ready when the clock strikes—"

"Seven" said a lilting voice from the doorway.

Surprised, Vinnie exclaimed, "Why if it isn't Mary Low, the first woman to enroll at Colby!"

"Oh Vinnie, you're so quick with words. You must be a sophomore."

Louise shook her head and laughed, "Did you knock?"

"No, I was having too much fun watching the two of you through the glass, but now it's time to get ready to welcome our new members. Ivy is bringing them over in Mrs. Bodfish's carriage. You know she drives a carriage better than most men."

Vinnie grinned. "At the blacksmith shop, they call her the Wild Horse Woman."

"I always listen to blacksmiths. They tend to be right," said Mary as she hung her coat up on the hall tree. "We better hurry. Ivy and the new girls will be here soon."

After the pledges took their oath to Sigma Kappa, the sisters gathered in Mrs. Hanson's dining room and helped themselves to big slices of pie and cups of hot cider or punch. While the sisters delved into cookies and Waterville drama, Mary and Vinnie stood by the fire and relished in their triumph. The sorority was growing.

Mary said, "I love to see our sisters gather near the halls of Colby, an institution that until four years ago didn't allow women to matriculate. For the first time, when I was walking here this evening, I felt the winds of change. Did you know I was born in Waterville?"

"Ayuh, I assumed you were a native because you live with your family here in town, but I wasn't sure."

"Well, it's true. Physically I haven't traveled far, but mentally I've circled the globe."

"I know exactly what you mean."

"I bet you do. Thomaston isn't all that far from Waterville, though it must seem as if it's five hundred miles away."

"At least two hundred," said Vinnie, raising her cup of punch.

"Ah yes, that's the beauty of education. It takes us further than we thought possible. Funny, I grew up skipping, running, and eventually riding along College Street, though I always felt invisible to the men who studied and taught in the ivy-covered buildings. But that feeling may soon be put to rest. This morning I learned I'm in contention for Valedictorian, Class of 1875."

"No, impossible!"

Mary laughed. "On the contrary, based on my academic performance, it's highly probable unless my mind runs away before I complete these last two terms."

"We have to celebrate. Let me tell the girls."

"No, not yet. Let's wait. I don't want to jinx my chances. Besides, I'd rather talk about you. I hear you're engaged. Will you stay the course? Will you graduate with your class?"

Caught off guard, Vinnie quickly shifted her glass of punch to her left hand and fixed her eyes on the two porcelain angels sitting on the mantle.

"Why are you hiding that sparkle on your ring finger? You can marry and still graduate."

Pressing her lips together, Vinnie nodded then dropped her gaze.

"What's wrong?"

"I wish I knew," she whispered. "I love Gray, but I'm afraid loving him will prevent me from keeping a promise."

"What promise and to whom did you make it?"

"When I was twelve years old, I made a promise to myself that I would work for justice. You see, both my father and mother died in the war. My father died on a battlefield and my mother died in a hospital tent, but they both died fighting to make life better for everyone. After my parents' deaths, my aunt and uncle took me in to raise me as their own. Except for my time at Colby, I've lived across the lane from the state prison, and whenever I hear the prison bell toll, I wonder if justice is really being served."

Mary took Vinnie's empty glass and put it on the mantle next to hers, then turned back and whispered, "You deserve to be loved. You can finish your studies, marry Gray, and work for peace and justice, too. It's all possible. Love is a gift. Receive it with a grateful heart."

Stepping closer, Vinnie opened her arms and gave her sorority sister a hug. "Thank you. I needed to hear that."

Vinnie woke to the smell of coffee and bacon. She rolled over and opened one eye to glimpse sunlight streaming through the window. It was Thursday, her morning off. With that happy thought, she burrowed deeper into her big warm four-poster bed. The knock on her door, though, prevented her from falling into another sweet dream.

"Wake up, Lavinia! It's eight o'clock and you're about to miss breakfast."

She pushed off her quilt made with blocks of lavender, pink, and white cotton, and rubbed the sleep from her eyes. "I'm coming," she squeaked in a dry, hoarse voice.

Cracking the door open, Mrs. Knight replied in a chipper voice, "Don't dawdle. You may not have class this morning, but you did mention a meeting with your advisor."

"At nine o'clock!" exclaimed Vinnie as she scrambled out of bed. "How could I forget!"

"Maybe you stayed out too late, maybe you've been burning the candle on both ends, and maybe you don't like to think about tomorrow, but tomorrow is here. Hurry up! I'll keep your breakfast warm on the stove."

"Thank you, Mrs. Knight. I'd be lost without you."

Placing her hand on the smooth banister, the mother of the house replied, "'Tis true. You'd be lost."

Before her bacon and eggs turned cold, Vinnie flew into the kitchen. Her honey-colored hair was swept up in a bun with a few strands slipping free. She was wearing a long black skirt and a white silk blouse with puffy sleeves. As soon as she said, "Good morning," Mrs. Knight, who was about to pull a tray of popovers out of the oven, stood up straight and took a deep breath.

"I hope I'm not too late," said Vinnie, looking apologetic. "If it wasn't for the smell of your coffee and those heavenly popovers, I might still be asleep. And that would be a tragedy in the making. I'm supposed to be meeting with Professor Beaumont, my new advisor, at nine o'clock sharp. Once again, Mrs. Knight, I'm in your debt."

"Nonsense! You're not too late, nor are you in my debt. You know I enjoy cooking a big breakfast. My husband always said it was the most important meal of the day. Now take a seat and I'll fill a plate for you."

"Thank you," said Vinnie, sitting down at the round oak table.

"You're welcome, dear. I have to say, you look different this morning."

"Different?"

"Yes, you look smart and…"

"And what?"

Mrs. Knight smiled, which made her eyes crinkle. "You look serene for a girl who was almost late for breakfast *and* could've been late for a meeting, as well."

"Oh, that's kind of you to say," said Vinnie, reaching for a napkin to cover her lap. "I'd like to make a good impression on my advisor this morning. My former advisor is on sabbatical, so the university assigned me to Professor Beaumont, who is also my Greek instructor, and you know I don't like Greek."

"Yes, I think I've heard you say that more than once," replied the lady of the house as she put a plate piled with eggs, potatoes, and bacon on the table. "Perhaps the new professor can change your mind. If you want to get off on the right foot, don't be late for your appointment."

"Lizzie has a class this morning, so her dad offered to take us both to Champlin Hall. We'll be warm and on time!"

"Mr. Hoag is a dear, dear man," said Mrs. Knight, setting a basket of popovers on the table. "Can I bring you some butter and jam?"

"Yes, please. I would never refuse butter and jam!"

Smiling, Mrs. Knight reached for the butter on the sideboard.

"I almost forgot..." She took two letters from the marble top and handed them to Vinnie. "I picked these up at the post office yesterday, but you were busy with the pledge ceremony..." She paused to clear her throat. "One's from Thomaston, and the other is from —"

"I'll read them after my appointment. I have to be able to focus this morning."

"I see," said Mrs. Knight, peering over her glasses. "Reading two letters from two gentlemen might cloud your judgment, especially when you're engaged to one of them."

Mapping Out a Plan

Vinnie arrived at Professor Beaumont's office five minutes early. The door was open, and her eyes swept
the room. Until recently, this had been the office of her
former advisor, who was now on sabbatical at Harvard.
Today, there was someone new sitting at the dark wal-
nut desk, which was still covered with the same stack of
books, paperweight, inkwell, and assortment of pens, but
looking oddly more inviting than ever before. Perhaps the
difference was the morning light. Someone had pulled
back the drapes that had covered the east-facing windows and tied them with white cording. Drenched in
sunshine, Professor Beaumont looked even younger than
his rumored twenty-eight years. For the first time, Vinnie
noticed his curly black hair, broad shoulders, and boyish
face. He was truly handsome. She stepped into his office
and said, "Good morning."

André Beaumont looked up. "Good morning to you,
Miss Wren. I didn't hear you come in. If you've been waiting, I'm sorry."

"Don't be sorry. I just arrived, and you're obviously
busy. I hope that's not my essay you're reading." She
blushed. "You were writing a long comment in the mar-
gin and that's usually not a good sign."

He cocked his head and laid his pen on the desk. "Please sit down, Miss Wren. Let me put your mind at ease. I wasn't reading your paper, but I'm notorious for writing long comments on every essay I read."

"That's good to know. I'll be prepared for lots of ink on the page."

He smiled and his coffee-colored eyes warmed. "Good. I think we've accomplished something already. Let's talk about your spring schedule and your plans for the summer."

Vinnie sat down, crossed her ankles, and folded her hands in her lap.

Professor Beaumont cleared his throat. "I hope I'm not being too bold, but is that an engagement ring on your finger?"

Though her cheeks turned red, Vinnie calmly said, "Yes. Why do you ask?"

"I'm surprised. Your file says you're interested in prison reform. That's not a typical ambition for a woman who plans to marry."

"My fiancé proposed on New Year's Eve, and he's willing to wait until I graduate."

"Congratulations," he said riffling through her file before fixing his eyes on hers. "Your fiancé is a smart man; you're a woman worth waiting for. I'm here to advise you regarding your studies at Colby as well as your plans for the future."

"Of course," she nodded. "What do you suggest, Professor Beaumont?"

"Well, according to the course catalogue, Colby students in the third term of their sophomore year must study Mechanics, French, specifically Dumas's *Napoleon*, English Literature, Botany, and Pneumatics. Since this is our first meeting as advisor and advisee, I don't know if you're excited about that schedule. However, I have some good news to share—"

"I certainly hope so," muttered Vinnie.

Detecting a note of sarcasm, the professor splayed his fingers on the desk. "Miss Wren, I'm about to give you some key information. Please listen to me."

Vinnie sat back.

"Sophomores in their third term are allowed two electives. I'm willing to recommend you for two advanced classes, Rhetoric and Ethics."

"Rhetoric! Ethics! That's what I *need* to study if I'm going to—"

"Work to reform our prison system?"

"Yes," said Vinnie.

The professor turned his gaze toward the window and the tides of the Kennebec. He said, "That brings me back to the ring on your finger. Miss Wren, you're a stellar student, one of five women enrolled at Colby—"

"Actually, I'm one of seven. There are two women in the freshman class. They just joined our sorority last night."

He cleared his throat. "Seven then. You're one of seven women smart enough to juggle Colby's rigorous academic schedule with outside interests. You have enormous potential. I think you could be as transformative as Dorothea Dix."

"Dorothea Dix?"

"Yes. Are you familiar with her work?"

"Yes, I'm well versed in her career. I know she was the first superintendent of Female Army Nurses. On a personal level, I know Miss Dix accepted my mother's application to become an Army nurse. My mother, Cora Wren, served in the tents with Sarah Sampson, Isabella Fogg, and Ruth Mayhew. She died of a fever in a field hospital near Richmond. Though I was only twelve years old, I came to know her sisters in nursing because they wrote to me. Mrs. Sampson even wrote to the Wiscasset Scholarship Committee on my behalf. She knew my parents were from there and felt I deserved their assistance. If it wasn't for their support, I wouldn't be here."

Professor Beaumont sat back and studied her. He noticed her heart-shaped face, long black lashes, and profoundly blue eyes. At that moment, his classically trained mind compared her to Aphrodite, and he was dumbfounded.

In silence, Vinnie lowered her gaze, folded her hands, and waited. Finally, her advisor cleared his throat.

"Rest easy, Miss Wren, I'm not suggesting you become an Army nurse. I was a senior at Bowdoin when General Chamberlain became President of the college, and I know he suffered daily from his wounds. If it was not for the skill of the surgeons and nurses in those tents you mentioned, he would have died in Virginia after the Battle of Petersburg. Your mother and father sacrificed their lives to save the Union and give us peace."

"And justice, Professor Beaumont. You can't have one without the other."

The professor leaned forward. "I agree. My father is a lawyer in Brunswick and Albert Gould is one of his dearest friends. With your permission, I'll write a letter of introduction, extolling your many talents, to Mr. Gould and his partner, Mr. Moore. I believe their law office is on Main Street in Thomaston, your hometown. Perhaps you could work for them this summer."

Vinnie blinked.

"Miss Wren?"

"I don't know what to say. That would be wonderful."

"So, I have your permission to write to Gould and Moore?"

"Yes, by all means. How can I ever thank you?"

"I'm not seeking gratitude. My goal is to help you realize your enormous potential, Miss Wren."

He took out his pocket watch to check the time then stood to signal the end of their meeting. When she rose from her chair, he offered his hand, and she shook it with a firm grip.

With a hint of a smile, he said, "You know, before Dorothea Dix became the first woman to hold an executive office in the federal government, she lobbied for better prison conditions. Her voice was heard by legislators, and her work helped to pass a relief bill in Massachusetts and nine other states, as well as two Canadian provinces. The girl from Hampden, Maine was a reformer, and I believe you are, as well."

"Thank you, Professor. I know you don't need my gratitude, but you have it anyway."

He grinned like a schoolboy. "You're always welcome, Miss Wren. I'll see you on Friday."

She turned to leave then looked back. "I'll be on time, and I'll do the reading."

"Of course. I know how much you love Homer's *Odyssey*."

His words left an indelible mark on her poetic soul.

Back at the library, Vinnie sat down in her chair, the one facing the Kennebec River, and placed her two envelopes on the ink-stained table in front of her. She studied the handwriting on both. The first was a tight, elegant script; the second, noticeably different, was neat and precise. They both made her smile, but she deliberately opened the elegant one first.

Dear Vinnie,

I'm writing to you from the offices of Gilchrist, Flint & Company at the South Street Seaport in Manhattan, and through my window I have a breathtaking view of a three-masted ship with a band of unpainted planking on the top portion of her hull, and yes, she's flying the house flag of Edward O'Brien. If *The New York Times* is correct, she's the *Alida*, the namesake of O'Brien's granddaughter; and she's resplendent in her 10,000 yards of sail. I cannot look at her without thinking of my hometown, nestled along the Georges River, and you.

When you grow up among shipbuilders, you learn at an early age that every port around the world is connected by mighty vessels under sail. The *Alida* connects me to you, and I'm grateful. On my walk to work this morning, I saw a variety of house flags flying over the ships at the dock, and I stopped to talk with the captain of a Thomaston-built ship that had just arrived from Messina, Sicily. I watched as the crew started to unload her cargo of oranges, lemons, hazelnuts, and birdseed. Looking up, I complimented the captain on his ship's fine suit of sails, and he exclaimed, "Dunn & Elliot makes the best sails I've ever seen!" Then I told him my name. He laughed and said, "I hear they make sails for Chapman and Flint, too." We talked for a long while. I told him I was born in Thomaston and spent my childhood fishing at the Crick. He mentioned that D&E has a rising star, Gray Rowley. The name surprised me, and the captain noticed. He said that Gray had recently proposed to Lavinia Wren. Then he asked me if I remembered that girl, and I replied, "Yes, I remember her well."

My dearest Vinnie, you're the smartest girl I know, and I've been around the world more than once. If the seafaring news from Thomaston is true, I beg you to wait. Before you become the sailmaker's wife, finish what you started.

Graduate from Colby, shine light on the deepest, darkest hole at the prison, and demand justice.

With love,
Charlie

P.S. I'm traveling to Bath next week to meet with John McDonald and a representative from D&E to discuss replacement sails for the W.R. Grace and a few other ships we employ in the guano trade. Unless I'm mistaken, the D&E representative is newly promoted. The maritime world is smaller than you imagine.

With the back of her hand, Vinnie wiped her tears away. She folded the letter, slipped it in the envelope, and looked out the window at the Kennebec River. Floating on waves of sweet memories, she held Charlie's letter close to her heart and considered its meaning. Those days at the creek catching frogs, skipping stones, and fishing in the morning light gave her hope and encouraged her to move forward. Charlie was indeed her first friend. He understood, perhaps better than anyone, where she came from and where she wanted to go. Most of all, Charlie recognized the importance of the journey and believed in staying the course. As a child, she always wanted to follow him. Though at this moment in time, she wondered if his way was the only way to proceed. As a man, Charlie had the freedom to fly straight like an arrow. She, on the other hand, was beginning to see her path as a series of circles leading to a happy ending, the circuitous route to a dream fulfilled.

Placing Charlie's letter on the table, she reached for the second envelope, the one with a Thomaston address written in the upper left corner. She wanted to savor it, and when she opened it, a flower fell to the table.

My darling Lavinia,

Last spring, I pressed this flower from the hawthorn tree in my mother's backyard and saved it for winter. I knew then that I wanted to marry you, though you would leave the Georges for the Kennebec again, and I would have to wait. Realizing that you would spend the coldest days of winter far away from Thomaston and me, I wanted you to have a sweet reminder of home. Since I can't give you a sunny bouquet, I hope this flower fills your heart with song until springtime comes again. When those brighter, longer days return, I'll be in Thomaston waiting for you.

The flower isn't the only gift I've pressed inside this letter. I'm sending you a second surprise, a bigger one. Do you remember Mr. Pease, the shopkeeper at the Upper Corner? I'm sure you do because you used to shop there every other day just to visit with him. He was my father's dearest friend. Though Mr. Pease has outlived most of his friends, including my father, his health is failing. He sold his store and is moving to Damariscotta to live with his daughter and her family. I'm telling you this because I offered to buy his house on Lowell Street, which may soon be Hyler Street because the town is voting to extend Lowell beyond Green to Wadsworth Street. And if Lowell runs from Knox to Wadsworth, they want to rename the street Hyler in honor of Polly Hyler, whose house is at the corner of Wadsworth and Hyler. Our town is a strange and storied place, but I love it, and I know you've always loved Mr. Pease's house, the Italianate built by Benjamin Lowell himself in the early fifties. Since then, it's been updated with an ell. Rest assured, from now until we marry, whenever I'm not working at the sail loft or sleeping, I'll be fixing up our castle. I can hardly wait to share it with you. This winter seems eternal, but at the end of May when you come home to Thomaston, we'll sit under the horse chestnut tree at 9 Lowell Street or "something" Hyler Street and count the flowers. It's a big tree so we'll be counting for a long time.

I really can't wait till spring to see you. Can you break away from your studies on a Sunday in February? Depending on the weather, I'll saddle up Shadow and ride to Waterville on the seventh or fourteenth of February. We can sit by the fire in Mrs. Knight's parlor, and I can show you my sketches of our home to be. My dad must be smiling. His best friend, Jonathan Pease, has made one of my dreams come true. When you finish your studies and we get married, we'll have a home of our own near the house where I was born and close to where we met.

May all your assignments be easy, and may all your tests go well. Until we're together again, my heart waits for you.

Devotedly yours,
Gray

As if a weight had been lifted from her shoulders, Vinnie's whole body relaxed into the hoop-back Windsor facing the river. Lost in reverie, she let the ochre-colored sheets of paper slip out of her hand to the table, which was etched with a scattering of initials. If she had had a pen knife, she would have added a heart and filled it with LW & GR, but she didn't so she closed her eyes and imagined her beautiful future.

Double the Trouble

On a sweltering Monday in August, Vinnie trudged up the dark, narrow staircase between the Thomaston Bank and the post office on the newest block in town, the C.W. Stimpson Block. Reaching the lofty second floor of the redbrick building, she wondered if justice under God was possible. She pulled a handkerchief from the pocket of her light-green dress, wiped her brow, straightened her hat, and proceeded to the door of Gould & Moore. As soon as she turned the knob, she officially started her fifth week as an apprentice. Despite the early hour, Albert Gould and Joseph Moore were already hunched over their roll-top desks in front of the tall arched windows overlooking Main Street. Though every window was open, the air was still and the heat was oppressive. At that moment, facing an eight-hour workday at a small table behind a mountain of paper and a stack of law books, she instantly missed the wind blowing off the Kennebec, the chilly recitation rooms of Champlin Hall, and the velvet voice of Professor Beaumont reading the *Iliad* aloud in mystical ancient Greek.

"Good morning, Miss Wren," said Mr. Moore, spinning his swivel chair around to see her. "I left a letter on your desk. Albert and I have already read it, but we think you should read it, too. It's from Governor Dingley."

Standing on the pumpkin pine floor under a ten-foot-high ceiling, and surrounded by an abundance of natural light, Vinnie felt fortunate to be apprenticing with two esteemed lawyers in her hometown, but she also felt the weight of their office. For the past two years, Gould & Moore had been working tirelessly to stave off the execution of two murderers found guilty of separate crimes. In March, when they received a letter of recommendation from Professor André Beaumont for Lavinia Wren, a Colby student from Thomaston interested in reforming the criminal justice system, they agreed to interview her, hoping she would assist their effort to abolish capital punishment. In June, when Vinnie arrived for the interview looking smart and bold in a gray dress with a crisp white collar and cuffs and a row of red buttons down the front, they liked her instantly, asked her a few questions, and offered her a paid position as their apprentice. Within a week, she was sitting at the oak table in the corner of the office, assisting Gould & Moore's effort to stop the double hanging of Gordon and Wagner.

"Good morning!" she said with a lilt, trying to be cheerful.

Mr. Gould looked up and nodded hello. "It's not a good morning, though."

"Oh," she said as she placed her hat on a hook and glimpsed the letter waiting for her on the corner table. "Why do I think that letter will explain the gloominess in this office today?"

"Because it will," replied Mr. Gould.

She sat down, took the sheet of paper, and focused on the governor's signature. Taking a breath, she read the two short paragraphs above it with an alarming sense of doom. When she finished, she set the letter down and closed her eyes.

Until recently, the work at Gould & Moore had filled her with hope. According to Maine law, a person guilty of murder within the state "should hang by the neck until he was dead," but only after a full year had elapsed. With statewide pressure to abolish capital punishment, Gordon and Wagner's legal counsel was able to extend one year to two years by filing appeals for a change in verdict. In the case of Wagner, Vinnie felt the appeals were justified.

Gordon had been convicted of arson and a triple murder in Thorndike. He was identified by a five-year-old nephew who survived the vicious attack and told police his uncle had struck him with an axe, though he didn't think he meant to do it. Wagner was convicted of attacking three women in their house on the island of Smutty Nose, one of the Isles of Shoals ten miles off the coast of New Hampshire, and the only one in Maine's jurisdiction. Like Gordon's nephew, one of Wagner's victims survived. She fled the house during the March 1873 attack and hid behind a snowbank. Later, she identified Wagner, and after a nine-day trial, the jury deliberated for fifty-five minutes and returned a verdict of guilty, though many of the local fishermen weren't convinced. They didn't think any man could row from Portsmouth out to Smutty Nose in the time period the defendant couldn't cover with an alibi. That sliver of doubt fueled everyone's hope, including Vinnie's, who favored "Imprisonment for Life" over capital punishment. After all, death by hanging was final, a wrong that could not be undone.

At half past five, Joe Moore stood up. "Miss Wren, it's time for you to go home. It has been a long day, and we all deserve a cool breeze and a peaceful stroll under the elms of Thomaston."

"Thank you, Mr. Moore. That cool breeze sounds wonderful, and perhaps it will help me forget…"

"Forget the letter? I wish a breeze could do that, but I know it can't. All we can do is come back tomorrow and keep searching for the best path forward."

She nodded, put on her hat, and waved goodbye.

"See you tomorrow, Vinnie! Don't forget to pick some daisies on the way home."

As soon as Vinnie stepped out of the building, she saw Gray waiting for her with a pink parasol in his hand.

Like a bolt of light, he grinned and opened the parasol. "Hello, sweet bird! Today has been the hottest day of the summer so I stopped by to check on your Aunt Susan. She told me you forgot your new French parasol, the one Amelia brought back from Le Havre, and she insisted I bring it to you."

"Oh, my word! Aunt Susan worries too much about freckles—"

"What's wrong, Vinnie?"

Her head dropped.

Wrapping his free arm around her waist, he pulled her close. "Why so glum? What happened today?"

Choking back tears, she stammered, "Governor Dingley sent Gould and Moore a letter. It's official. The governor has signed two death warrants. There will be a double hanging this fall. The date hasn't been set yet, but Gordon and Wagner will swing together for separate crimes."

"I'm sorry, Vinnie. I know you were hoping for a different decision, but your work has not been in vain, and your research has strengthened the argument for reform. Mr. Gould, Mr. Moore, and you have shed some light on a serious issue. Or should I say *injustice*?"

"*Injustice* is the right word."

"Oh, Vinnie, I'm worried about you. We lost Uncle Emery a month ago. His passing was a shock. A fatal heart attack is both merciful and cruel. For the departed, it's quick, but for loved ones left behind…"

"It steals our goodbyes and leaves us with words unspoken."

"Your uncle knew he was loved. You didn't have to say anything. No one did. Your uncle lived well, and he died with no regrets."

Pressing her face into his chest, she started to weep. When her shoulders stopped heaving, she pushed back, pulled a handkerchief from her sleeve, and blew her nose like a trumpet.

"He had one," she murmured.

"One what?"

"Regret. He told me he wished he had died instead of my father."

"Oh, Vinnie, I don't think he meant that."

"No, he did. I believe my uncle was a casualty of the war. You couldn't see his wounds, but they were there. Some soldiers die on the battlefield, speared with a bayonet, blown up by a cannonball, or peppered with gunfire. Others die slowly, haunted by the carnage. It's the survivors who suffer the longest."

He looped his arm around her shoulders and squeezed her tight. "I'll walk you home and we'll have some tea with Aunt Susan. You can talk about all the good times you shared with your uncle, and in time that's all you'll think of when you think of him. Vinnie, you and Aunt Susan made him happy. I know you did."

Commencement

On a field of green, twenty bright stars lined up in alphabetical order to pass through the arch of Monument Hall. Stirred by the sound of Beethoven's "Triumphal March," the class of 1877, robed in black, entered the gleaming white chapel of Colby University. In single file, the eighteen men and two women followed the graduate marshal up the center aisle. Vinnie kept her eyes forward, though she was fully aware that Aunt Susan, Gray, Gray's mother and sister, the Honorable Mr. Gould, Mr. Moore, and Captain and Mrs. James Sutton were all present. She walked slowly, focused on the music, and prayed her cap would stay put. At her seat, she remained standing with her classmates until the music stopped, then they all sat down together for one more lesson.

Vinnie listened serenely to speech after speech, but none of them affected her until the dean of her class took the podium. When she heard Dean Beaumont's deep, velvety voice, she thought he was speaking directly to her: "Today we gather to celebrate the class of 1877. Graduates, in a few minutes the president of Colby University will present you with the last gift of a fortunate childhood, a college degree. It's time to say goodbye to schooldays. From now on your performance will be evaluated by your family, neighbors, and God, not a professor. I urge you to follow your conscience and always be guided by love. As you embark on your separate journeys, know that our prayers and hopes for tomorrow go with you."

She blinked, and her tears escaped unchecked. As her advisor began to read the names of her classmates, *William Henry Brownson, Louise Helen Coburn...*, she remembered the day she had entered his office seeking his counsel and he gave it freely along with a kiss. In a moment of weakness, grieving the loss of her uncle, discouraged by the double hanging in Thomaston, and feeling conflicted about her future plans, she had kissed him back. Hearing the name *Lyford*, she closed her eyes and blew as if she was making a wish: Stop the memory. One kiss is not a sin. Her love for Gray was true. Soon she'd be wearing a white gown and a bridal veil.

She heard Dean Beaumont's voice say "Lavinia Wren," and Vinnie stepped onto the platform to accept her degree and shake the hand of the president, Reverend Henry Robins. As soon as she turned, her eyes found Gray, and every other thought disappeared. She raised her diploma in the air, and as the morning light touched her diamond, she imagined her future—a home filled with children and love, an upstairs office filled with law books, and a nearby sail loft with a large expanse of floor and miles of clean duck. Gray raised his arms and clasped his hands in victory. Vinnie knew for certain she had made the right choice.

An hour later, the graduates mingled with their friends, family, and mentors under a white canopy on a carpet of lush green grass between the chapel of Monument Hall and The Bricks—South Campus, Chaplin Hall, and Champlin Hall—overlooking the Kennebec River. Standing in a circle with Gray, Aunt Susan, Amelia,

James, and her other invited guests, Vinnie raised her glass and turned toward the river as if she wanted to toast its majesty.

Aunt Susan followed her niece's gaze. Then she cleared her throat, lifted her glass, and exclaimed, "The Kennebec is sparkling today, and so is Lavinia!"

Gray draped his arm around Vinnie, raised his glass, and boomed, "Hear! Hear! Lavinia Wren has received her Bachelor of Arts degree! Right now she's shimmering in Waterville, but tomorrow she'll be strolling along Water Street in Thomaston. She's coming home. Hooray!"

"Oh, stop! You're making me blush!"

He laughed. "That's the idea, my love."

She laughed, too, and that happy sound set off a wave of laughter that flowed from Amelia to James to Mr. Gould to Mr. Moore and continued until Professor Beaumont appeared.

"Congratulations, Lavinia!" he exclaimed. Then, scanning the faces around the circle, he smiled. "I'm so glad your family and friends were able to see you graduate."

Aunt Susan stepped forward. "I don't think we've met. I'm Susan Payson, Lavinia's aunt."

The professor took her hand and kissed it gently. "It's a pleasure to meet you, Mrs. Payson. I've heard so much about you. I'm André Beaumont. I was Lavinia's advisor."

"I'm sorry...where are my manners?" stammered Vinnie. "Aunt Susan, this is Dean Beaumont. He encouraged me to enroll in Rhetoric, Ethics, and classes that would further my understanding of peace, justice, and the law, and he introduced me to Mr. Gould."

"Yes, he did indeed," said Mr. Gould, extending his hand, "and I'm so glad he did! Thank you, Professor Beaumont!"

"Please call me André," said the professor with a smile as he shook the esteemed lawyer's hand.

Gray cleared his throat. "I trust you've heard about me, André. My name is Gray Rowley. I'm a sailmaker with Dunn and Elliot, and I'm Vinnie's fiancé."

The color of the professor's neck deepened, but his face remained unchanged. "Yes, of course. Vinnie's engagement ring was hard to miss, so I asked her about you."

Glancing at Vinnie, Gray folded his arms. "Really? I'm curious. What did she say?"

"I can't remember her exact words, but she told me you were smart, strong, and handsome."

Now it was Gray's neck that changed color.

André savored the moment and quietly added, "In truth, she talked a lot about you, but she left something out."

"What's that?" asked Gray, cocking his brow.

"She never mentioned how tall you are!"

Speechless, Gray stared at the professor then burst out laughing.

André bowed and Vinnie giggled, and that started another wave of laughter, which continued till the food and punch disappeared, the sun went down, and the class of 1877 had to say goodbye to the ivy-covered bricks of Colby.

Part Three
1883–1889

Love in October

At the end of October, on a crisp, golden afternoon, Aunt Susan set a tray of tea and biscuits on the table next to Vinnie's rocker and sighed.

"You've been knitting booties for the last two weeks. You must have over a dozen pairs by now."

"Thirteen to be exact. I'm too big and uncomfortable to do anything else."

"Oh, my dear, when the boys are at school and Olivia is napping, you should put your feet up and close your eyes. When your fourth little one arrives, you won't have time to eat or sleep."

Dropping the bootie and needles to her lap, Vinnie reached for a biscuit and winced. "I can't wait for this baby to come. This pregnancy has been harder than all the others combined."

"Well, maybe this will distract you," said Aunt Susan, pulling an envelope from her pocket. "It came in today's mail."

Vinnie glanced at the envelope and whispered, "A letter from Charlie?"

"Yes, his handwriting is remarkable, isn't it?"

"It is, but I'm surprised you're so familiar with it."

"Well, I am. The truth is I've always considered Charlie part of our family. He spent his boyhood with us, and he grew up to be a good man. I'm as proud of him as I am of you. Now read his letter. If you need me, just call. I'll be in the kitchen peeling apples."

Vinnie turned the envelope over and looked at the return address. Smiling, she opened the envelope, unfolded a thin sheet of paper, and read the flowing script.

Dear Vinnie,

Yesterday, I received a letter from your aunt. Don't cock that eyebrow. Susan and I have been corresponding for quite some time. Her letters are filled with news about Thomaston and family, and they never fail to brighten my day. Yesterday's letter was no exception. Your aunt told me you're expecting your fourth child. Congratulations!

I know you have always dreamed of filling every seat around your table, and now your dream is coming true. I'm so happy for you and Gray. You're building a family. May God bless you.

Sitting in my office in Lower Manhattan, I'm counting my blessings, as well. I've met someone who is willing to put up with my crazy schedule, constant travel, and thirst for adventure. Her name is Emma Kate Simmons, but she prefers Kate, and I plan to marry her. I can't wait for you to meet her. She's a composer. Can you believe it? I can barely carry a tune and can't play an instrument, but she composes music for voice and piano. She's also sweet, beautiful, and generous. I know this must seem sudden, but we've been dating for a while. Shortly after we met, I took her up the Hudson on my yacht, Gracie, and that's when I realized she is my best partner. We're both thirty-three years old, and we're ready to start our life together.

I'm sorry I didn't tell you sooner, but I've been trying to consolidate light and power, and it isn't going well. As the President of U.S. Electric Lighting Company, I'd like to join forces with Thomas Edison and C.F. Brush. Edison invented the light bulb and founded a lighting company. C.F. Brush developed an electric street lighting system and founded an illuminating company, as well. I doubt the merger will happen, but I know Kate and I will be wed on November 21, 1883.

We're planning an afternoon wedding at St. Thomas's Episcopal Church on Fifth Avenue. Kate's father died some years ago so her brother, Dr. Charles Simmons, will give her away. Her mother and my parents will be present along with close family and friends, including Mr. and Mrs. Wm. R. Grace. We'll have wonderful music and beautiful flowers, but we won't have a bridal party or a big reception. I'll have a best man, but Kate prefers to walk down the aisle without bridesmaids. It will be a New York event, though. The bride will wear a white satin gown, a tulle veil, and some diamond ornaments. The groom will provide the ornaments!

I wish you and Gray could join us on our wedding day, but you'll have your hands full with a new baby. Hopefully Kate and I will be able to visit Thomaston after the honeymoon. It's a secret, but I can give you a hint. We're headed south.

Be sure to give the newest Rowley a kiss from Uncle Charlie as soon as he or she arrives. You and your family are forever in my heart.

With love,
Charlie

Vinnie folded the letter and closed her eyes. Minutes later, Aunt Susan returned and covered her with a quilt. She was sound asleep.

Pacing by the stairs, the dog barked, and Gray snapped, "Lie down, Whit! You're not helping." The springer obeyed and Gray sat on the bottom step, rubbing the dog's ears, which seemed to soothe them both until they heard the next scream. Gray ran up the stairs two at a time with Whit at his heels, but as soon as they reached the second floor, Aunt Susan barred their way.

"The baby's coming feet first. The midwife wants you to get Doc Spear. She's doing everything she can, but it's going to be a difficult delivery. Vinnie may need—"

"I'll get 'im."

"Go quickly! Tell Amelia to take the children over to my house. I don't want them to hear this."

Flying down the stairs, he called back, "I will!" Though when he reached the kitchen, he didn't have to say a word. Amelia was buttoning up Olivia's coat, and Emery, the five-year-old, was helping his little brother, Galen, put on his boots.

"Just go," she said in a soft voice without a hint of alarm. "James has Owen and Maria at my mother's. I'll take your three over to Susan's and stay with them. Everyone will be safe and cozy. Send word when you're ready for visitors. We're all anxious to meet the newest Rowley."

"Thanks, Amelia."

As soon as he opened the door, a blast of cold air came in and he ran out, followed by Whit.

With Olivia in her arms, Amelia shouted into the wind, "I guess Whit will be going with you."

Jumping into the sleigh, Gray called back, "He's going to help me find Doc!"

As soon as Gray pulled back on the reins, the horses, Cinder and Spark, came to a hard stop in front of the rambling white house at 20 Hyler Street. Whit jumped out of the sleigh and into the snow with Gray and Doc following. Together, they ran into the house. As they ascended the stairs, Vinnie screamed. The chilling sound filled the air and struck their hearts. A terrifying hush fell over the house. Gray and Whit froze in their tracks when the doctor opened the door to the birthing room and rushed to the foot of the bed.

"Step aside, Mrs. Slocum."

The midwife moved a half-step, just enough to let the doctor spy a wondrous birth. Vinnie was on her hands and knees on the bed with the baby's legs, buttocks, and torso dangling from the womb. Mrs. Slocum, ready with a clean, white towel, said, "One more push, my dear, and your daughter will arrive."

In a blink, the baby's head slipped through her mother's cervix, and her legs and buttocks landed on the bed as if she was gently sitting down. The baby girl had a small head, and only the doctor and midwife fully appreciated the magnitude of that blessing. When the baby's legs were dangling, her head leaned back and that helped it move through the canal. If the head had been any larger, it might have stuck, and the outcome might have been different. Because Mrs. Slocum was an experienced midwife, she didn't pull on the baby's legs or interfere with the mother's pushing; rather, she encouraged Vinnie to kneel on all fours and let nature take its course. By the grace of God and the gift of midwifery, Vinnie delivered a healthy baby girl on Friday, November 23, 1883.

The next morning, Aunt Susan gingerly opened Vinnie and Gray's bedroom door and peeked inside. "Are you up for receiving visitors?"

Standing next to the four-poster bed with his baby girl asleep in his arms, and Vinnie sipping a cup of tea in the middle of a lot of pillows, Gray smiled.

Aunt Susan nodded and pushed the door wide open so Amelia could enter with Olivia, Galen, and Emery in tow.

"Good morning! We're all here to meet our November baby!" exclaimed Amelia, picking up Olivia so she could have a better look at her new sister.

Gray lowered his arms to reveal a sweet little face with a rosebud mouth, button nose, and long, feathery eyelashes.

Amelia laughed, "My goodness! Where did she get all that black hair?"

"We don't know," murmured Vinnie, "but I hope she grows up to be as pretty as her godmother, who also has dark hair."

"Her godmother?"

"Yes, Gray and I would like you and James to be Corinne Marie's godparents."

Flashing a smile, Amelia exclaimed, "I love the name! And I can't wait to tell James. I know he'll be as thrilled as I am."

Olivia squealed, "Baby."

Gray laughed out loud. "Yes, Liv, this is your baby sister. Would you like to give her a kiss?"

As Olivia reached for her baby sister, Amelia stepped closer. "Be gentle, Liv. Corinne is very little."

Olivia gently pressed her mouth against the newborn's soft, creamy cheek then giggled, "I love Cowin."

"Can I hold her?" asked Galen.

Gray cocked his head and winked. "Not yet, my little man. Maybe in a week or two, but you can touch her hand."

"Really?" said Galen, his blue eyes opening wide.

Aunt Susan chimed in, "Go ahead, Galen."

When Corinne opened her fist and closed it around Galen's finger, everyone laughed except Emery.

"Em, what do you think about having *two* little sisters?" asked Vinnie, handing her teacup to her aunt.

He bit his lip and kicked the floor with the tip of his shoe. "I think she sounds funny, and she just spit up on Papa's sleeve."

Wiping his sleeve with a cloth, Gray chuckled. "You're right, but that's easy to fix. It's not a problem. Babies spit up a lot because they're so tiny and they have trouble holding all the food they eat inside their small tummy. As they get bigger, they get better at eating. Corinne is just doing what babies do."

"Would you like to wiggle her toes?" asked Vinnie.

Emery nodded but didn't move. "I have a question."

Gray and Vinnie exchanged glances. "Ask me anything," said Vinnie, sitting up as straight as her pain would allow.

"Why are you still in bed, Mama? It's almost lunchtime, and you're still under your quilt. Are you sick?"

Not expecting such a serious question from her five-year-old son, Vinnie was rendered speechless. In that awkward moment, Corinne started to fuss, and Vinnie shifted her focus.

"I'll take her," she whispered. "I think Corinne knows it's lunchtime."

As she untied her nightdress, Gray handed her the baby. As soon as Corinne was nestled in her arm, she patted the bed. "Emery, why don't you sit beside me. We can talk while I feed your baby sister."

As Emery climbed into the big maple bed, Gray encouraged the rest of the family to retreat to the kitchen, where Amelia's mother, Madeleine, was already preparing a hot lunch. Following Aunt Susan, Gray was the last one out the door. As he closed it, he heard Lavinia's mellifluous voice, "Sweetheart, you don't have to worry about me. I'm not sick. Having a baby is a lot of work, but it's worth it. I'm tired, but all I need is a little rest. I'll be up and making lunches in no time."

"How about breakfast and dinner?"

Vinnie stifled a laugh because she knew it would hurt. "I'll be up for that, too."

Emery laid his head on his mother's shoulder and touched his sister's hand. When she opened her fist and closed it around his index finger, he smiled.

"I'm glad you'll be up soon, and I love Corinne."

Vinnie closed her eyes and leaned back on the downy-soft pillows. "I love her, too; and I love Galen, Olivia, and you just as much. My heart keeps getting bigger."

Emery scooted up in the bed, cupped his hands around his mouth, and whispered in his mother's ear, "Mama, do you think my heart will ever be as big as yours?"

She turned her face toward her son, "My darling boy, I believe that someday your heart will be bigger than mine because love grows."

Lost at Sea

On New Year's Day, Vinnie and Gray sat by the fire with Amelia and James, Madeleine and Harvey, and Aunt Susan. They raised their glasses in a toast to good health, friends, family, and many blessings, especially the blessing of children. Baby Corinne was asleep in her cradle a few feet from her mother's chair, and the rest of the children, including the Suttons' mischievous pair, were playing upstairs under the watchful eye of Lisbeth, Gray's sister. While the snow was swirling outside, the circle of friends and family inside was relishing the crackling fire on the hearth.

"I'm almost sorry to see 1883 pass by," said Harvey raising his glass of whiskey. "I was worried when Amos Walker retired three years ago, but I must say the shipyard hasn't lost its vigor. The Dunn and Elliot Company had an exceptional year, especially when you combine their shipbuilding and sailmaking revenues. If it wasn't for the loss of the *Minnie M. Watts*—"

Aunt Susan's eyes widened. "What are you talking about? Her master is Edwin Watts. She set sail for Oregon last May, and I read in the paper that she spoke off Cape Horn. Her flags reported her all well at the end of July. I know Captain Watts is sailing with his family. His son is the first mate." She took a breath and solemnly added, "His wife is a good friend of mine."

"I'm sorry, Mrs. Payson," said James, "but Harvey is right. I was at the loft this morning checking on the replacement sails for my ship, and George told me the *Minnie Watts* had been reported missing—"

Harvey cleared his throat. "As I was saying, the Walker and Dunn shipyard has continued to thrive under the leadership of Thomas Dunn and George Elliot. With the help of a good master builder, they've managed to expand the fleet and grow their business."

Shaking her head, Aunt Susan took out her handkerchief and wiped her tears. "I remember talking about the dangers of Cape Horn with my sewing circle, and one of the ladies commented on how many times the *Minnie Watts* had rounded the Horn."

"I didn't know that," said Amelia, "nor was I aware that the *Minnie Watts* had gone missing."

James, the seven-year captain of the *Alexander Gibson*, reached for his wife's hand and sat up taller on the soft green settee. "Families that go to sea know how fickle the winds can be. They know the perils of Cape Horn, and they face them over and over again. Captain Watts was a courageous Cape Horner. If *he* couldn't bring his crew and family safely home, no one could."

"I agree," said Gray, looking at his friend, "and I agree with Harvey, too. Thomas and George know how to build and grow a shipyard. From 1867 to 1880, Walker, Dunn and Company built an impressive fleet of schooners, three-masters, a barkentine, and a bark—*Minnie M. Watts*, the pride of the fleet. Now the partnership of Dunn and Elliot is getting their business ready for the next century. They're formidable men. I know because I work with them."

At that moment, Lisbeth appeared at the foot of the stairs with five little ones ranging in age from two to six.

"As some of you know, Owen and Maria received four puppets for Christmas," Lisbeth announced stepping into the parlor. "They told me they're going to bring them on their long voyage this March, the one that will take them from Boston, around Cape Horn, up to San Francisco, over to the China Sea, around the Horn again to France and England, then back across the ocean to Boston. At least that's what Owen told me. I'm shocked he could remember all that—"

Maria giggled and the parlor instantly filled with laughter. Forgetting Corinne was sleeping, James called out, "I think I'll make him my navigator!"

Corinne stirred in her cradle and the room fell quiet. Though when she didn't cry, Lisbeth continued. "The children and I have been busy creating a puppet show, and we'd like you all to come upstairs to see it."

Madeleine cleared her throat. "What's the name of the show?"

Six-year-old Owen piped up, "The Parrot—"

The chorus of Maria, Galen, and Olivia tried to chirp like birds—clicking their tongues the way Lisbeth had taught them. Emery concluded, "—the Pirate and the Lost Toys."

Springing from her chair, Aunt Susan clapped her hands as quietly as possible, not wanting to wake the baby. "Sounds like a great adventure. I love the little parrots."

With Corinne beginning to fuss in her cradle, Harvey chuckled, "I hope this show has a happy ending. I think Baby Corinne is going to be looking for a few good toys very soon."

Lisbeth smiled. "Don't worry. Maria and Olivia insisted the toys be found and returned to their owners."

"Let's go up to the 'theater'—also known as Emery and Galen's room," said Vinnie, touching her breast and stepping toward the cradle. "Corinne and I will be up in a minute. I think she's hungry."

As everyone filed upstairs, Amelia hung back to help her friend. "You don't have to stay behind to feed Corinne. My children have seen a breast before, and so have yours."

Vinnie winked. "It's not the children I'm worried about."

"The adults are familiar with breastfeeding," said Amelia, nodding toward the stairs.

"So true," she laughed, cradling her baby in her arms. "How will I survive without you?"

"And how will I survive at sea for three years without *you*? Why did I give my heart to a sailor?"

With Corinne latched to her breast, Vinnie wrapped her free arm around her friend. "You had no choice. Once a woman finds love, she gives everything to keep it."

Amelia patted the baby and smiled. "You're right, of course. Our husbands don't realize how daring we can be. We're as enterprising as Amos Walker, Thomas Dunn, and George Elliot."

"And don't forget Edward O'Brien, God rest his soul."

"How could anyone forget Thomaston's *first* millionaire? James and I owe him so much; James has been sailing under the O'Brien house flag since he was twenty. In a few months, we'll be sailing around the Horn on the *Alexander Gibson*, built on the other side of the bridge at the O'Brien Shipyard."

Moving Corinne to her shoulder, Vinnie grinned. "I think a lot of people have Edward O'Brien to thank for their livelihood. Gray and I attended his funeral. It was a ceremony fit for a king. A stately ship with a hull of white carnations, a deck of roses, masts of violets, and sails of white pinks carried the great builder of Down Easters to his final resting place. Four of his deep-water captains served as pallbearers, and others were among the six under-bearers. I'll never forget the pageantry of that spring day."

The baby burped and Amelia sighed.

"Oh, Vinnie. We shouldn't be talking about funerals in the presence of a beautiful newborn. Let's go see the show, 'The Parrot, the Pirate, and the Lost Toys.' Shall we?"

"Yes! If we hurry, we'll catch the applause."

Justice and the Ladies Library

On November 25, 1885, a chilly Wednesday morning, Vinnie heard the prison bell and shivered. She was standing at the sink peeling apples, waiting for Emery and Galen to burst through the door hungry for lunch, but the tolling stopped her. Instantly, she knew the execution was about to begin. She dropped her paring knife and Olivia started to cry. At first, Vinnie thought it was the noise, but as she bent down to comfort her, she realized little Corinne had taken her sister's rag doll.

At a quarter past twelve, like clockwork, Emery opened the door and shouted, "What's for lunch? I'm so hungry I could eat green beans!"

"I'm so hungry I could eat green biscuits," added Galen, his shadow.

In a single swoop, Vinnie picked up Corinne and gently returned the beloved doll to its rightful owner. Glancing at her boys, she said, "Wash your hands! You're not touching food until those fingers shine like the stars at night."

"Oh, Ma, why do you talk like a poem?" said Emery, spinning on his heels and heading for the sink.

As she put Corinne in the maple highchair that Gray had made for Emery's first birthday, she heard the bell again and said a silent prayer. Daniel Wilkinson, the man convicted of killing Constable Lawrence of the Bath Police Department, had been hanged.

"Me, too," said Olivia. "I want to sit in Papa's highchair."

A lock of silky hair fell over Vinnie's eyes as she turned to look at her four-year-old. "Liv, darling, you're old enough to sit in the big-girl chair. Now climb up and I'll give you a biscuit with lots of butter."

"Do I have to eat chowder, too?"

"Yes, you do," said Galen pulling out the chair next to her. "You can't just eat a biscuit for lunch. Your bones will turn to mush."

"No, they won't," said Emery with authority. "At least not right away."

Galen puffed out his chest. "Maybe not, but chowder makes you strong. Right, Mama?"

Vinnie didn't answer. The question hung in the air until Aunt Susan slipped into the kitchen.

"That's right," she said in a lilting voice. "Are we feeling happy and strong today?"

Hearing their Aunt Sue-Sue, the children giggled, and Galen jumped up and wrapped his arms around her. "Yes, we're very strong!" he shouted.

"And happy?" she pressed, looking at Vinnie.

"We're always happy to see Sue-Sue. Would you like some chowder?"

"I'd love some," she replied, taking off her coat and hanging it on a peg. "I could smell it before I opened the door."

Before Aunt Susan could sit down, Gray burst through the door. "I'm home!" he exclaimed as if he were returning from a long voyage, not a morning at the sail loft.

Vinnie pursed her lips.

"What? No kiss?" teased Gray.

"Home for lunch?" queried Vinnie. "I don't believe it."

Unwrapping his scarf, he stepped close. "Believe it," he whispered as he kissed her.

A few hours later, after the boys had returned to school and the girls had gone down for a nap, Vinnie and Aunt Susan sat in the parlor working with deft hands. Vinnie was knitting mittens for the coming winter, and Aunt Susan was hooking a new rug for Amelia and James to take on their next voyage twice around Cape Horn on the *Alexander Gibson*. Even though they were accustomed to spending a quiet hour together every afternoon, Vinnie was clearly restless. She was happy to be raising her children on land, sitting in a warm, dry house with a steady floor beneath her feet, but today she felt like a servant confined to 20 Hyler Street. Her friend Amelia had married a sea captain and spent her days crossing the ocean under sail with only the sun, moon, and tides setting her schedule. Today, Vinnie yearned for the open sea.

"If that ol' rocker moves any faster, you may fly like a bird," said Aunt Susan as she sat knitting in Vinnie's new Eastlake chair just a few feet away.

Vinnie shook her head and muttered, "I'm sorry. I'm not the best company today. If I could, I'd like to fly away."

Aunt Susan raised her eyes, framed by white brows and fine lines, and focused on her niece's face. "What are you talking about? You'd never leave Gray or the children."

Vinnie's lower lip started to tremble. Fighting back tears, she whispered, "Of course not. I love them more than anything, but—"

"But what? Is this about that darn bell?"

"I just feel as though I've failed."

"How have you failed? You have a good husband, four beautiful children, a lovely home—"

"That's all true," said Vinnie dropping her needles with half a mitten onto her lap. "I'm talking about my

Colby education. I was supposed to help Mr. Gould and Mr. Moore end capital punishment."

"You did. Two years after that ghastly double hanging, the death penalty was abolished. You helped make that happen by working for Gould and Moore while you were still enrolled at Colby. Remember?"

"Yes, but—"

"No, no buts. You were the one who opened my eyes to the possibility that a life sentence in the case of murder was better than death by hanging. Along with Albert Gould and Joe Moore, you convinced me that a man or woman could be found guilty when in fact they were innocent. By the end of seventy-six, you had convinced lawmakers that a life sentence in prison is more humane than a death sentence. It allows for an error in judgment."

"And seven years later, the death penalty was revived for murder in the first degree. This year, *three* men have been hanged. What have we accomplished?"

Aunt Susan placed her hands on the soft green fabric covering the arms of the chair and pushed herself up. Watching, Vinnie realized her once nimble aunt was aging. Her dark hair was streaked with white, the lines on her face were multiplying, her bright eyes were fading, and when she stood and made a fist, she winced. Her voice, though, was as strong and vibrant as ever.

"Lavinia, you've never given up before. Don't start now."

"I'm not giving up...I'm just tired and confused," said Vinnie, picking up her knitting. "I don't know which way to turn."

"My dear, that's an easy problem to solve. Don't turn to the right or the left. Keep moving forward."

"I'll stay the course. Don't worry," smiled Vinnie.

Her aunt gave her a wink and headed for the stairs.

"Where are you going?"

"To check on Olivia and Corinne."

Vinnie jumped up. "I'll go. You can put the kettle on and enjoy a cup of tea."

"All right, but tomorrow afternoon, when the girls are napping, I want you to visit the law office of Gould and Moore. I think you're ready to help end the death penalty *again*. When you speak with Albert and Joe, please tell them your aunt would like some prison reform, too."

With her foot on the bottom step and her hand on the newel post, Vinnie paused. "I'm not sure that's possible. Don't forget, I have four children and a husband."

"I haven't forgotten, but I believe anything is possible. Most of all, I believe in you. Maybe you can write letters from home. Of course, if you need to be in the office, I can watch the children. Since we're both members of the Ladies Library, where there's a trove of journals, books, and newspapers, I bet the ladies can help you with your research."

Vinnie's eyes opened wide. "How could they refuse? You're on the executive committee, right?"

"Yes, and tomorrow—"

Corinne let out a high-pitched wail, and Vinnie lifted her skirt to fly up the stairs. "Tomorrow we'll change the world, but today I have to console a two-year-old, and Olivia is probably awake now, too."

On Monday while the girls were sleeping, Vinnie and Aunt Susan walked to the barn.

"I expect they'll sleep for at least two hours, so enjoy the peace while it lasts," said Vinnie, leaving her aunt alone to take care of her children. "I'll be back before the boys get home from school."

"Don't hurry. I can handle the four of them. I raised *you*, didn't I?"

"Yes, that's my worry," Vinnie replied, opening the heavy barn door. "There's four of them, and there was only one of me. You're outnumbered."

"Never you mind. I'm perfectly capable of caring for my grandnieces and grandnephews."

Vinnie reached into her coat pocket and pulled out an apple for Cinder. Rubbing the stallion's smooth black neck, she smiled. "I'm joking. Sometimes I think my children behave better for you than for me."

Aunt Susan pursed her lips and paused. "That's not true. You're good with children *and* horses. Be careful riding uptown. There's a dusting of snow on the roads, and since becoming a mother, you're more accustomed to riding in a carriage than in a saddle."

"You're right, but Cinder is fast and sure-footed. I'm meeting Mr. Moore at his office in less than fifteen minutes. I have to hurry!"

"All right then. Mount up and godspeed."

Upon arriving at the Stimpson Block, Vinnie dismounted and tied Cinder to a granite post in front of the bank. She straightened her velvet hat, tucked a strand of her golden hair behind her ear, and tried to calm her racing heart. Climbing the stairs to Gould & Moore's second-floor office, she paused to reminisce. As a rising senior at Colby, she had worked here, fighting for justice while dreaming of a career in law. Reaching for the doorknob, she peered through the glass and sighed. She saw Mr. Moore at his rolltop desk and remembered the battle they had won nine years ago. Could they do it again? She knocked and let herself in.

Looking up, Mr. Moore exclaimed, "Why if it isn't Lavinia Wren!"

"Lavinia *Rowley*," she blushed.

He stood and cleared his throat. "Yes, of course. It's wonderful to see you Mrs. *Rowley*. You haven't changed a bit."

"You're kind to say that, though I assure you I've matured in every way."

He laughed and pulled up a chair for her. "May I take your coat?"

"No, thank you. I won't be long," said Vinnie as she sat on the black leather seat.

"What can I do for you, Mrs. Rowley?" asked Mr. Moore, sitting down next to her in his swivel chair.

"Well, sir, I was hoping I could do something for you."

Resting his chin between his thumb and index finger, Mr. Moore leaned back and focused on the young mother facing him. "What exactly do you have in mind?"

"I'd like to help you and Mr. Gould convince our state legislature to abolish capital punishment once and for all."

Mr. Moore dropped his hand. "So, you've heard about the botched execution?"

"I heard the bell and know Daniel Wilkinson was hanged on Friday."

Mr. Moore fixed his gaze on a red-winged blackbird perching outside his window and cleared his throat. "That's true, but the noose was tied incorrectly so the strangulation of Wilkinson took longer than necessary."

Vinnie gasped. "Oh, my Lord! How could that happen?"

"A human mistake. Though a botched hanging proves that we are all fallible. Anyone—a witness, a sheriff, a juror, a judge, or an executioner—can make a mistake. If there was ever a time to push for a life sentence instead of a death sentence, it's now."

"I'm ready. When can I start?"

"You already have. Mrs. Rowley, what about your children? Don't they need you, too?"

"Yes, they do, but my aunt has offered to help, and my husband is willing to lend a hand, as well. I'd like to work at home as much as possible. Is that all right with you?"

"It's more than all right; it's brilliant. Thank you for joining us again."

"I'll come back tomorrow to discuss my schedule," said Vinnie, standing to leave.

"Splendid," said Mr. Moore as he walked her to the door. "Mr. Gould will be here tomorrow, too. Together, we'll make a plan to change the hearts and minds of legislators."

Smiling, they shook hands and parted.

On her way home, Vinnie rode by the O.W. Jordan Building and decided to stop. The Ladies Library, a private collection of almost 3,000 volumes, was housed on the second floor in a large room with a ten-foot ceiling and tall windows. For Vinnie, it was a peaceful place filled with quiet wisdom, and today she was looking for guidance. Hopefully, her favorite librarian, who was once her teacher at Bailey School, would be at the front desk, ready to help her.

While she was tying Cinder to a post for the second time that afternoon, she heard a high-pitched voice say, "Hello," and turned to see the warden's chatty wife.

"Good afternoon, Mrs. Bean."

"You look well, Lavinia, though I must say I'm surprised to see you out riding at this hour on a weekday. Don't you have children at home?"

"I do indeed. At this hour, I have two at home and two at school."

Mrs. Bean fixed her small eyes on Vinnie, then lifted her chin as the folds of her skin moved like a jellyfish. "I suppose your aunt is watching Olivia and Corinne."

As she stepped onto the boards, Vinnie replied, "Yes, my Aunt Susan is always generous with her time. Good to see you, though I really must run. The library's my last stop."

The dour Mrs. Bean walked away, and Vinnie hurried into the Jordan Building. When she entered the library, she was relieved to find Mrs. McNeil reshelving books.

"Hello, Vinnie! I haven't seen you in a while. What brings you to my kingdom?"

Vinnie pressed her hands together, raised them to her lips, and whispered, "I need some help."

"Well, that's what I'm here for, so tell me what you need."

"I'm going to be working with the law office of Gould and Moore again. If you haven't heard, I'm sorry to be the one to tell you, but the hanging of Daniel Wilkinson last Friday was botched. The deputy sheriff, Warden Bean, the prison doctor, and a few others watched him slowly strangle to death because the noose wasn't tied correctly."

"Oh, no," Peggy gasped. "I read about Wilkinson. His conviction was in all the papers. I know he shot a constable in Bath at point-blank range, and he was sentenced to death, but I wasn't aware his execution went wrong."

"It was gruesome, and I'm determined to let people know, elicit their support, and convince our legislators that 1886 is the year to end capital punishment for good."

"How can I help?"

"Can you look for articles in newspapers or scholarly journals that illuminate how justice is better served by a life sentence in prison than a death sentence?"

"I'll start this evening. Hugh's at sea, and John, our oldest, is with him, so I have some spare time. I'm sure my twin girls will want to help, too. They're in their last year at Thomaston Academy, and they're twice as smart as I."

"That's only because there are two of them," said Vinnie, hugging her favorite teacher with delight. "I don't know how to thank you."

The librarian laughed. "You don't have to. It's my pleasure. After all, you were my best student at Bailey School, and one of the first women to graduate from Colby

University. But since we're talking about schooldays, do you ever hear from Charlie Flint?"

When Vinnie didn't respond, Peggy smiled. "I only ask because he was mentioned in the *Courier-Gazette* for the hundredth time, this time on the front page. He's joined Flint and Company, an offshoot of Chapman and Flint."

"I'm aware, though Charlie is *not* a shipbuilder. My uncle Emery used to work for Chapman and Flint when their yard was at the bottom of Ship Street."

"I remember," said Peggy, giving Vinnie her full attention.

"On their quest for riches and fame, Flint and Company became a merchant banking firm. They're interested in general merchant trade, especially in South America."

"You do hear from him then."

"A few years ago, Gray and I sent one of Aunt Susan's coveted hooked rugs to Charlie and his bride as a wedding present. After their honeymoon, they sent us a thank-you note with each of them writing a paragraph in their own hand. That was the last time I heard from Charlie, but I intend to write to him this week. I'm going to ask him to use his redoubtable talent for bringing competing groups together to help us convince the state legislature to abolish capital punishment *again*."

"That's a marvelous idea," said Peggy with a glint in her eye. "And I can't imagine Charlie saying no..."

"Really? I'm not so sure."

Peggy put her hand on Vinnie's shoulder. "Everyone in Thomaston knows Charlie would never say no to you."

Vinnie bit her lip and hurried to the door, but before turning the knob, she glanced back and murmured, "I'll write the letter, and he'll say yes...that's what friends do."

"Yes, Vinnie. That's what best friends do."

Winter

As the sun came up on the twentieth of February, a blanket of pearl-white snow covered the old Knox pasture from the prison wall to the edge of the Georges River. By noon, the hill was dotted with children, sleds, and a few daring parents. Vinnie held Corinne's mittened hand while Emery jumped on his sleek clipper with rounded steel runners. Coasting off, he shouted, "Last one down the hill is a toad!"

Racing after him, his friend Arthur cried out, "I'm not a toad!" Arthur's brother Frank sped after them with Galen on his tail.

Gray shouted, "You're flying, Galen! You can catch 'em!"

"Don't encourage reckless behavior," chided Vinnie.

Gray took her hand and smiled. "He's not in peril. He's just having fun." A split second later he pointed toward the bottom of the hill. "Look! Galen just beat Frank!"

"He's jumping up and down like a frog," she said under her breath and then laughed out loud.

Taking her hand, he pulled her close. "Ah, Mrs. Rowley, when it comes to words, you always win."

Leaning into him, she whispered, "Only because you let me, darling."

He turned and his lips brushed her cheek. "How about I give Olivia a ride down on my back, then come back for you?"

"Well, that sounds dangerous, and who will watch the girls?"

"Emery is eight years old, and he just won a big race. He can watch his sisters play in the snow for a bit while we coast on a handsome clipper."

Vinnie's face sparkled in the sun. "How could I refuse a midwinter ride with the best sailmaker in town?"

He cocked an eyebrow. "You couldn't."

As heavy clouds moved in and the temperature began to drop, Gray announced it was time to pack up and go home. Vinnie pulled Olivia and Corinne in a cozy sled with back and side rails while Gray and the boys carried their clippers to the family's sleigh. After loading the sleds in the middle, all the children climbed in except for Corinne, who was still too little to manage by herself. Though she didn't cry, she pouted when she was forced to sit in her mother's lap on the front seat. Olivia, on the other hand, squealed with delight when the only way she could fit was to sit on Arthur's lap.

"Well, did we all have fun today?" boomed Gray as he picked up the reins.

They all shouted "Yes!" in unison. When Arthur tickled Olivia, she started to giggle—which started a chain reaction until Vinnie suggested they sing.

"What shall we sing?" asked Galen.

"I know," said Frank. "Let's sing 'Row, Row, Row Your Boat.'"

They all agreed and didn't stop until Gray reined in the horses in front of the grand three-story home of George and Mary Ella Elliot.

As Olivia slid off Arthur's lap, she whispered, "Do you live here?"

Arthur replied, "Yes, this is where I live, Ten Elliot Street—ten like my age and Elliot like my name. It's easy to remember. You're welcome to visit any time."

At that moment, the boys' father, George, stepped outside and waved. "Thank you, Gray! Thank you, Lavinia!"

"You're welcome. We had a good time. See you on Monday morning!"

"I'll be there, rain or shine!"

"Your boys were angels," called Vinnie. "Thank you for letting them come."

"You can borrow them anytime," he called back.

Driving north on Knox Street, they passed Mr. Moore driving south.

"Just received a letter from Augusta!" he shouted. "Charlie Flint is changing the tide. Our wish may come true!"

If Corinne had not fallen asleep in her arms, Vinnie would have stood up. Instead, she shouted back, "Hooray!" and beamed a smile.

Though Corinne stirred, she didn't wake, and the others were too tired to notice her jubilation, except for Gray. He glanced at her and mumbled, "I guess your first love responded well to your letter."

She looked at him and softly said, "Yes, he did. Listen Gray, you won my heart fair and square a long time ago. You're my one and only."

"So, did you have fun today?"

Putting her hand on his leg, she smiled. "Oh, yes, today was a gift I'll treasure forever."

A Twist of Fate

When Gray entered the kitchen, Vinnie was fishing for the last spoon at the bottom of the sink while Aunt Susan stacked plates on the sideboard, humming "Buffalo Gals," her favorite song.

"I can't believe it's not dark yet," said Gray with a yawn. "I must have read *Five Little Peppers* five times before the girls fell asleep." He stood behind Vinnie, squeezed her shoulder, and asked, "Where are the boys?"

Wiping her hands on her frilly white apron, she gazed out the window. "They're in the barn, feeding Cinder and Spark."

"Well, since you two ladies have the kitchen under control, I think I'll join them."

"Not so fast, my darling. Tomorrow is the tenth of May, a milestone birthday for Aunt Susan. I'd like you to convince her to stay with us tonight to celebrate her sixtieth birthday from dawn to dusk. I don't want her to volunteer at the prison like she usually does on Sundays."

In a huff, Aunt Susan turned around to face them. "Why are you talking as if I'm not in the room? I can hear you plain as day."

As Vinnie stepped forward, Gray stepped back.

"I know you can hear me, but my words don't seem to get through to you. How I wish they would! You don't have to teach the female inmates how to hook a rug on your birthday, and you don't have to spend every Sunday inside that gloomy prison. Please stay with us tonight and enjoy tomorrow with family and friends."

Aunt Susan took a deep breath and exhaled slowly. "Oh, my dear, you're right. I should spend my birthday with you, though it lightens my soul to spend a few hours each week teaching the women at the prison how to make something useful. The time I spend inside those walls reminds me how blessed I am to be free."

The softly lit kitchen fell silent. When Vinnie dabbed her eyes with the hem of her apron, Gray came up beside her and placed his hand on the small of her back.

Addressing Aunt Susan, he said quietly, "The sweetest part of a birthday is being with those you love. Maybe Vinnie could go with you tomorrow morning and help teach your class. While you're there, the children and I will prepare a special lunch. Later, we'll have a party with music and dancing. I saw James at the sail loft yesterday and invited the whole Sutton family, including Madeleine and Harvey Counce. He said they'd be delighted to join us. Apparently, after rounding the Horn twice in three years, Amelia's more than ready to dance on solid ground."

Vinnie and Aunt Susan looked at Gray, then at each other.

"How can I refuse?" Aunt Susan said with a smile, "but I'm going home tonight. I sleep best in my own bed."

The next morning, Vinnie packed a basket of rug hooks, scissors, and thread, omitting her scraps of fabric because she knew the warden's office provided worn-out uniforms, and the women enjoyed ripping them to shreds.

Gray saddled Spark and brought her up to the side door. Before mounting, Vinnie rubbed the mare's white star and whispered, "You're a black beauty!"

"Don't I get a kiss, as well?" asked Gray.

She turned and kissed him on the lips.

"Be still my heart," he laughed. "I'll miss you. Don't stay too long at the prison."

"Don't worry. I won't," she replied, picking up the reins.

A few minutes later, she dismounted in the barnyard of her aunt's house on Wadsworth Street.

"Are you ready for class?" called her aunt from the kitchen door.

"Yes. It's your birthday, and I'll follow your lead."

"All right. Let's walk over then."

As they passed through the prison gate, Vinnie's face paled.

"Are you okay? You haven't been inside these walls for a long time."

"Not since the day Harlowe put a knife to my throat and threatened to kill me if I didn't help him."

Aunt Susan fixed her eyes on the carriage shop just forty yards away and whispered, "He's over there working on a buggy. I stopped at Warden Bean's house after I left your place last night, and I asked him if we could speak with Sam."

"What did he say?" asked Vinnie, coming to a full stop

"He said yes."

Shaking her head, she replied, "No, the warden would never—"

"Oh yes, he would."

Vinnie shook her head. "Why?"

"Because Sam Harlowe is still haunting you. I don't want you to be afraid anymore. If you want to stop fear, you have to face it."

Taking her hand, Aunt Susan led Vinnie over to the workshop where Warden Bean was waiting for them.

Tipping his hat, the warden said, "Good morning, ladies! I wish we were going on a picnic or down to the river to see a bark slip over the ways. Instead, we're going to see a hardened criminal."

"Hardened or reformed?" said Aunt Susan.

Opening the door, the warden gave them a half-smile. "I'm not sure, though I hope he's reformed." Then he stepped aside and murmured, "After you, ladies."

Vinnie followed her aunt. She kept her head down and her eyes fixed on the dirt floor. The workshop was noisy, but over the din she heard a gravelly voice bark an order: "Harlowe, stop what you're doing and get over here." Lifting her gaze, Vinnie saw a tall, lean man with a mop of gray hair move quickly toward them. Before he could reach them, there was a loud crash and all eyes turned to the far corner of the room where a stocky man dressed in red and black was pummeling the face of another man wearing the same red-and-black garb. The overseer grabbed Harlowe and shouted, "Guards!"

Seconds later, a group of men armed with clubs descended on the raging prisoners, but not before three others rushed the door. In the chaos, Aunt Susan was knocked hard by a fleeing prisoner. As she fell, her head hit the corner of a workbench and blood gushed from her temple, soaking her hat and streaming down the left side of her thin face.

Vinnie dropped to the floor and took her aunt's limp hand. "Aunt Susan! Aunt Susan! Can you hear me?" In a panic, she wiped the blood from her aunt's face and pleaded, "Don't die on me!" Then she looked up at the rafters and shouted, "Help!"

Using all his strength, Sam Harlowe shoved the warden and broke free, coming to Vinnie's side. He lifted her aunt and ran out the door. Once outside, he kept running with Vinnie close on his heels. The prison bell was ringing, alerting the guards of the prison break, but Harlowe wasn't in their line of sight because he wasn't running away. Instead, he was running into the infirmary and was standing at Aunt Susan's side when the doctor arrived.

"Step aside," said the doctor, moving quickly. He placed his fingers on the inside of her wrist and then on the side of her neck. He gently lifted her eyelid then closed it. "I'm sorry. She's gone," he said, turning to face Vinnie. He shook his head. "There's nothing you could have done. It was a fatal injury."

The warden, who was waiting close by, reached for Vinnie's hand. "Your aunt was a dear friend of mine, and a friend to every soul at this prison. What a tragic loss! I was going to tell you both that the state legislature voted to abolish capital punishment. I wanted to share the news on Susan's birthday as a tribute—"

Vinnie's knees buckled, but Sam caught her before she hit the floor.

Man Overboard

In April 1889, Amelia Sutton and her children stood on the dock in San Francisco's harbor and waved good-bye to the *Alexander Gibson.* Though last year Captain James Sutton and his family had made the passage to Seattle together, this year Amelia had asked if she and the children could stay behind to enjoy a few more weeks on land. James was the *Alexander Gibson's* first captain, and for the last twelve years he and his family had been rounding the Horn. This winter, however, their passage from Liverpool to San Francisco, loaded with coal, had been harrowing, so extending his family's stay in San Francisco was completely justifiable. Without a moment's hesitation, the captain procured an apartment at 627 Folsom Street, where his family would be safe and comfortable in his absence.

Maria took her mother's hand and murmured, "When will he be back?"

"Soon, sweetheart," she said, meeting her daughter's woeful brown eyes.

"Not that soon," grumbled Owen, her twelve-year-old.

"Soon," she repeated with a lilt, "about a month. In the meantime, we're going to explore every corner of San Francisco, including Chinatown."

"Can we go to one of those restaurants with a dragon above the door?" asked her nine-year-old.

"Oh, I think that can be arranged. Now, what do you say we take a ride on a cable car and visit the new Golden Gate Park?"

Owen piped up, "I'd like that very much."

"I thought you would," she smiled. "We're going to have lots of fun. San Francisco is amazing and we're lucky to be here."

Owen took her hand and tugged her arm. "Come on, let's go!"

Four weeks later, Amelia and her children were at their apartment on Folsom Street getting ready to go to Chinatown for tea and cookies at a restaurant near the Tung Foo Company, when they heard a knock.

"Good afternoon, Mrs. Sutton," said the stranger. "I'm Claude Lamont, an agent with J.W. Grace and Company, and I'm here on behalf of the company to inform you—"

"No!" she screamed.

The agent continued to deliver his message in a calm, steady voice. "Your husband was lost at sea on the twenty-second of May off the coast of Cape Blanco, Oregon, at ten after six in the morning. I'm sorry to be the bearer of such tragic news, but I have a copy of the full report taken from a representative of The Call this morning, the twenty-fifth of May."

The agent handed her an envelope and bowed his head. "I'm truly sorry for your loss. Would you like me to stay and review the details with you, or would you rather read the report on your own?"

Owen came running to her side and Maria followed, crying.

"Ayuh...prefer—"

She started to buckle, but Owen wrapped his arm around her waist, and she found the strength to keep standing.

"My children are here. You can go."

"Are you sure, ma'am?"

"Please."

The stranger put on his hat and left Captain James Sutton's family to grieve alone in a small apartment in a city they had never called home.

Hours later, after they had run out of tears and words, Owen and Maria fell asleep on their mother's bed. Amelia got up, washed her face, and opened the envelope to read the report. At first glance, she read the headers: Full Details; The Official Log; Altering the Course; Spring Overboard; A Boat to the Rescue.

"Oh, my God," she whispered, and sat down to absorb the shock of a life extinguished too soon. When her head started to clear, she turned on the reading lamp beside the chair and focused on the official log:

The Alexander Gibson *left Seattle on Saturday, May 18, 1889, at five o'clock in tow of the steam tug* S.L. Mastick. *She let go the hawser and made sail at noon the next day. When casting off the hawser, the end struck the mate's leg, causing a bad bruise which kept him off duty for twenty-four hours. During that time, the captain stood the mate's watch. At eleven o'clock on Tuesday morning, the captain began to show signs of mental weakness. He imagined there were strange persons aboard and several times opened the cabin doors to invite them in. He was quiet, not belligerent, but out of precaution the mate took charge of his gun and prepared to secure him if necessary.*

At ten o'clock Tuesday evening, the captain came on deck, altered the ship's course, and let go the weather braces.

The mate opposed his action and threatened to tie him up if he didn't go below, but the captain refused, shouting, "I'll look out for myself." The mate and his crew shut him in the cabin. He remained quiet, but at two o'clock Wednesday morning, the 22nd, he went quietly on deck, talking sensibly and in good humor, and the crew on duty thought his weakness had passed. At five o'clock Wednesday morning, he came on deck, and after standing a few minutes, went below again. At six o'clock Wednesday morning, the mate saw the captain in the passageway leading to the cabin. At ten after six, the captain took an axe from the mate's room, stepped out to the mizzenmast, made a spring on the rail, and went overboard. Only the cook saw him jump, and he immediately called out, "Man overboard!"

A boat was put over in six minutes. Pulled by three men, the boat pulled in the direction of the drowning man. They searched for fifty minutes before returning to the ship. The drowning occurred at latitude 43° 51' north, longitude 125° 15' west, the 22nd of May.

Perusing the signatures, Amelia recognized the names of the seventeen crew members, beginning with Chief Mate Henderson. She closed her eyes and started to rock, not making a sound. James had jumped and she would never know why. Was he exhausted from standing a double watch, or was it a mental illness caused by a wretched disease? If only she could talk with him one more time. If only she could touch his brow, cup his cheek, kiss his lips, feel his breath one more time. Like a ghost, she stood, walked to the bed, and lay down beside Maria and Owen.

"I must be strong," she whispered, draping her arm around her children.

Part Four
1899–1905

Through the Glass Door

At ten o'clock on a clear, cold morning, the Rowley family sat down with a few close friends at their dining room table to enjoy a late breakfast of ham, eggs, potatoes, popovers, cornbread, coffee with cream and sugar, and apple cider—the official start to New Year's Day at the Rowley house. When the last popover disappeared, Lavinia stood and started to clear the dishes.

"Please don't get up," she said. "It's the first day of 1899, the beginning of the end of the nineteenth century, and we should savor the moment."

Reaching for her hand, Gray smiled. "So why don't you sit down and let our daughters clean up?"

Amelia chimed in, "Maria can help. She's well versed in all the social graces, though she's spent the first half of her life at sea."

Maria blushed. "Mother, please. I'm almost nineteen. You're embarrassing me."

Gray gave her a wink. "Ah, Maria, your mother is just doing what every parent does. It's our job to embarrass our children, no matter how old they are." Glancing at Amelia, he paused, cleared his throat, and continued, "Of course, your mother can't take all the credit for your social grace. Your father invited many sea captains and their wives to dine with him and his family aboard the *Alexander Gibson*, and I'm sure you've inherited some of his charm. He'd be so proud of you."

With a gentle smile, Amelia said, "Thank you." She looked up at the gilded chandelier and sighed. "With every hour, I miss him more and more. What you say is true, though. Because of their father, my children observed Yankee hospitality around the globe."

She pressed the arms of her chair, leaned forward, and met her daughter's big brown eyes. "If we don't get moving, we're all going to be late for the Thomaston Public Library's grand opening."

Olivia, Corinne, and Maria jumped up. The young men, Arthur, Owen, Emery, and Galen, were about to follow their lead when Vinnie held up her hand.

"Wait! Before we leave the table, I want to tell you how much it means to share today with all of you. I pray the new year brings you many blessings. I'm excited that Owen is sailing before the mast on the *J.B. Walker* and Arthur will be sailing as first mate on the *D.H. Rivers*."

"I'm not happy about that," pouted Olivia.

Vinnie gave her a look and a hush fell over the room.

"I wish Aunt Susan was with us," said Gray, coming to their rescue. "She told me once that she was a past president of the Thomaston Literary Association and one of the founders of the Ladies Library. For Aunt Susan, a public library is a victory."

"Where exactly is our new library?" asked Owen with a glint in his eye.

"It's in the Vinal Building on the north side of Main Street," said Vinnie. We have a ten-year lease, and William Vinal is Vice President of the Board of Trustees."

Arthur Elliot, now twenty-two years old, smiled and stood up.

"Mrs. Rowley, my family and I miss your Aunt Susan.

She was kind to everyone, and my mother thought she was the best rug maker in Knox County. I bet she's smiling in heaven. Her family meant the world to her, and now she can see that you're thriving. Emery is studying medicine at Bowdoin, Galen's at Harvard, Olivia's at Colby, and Corinne told me she wants to be a nurse or a midwife."

"That's supposed to be a secret!" gasped Corinne with bright red cheeks.

"Sorry," mumbled Arthur, shoving his hands in his pockets. "I just want you all to know how important you are—"

"Stop," said Emery in his lowest voice. "We know how you feel about us, Arthur, and we know you've just returned from a long voyage, but you're on the verge of being emotional."

"Ayuh, I see what you mean," said Arthur turning almost as red as Corinne.

Vinnie's eyes swept the room before landing on Arthur. "I appreciate your kind words, and I'm certain Aunt Susan is smiling down on all of us, including you."

"I agree," said Gray. "Now let's get ready for the grand opening, shall we?"

Vinnie looked up to admire the roofline balustrade of the three-story brick W.E. Vinal Building. Then she dropped her gaze to the second floor, the home of the new library, and exclaimed, "Glory be!" Looping arms with Gray, she glanced at her children and felt a glow of happiness. They were standing with Owen, Maria, and Arthur, whose parents were there, too. It was rare to see so many townsfolk gathered on Main Street. George and Mary Ella had eight children, five sons and three daughters; their family alone could fill a small room and challenge the patience of the most seasoned librarian.

The mere thought made her wonder, *Is Thomaston ready for this library?* When she scanned the crowd, she recognized countless friends, including Peggy and Hugh McNeil with their twin daughters. Their son was somewhere in the South Pacific aboard the *Edward O'Brien*, or he would have been there, too. Despite the cold weather, families had come out to support the new library. Vinnie felt warm as toast and imagined her Aunt Susan at her side.

Just a few months ago, the taxpayers of Thomaston had voted to establish a public library with the bequest of $13,558.60 from the last will and testament of George R. Fuller. In accordance with that decision, the Ladies Library had turned over 3,469 books to seed the collection. Now, sixty-five years after the formation of the Thomaston Ladies Literary Association, Peggy McNeil, the director of the Ladies Library, and Anne Gerry, the head librarian of the Thomaston Public Library, were standing in front of the Vinal Building's glass door ready to begin the grand opening. In honor of her library service, the board had asked Peggy to say a few words before Anne cut the ribbon and opened a community treasure filled with volumes of history, art, philosophy, science, and adventure.

When Peggy turned to face her neighbors on Main Street, she was surprised to see so many grandmas warming hands in furry muffs, grandpas smoking pipes, mothers holding babies, and fathers keeping an eye on their sons and daughters. She took a deep breath, spotted her husband in the crowd, and found her voice:

"Happy New Year and welcome to the opening of the Thomaston Public Library. I feel as though I've waited half my life for this day; I suspect you feel the same. From the time I learned to read, I longed for a library, stacks of books that I could peruse in search of beauty, inspiration, and adventure. In my twenties, I taught at the Bailey School. Some of you may remember me as Miss

Catland. If you spent any time at all in my classroom, you know how much I adore books. Education is the key to our future. Can you imagine words strung together, printed on paper, bound together between two covers, pulling you through a keyhole to a place where anything is possible? If you can, I invite you all to step inside our library whenever your mind seeks light. Words may not be enough, but they're a good place to start. Today, the Thomaston Public Library will open because so many of you imagined it for decades. In truth, you did more than imagine. You worked to make it happen. Thank you to everyone who gave their treasure, talent, or both to make our library possible, especially Mr. George Fuller, whose estate provided the seed. Applause for the thousands of books donated by the Ladies Library and the library of the Monk-Humphrey House! Our town is richer today than yesterday because of you."

The crowd erupted. Hugh McNeil hooted like a schoolboy, as did Gray, and Vinnie and Amelia hugged until Mr. Vinal blew a whistle. When a hush fell over the street, he announced that Madame Librarian Anne Gerry would cut the ribbon on a count of ten. As soon as he started the countdown, the crowd joined him. Vinnie, hoping to capture the euphoria in her mind's eye, looked at her children just as Owen Sutton reached for Olivia's hand.

As Will Vinal shouted "*One!*" above the roar, Anne cut the ribbon. The hooting and hollering continued as a line formed in front of the door leading to the stairway. Then Madame Librarian put her finger to her lips and gave a familiar command: "Shh! Quiet, please! Be careful on the stairs. They're a bit too narrow for my liking, but the reading room is sunny and worth the climb."

When the crowd began to thin upstairs, Peggy walked up to Vinnie and tapped her on the shoulder. "Do you have a minute?"

"Of course," she said, holding up a pristine copy of *Uncle Tom's Cabin*, "I just peeked inside the cover of this gem. If the bookplate's correct, it's a donation from the private collection of the Monk-Humphrey House."

"A bookplate would never lie," said Peggy in a hushed voice. "That book is a gift from the Swinburne sisters, the stewards of that collection."

"Now that's what I call a treasure: a book from a mansion built by General Henry Knox, a bookbinder by trade, a patriot by calling, and America's first Secretary of War."

"Oh, Vinnie, you talk like a librarian. I had a chance to meet with Will Vinal. He told me he's thinking about hiring a few more librarians. The whole town is eager to borrow books, and the board is concerned about the workload. They fear it may be too much for one person. Ella Gilchrist is interested in working part-time and the board will probably approve her appointment, but that won't be enough. They'll need more help by summer. Would you be interested?"

Vinnie's eyes widened.

"I'd like to recommend you, Lavinia."

"I know you would, and I appreciate your confidence, but I still have some legal work to do with Mr. Moore. Warden Hillman Smith has requested a plan that would specify where Sam Harlowe would go and how he'd support himself if he was pardoned. It's quite a task considering the fact that Sam has spent more than half his life in prison."

"I'd say it's a job for Hercules."

"You'd be right," said Vinnie, "but we're determined to find some mercy. Since Albert Gould died ten years ago, Mr. Moore is even more committed to winning Harlowe's release. I'd like to see him walk out that prison gate, too. He's been incarcerated for over thirty years, and it's almost twelve years since he tried to save my aunt's life."

"I didn't realize it had been that long, though I remember Harlowe's attempted escape in the seventies when he attacked you in your aunt's home."

"Yes, that was a horrible day, but he was punished for that crime...fourteen months in the dog-hole."

Peggy gasped, raising her hand to cover her mouth.

"He was a young boy when his father went into the northern Army, and he lost his way in his father's absence. Jailed for petty theft, he killed a watchman in a fit of rage, and he's been paying for that crime ever since. For over twelve years, he's been a model prisoner. I think his good behavior has earned him a second chance."

"I see you have a lot to do, but when you're ready, I hope you join the library's staff, and I hope Harlowe is granted a pardon before he's too old to appreciate freedom. Your aunt favored mercy and so do I. If Susan has her way, heaven will intervene and Sam Harlowe will be working as a carpenter in some big city. Did you know the inmates at the prison built all our bookcases?"

Vinnie laughed. "No, but I'm not surprised!"

"Oh, Vinnie, it's good to hear you laugh. Sometimes I think you carry your aunt's desire."

"What's that?"

Folding her hands, Peggy murmured, "You want to help wherever you go."

"That's not bad, is it?"

"No, but it's exhausting," said Peggy.

Nodding, Vinnie said, "Yes." She looked past Peggy's shoulder and saw Gray waving.

"I'll think about the job, although between home and the law office I have my hands full."

Stepping to Vinnie's side, Gray tipped his hat. "Hello, Mrs. McNeil. The library looks wonderful."

"Why thank you, Gray! I think it's almost perfect. Now if I could only convince your wife to join the staff."

"How can I be of service?" asked Gray.

"Please tell Vinnie how much our library needs her."

"Oh, Peggy, you'll always be my favorite teacher," replied Gray.

The *madame librarian* tilted her head and smiled. "Coming from you, that's quite a compliment. After all, you and I had some rough days at Bailey School."

"Yes, I remember, and I'm eternally sorry."

She stepped beside him and whispered, "I forgive you, Gray." She picked up a copy of *The Adventures of Tom Sawyer* from a nearby table and turned on her heels. "I better put this one on the shelf right away. It's a favorite with the boys, you know."

Owen

Vinnie heard knocking at the door and rushed downstairs. Just as the clock started to chime, her foot landed on the carpet in front of the double doors, and she spotted Owen through the glass. It was five o'clock on the dot. Owen was definitely a chip off the old block. He paid attention to time and tides.

A few nights ago, Gray had mentioned that Owen had stopped by the sail loft to talk about the *Hattie Dunn* and her need for a new suit of sails and a second mate. After chatting for a while, he asked permission to take Olivia on a sleigh ride at five o'clock on Thursday. Now, Owen was at the door, and his Morgan stood patiently by the curb hitched to a sleek black sleigh, the handiwork of the prison's most skilled inmates.

As she turned the knob, Twain, the family's six-year-old English springer, barked a greeting.

"Good evening, Mrs. Rowley. I'm here to take Olivia on a sleigh ride."

"Yes," she grinned. "Mr. Rowley told me to expect you. Please come in."

When he took off his hat, a lock of his wavy dark hair fell into his eyes and she noticed how much he resembled his mother. She paused, remembering how Amelia had fallen in love with a mariner despite her fervent desire to marry a man who preferred land over sea.

"Your home is so cozy," smiled Owen. "The sun is gone for the day and it's getting colder by the minute. I brought an extra blanket for Liv, though."

"You think of everything, don't you?"

His mouth opened, but before he could reply, she had pulled the tassel on the bronze lamp and was headed upstairs.

"I'll get Olivia," she said, glancing back. "Why don't you wait in the parlor and keep Twain company. If you rub his ears, he'll be your friend forever."

He laughed. "I'd be happy to have him as a lifelong friend." He bent down and rubbed the dog's ears as if he meant it.

Tucked in the sleigh under an old quilt and a heavy wool blanket, Owen tapped the horse, Copper, and clicked his tongue.

"Where are we going?" asked Olivia.

"Does it really matter? I've been waiting to sit beside you all week."

"I've been waiting longer than that," she replied.

"You have?" he asked, keeping his eyes on the lane ahead.

She slid a little closer and leaned her head on his shoulder. "Yes. As a matter of fact, I thought you'd never ask my father's permission to…"

"To what?"

"To take me on an outing," she said, turning her face toward the wind and letting her hair blow across his face.

He chuckled. "Well, I did. I asked him for an hour without a chaperone. I know your dad, and he knows me, so I'll try to behave myself.

"Oh, you will, will you?"

With both hands on the reins, he steered Copper toward the cemetery, where no one would notice if they misbehaved just a little.

Next to a snowbank in the shadow of Edward O'Brien's monument, Owen said, "Whoa," hopped out of the sleigh, tied the reins around a low-hanging branch, and climbed back onto the seat. Putting his arm around Olivia, he pulled her close. She tilted her head back and they shared a kiss that bespoke their passion.

Taking a breath, Owen tucked a wisp of Olivia's silky blond hair behind her ear and whispered, "You taste sweeter than honey."

She met his eyes and teased, "You kiss like a sailor who's about to go to sea." Then she sat back and sighed, "I wish you wouldn't."

"Wouldn't what?" he asked, kissing her neck.

"Go to sea."

He paused and sat up straighter. "My maternal grandfather was one of the best ship carvers in Thomaston, and my father sailed on O'Brien-built ships for over twenty years—not to mention he was the captain of the *Alexander Gibson* for the last years of his life. I'm an Able-Bodied Seaman, but soon I'll be the second mate on the *Hattie Dunn*. If you don't want a seafaring life, I should probably take you home right now."

Feeling a chill travel up her spine, Olivia clutched the top blanket and pulled it up to her chin. "No, I don't want to go home. I want to be with you and that's my dilemma. All I do is think of you, but all you think about is coasting—taking ice from the Kennebec and Penobscot to Philadelphia, Baltimore, and Washington, then returning north to ports east of Cape Cod loaded with coal, and ready to do it again."

"That's not entirely true," said Owen, hugging her tight. "In the winter when there's no fear of hurricanes, we'll sail farther than the capital. We'll coast to Charleston, New Orleans, and Vera Cruz."

Light fluffy snow started to fall, softening the rows of tombstones and towering monuments.

"Talk to me, Liv. I think about you every morning, noon, and night." He took her mittened hand and held it on his lap. "It doesn't matter whether I'm coasting on the Atlantic or walking the boards on Green Street, you're in my heart."

She hushed him with a kiss and murmured, "Promise you'll always keep me there."

With melting brown eyes, he whispered back, "I promise."

When Owen turned the sleigh onto Hyler Street, Olivia noticed a Morgan tied to a granite post in her family's dooryard.

"Is that Whiskey?"

"I think so, and that looks like Arthur standing next to him."

"Why would Arthur be visiting my folks in a snow-storm at dinner time?"

"I don't know, but I wouldn't call this a snowstorm," mumbled Owen.

As soon as Owen said, "Whoa" and Copper came to a stop, Arthur appeared. "If you don't hurry, you'll be late for dinner," he chuckled, offering Olivia his hand.

Before she could take it, Owen jumped down, rushed to Arthur's side, and offered his hand, as well.

Olivia shook her head. "I think I can manage to step down without the help of two mates."

"Make that a first mate and an A.B.," said Arthur with a wink.

"No," said Owen, cocking an eyebrow and reaching for Liv's hand. "*Two* mates. I'm catching up fast. I'll be sailing as a second mate the next time out."

"Yeah, I can see you move fast, O, and I think you should be heading home for your supper. Unless you're dining with the Rowleys tonight?"

"No, Arthur, he's not," replied Olivia, "but he had my father's permission to take me on a sleigh ride. Not that it's any of your business."

"You're right," he shot back, raising the envelope in his hand. "I'm here to deliver some documents. When it comes to filling new orders, Dunn and Elliot relies on your father's judgment."

Fighting back tears, she stammered, "Ayuh...I'm sorry, Arthur. I know our families are close."

"They are, and I thought we were, too," he said sharply as he headed for the Rowleys' porch, leaving Olivia and Owen standing in the quiet of falling snow.

Looping his arm around her, Owen muttered, "Don't worry. We surprised him, that's all. He'll get over it."

"I hope so," she whispered, "because I choose you."

He cupped her cheek with his hand and sealed her lips with a kiss. Then he reached in his pocket and pulled out a red velvet pouch. "Will you be my Valentine, Olivia Rowley?"

She giggled. "I will."

Pressing the pouch into her hand, he brushed her lips with another kiss. "Happy Valentine's Day."

She opened the pouch, slipped out a cameo brooch, and gasped, "It's beautiful!"

He placed his hand on hers. "It was Mémè's."

"Your grandmother? This belonged to Madeleine Counce?"

"Yes, do you remember her?"

"Of course I remember her. She had luminous eyes and a crown of silver hair. I can only imagine what she was like when she was young."

He kissed her softly and whispered, "I imagine she was a lot like you."

Vinnie was halfway up the back staircase when she heard a tapping at the door. Hurrying to answer it, she wondered who would visit at suppertime. Owen and Olivia were due home any moment, but they wouldn't knock. Corinne was setting the table for four, not six. Emery and Galen were away at school. As she reached the door, Corinne stepped out of the dining room.

"Who's knocking?"

"We're about to find out," Vinnie said, catching her breath.

As soon as she opened the door, Arthur took off his hat.

"Arthur, what a surprise! Please come in."

"Good evening, Mrs. Rowley. I'm sorry to bother you… I have some papers for Mr. Rowley."

"Are you all right?"

He looked down, stomped the snow from his boots, and stepped inside.

"I'm okay. Why do you ask?"

At that moment, she looked into his brown eyes and thought of Charlie Flint. "I recognize sadness when I see it."

Handing her the envelope, he nodded. "You're a smart woman, Mrs. Rowley. My heart hurts, but the sea will cure what ails me. I haven't told anyone yet, but I've been asked to take command of the *Phineas W. Sprague*. She's a three-master docked in Boston, but next month she'll set sail for the West Indies, and I'll be on the quarterdeck. On Friday, I'm taking the train down to Boston, and I won't be back for a long time."

Standing on tiptoes, she kissed his cheek and murmured, "Congratulations, Captain, and godspeed. My family and I will miss you."

He swallowed hard, gave her a brave smile, and walked out the door.

Later that night, when the Rowley sisters were tucked under their grandmother's quilts in their matching wrought-iron beds, Corinne whispered, "Liv, are you awake?"

"Yes," she sighed, "but I wish I wasn't."

"I can't sleep. I keep seeing Arthur, standing in the hall with woeful eyes."

Rolling to her side, Olivia muttered, "What are you talking about?"

"I think you broke Arthur's heart today."

Olivia sat up as if she heard a bell ringing. "I did no such thing!"

"Oh yes, you did," said Corinne, pushing back the soft quilt and swinging her feet onto the cold floor.

With a big huff, Olivia did the same. "Why are you being so cruel?"

Sitting on their beds, they stared at each other in silence amidst the shadowy darkness until Olivia sniffled and dabbed her eyes with the edge of her quilt.

"I'm sorry, Liv, but everyone can see how Arthur feels about you, except you."

"I know. He loves me like a sister. He loves you, too. He treats Em and Galen like brothers. He cares about all of us."

Though Olivia couldn't see it, Corinne's eyes filled with tears, too. "That may be true, but he doesn't love you like a sister. You may be older and smarter than I, at least when it comes to books, but you're blind if you think Arthur loves you like a sister."

Olivia buried her face in her hands and let the tears fall. Corinne went to console her. She draped her arm over her sister's shoulders and softly said, "Unrequited love is not your fault, but it's the primary source of poetry and heart-break. I know you love Owen, and he loves you. Arthur will survive. He'll be going back to sea soon. Ma told me he's waiting to take command of a schooner."

Olivia dropped her hands. "He is?" Wiping her nose with her sleeve, she murmured, "Those three-masters sail as far as South America."

"Yes," said Corinne with a smile, "and time and tides will patch his heart. Besides, Lilla Burbank is hopelessly in love with him. He just doesn't know it yet."

Working for a Pardon

Seated at a small desk, closer to the three-quarter glass door than the tall windows facing Main Street, Vinnie looked up to see George Elliot enter the law office with his top hat in hand.

"Good morning, Mr. Elliot."

"Oh, Vinnie, please call me George. We're friends, you know."

She laughed. "Ah, but in this setting, George doesn't seem appropriate."

He laughed. "George is always appropriate. It's my name. Now, if you called me Thomas, I'd be offended."

Vinnie blushed. "I suppose you're right."

"I'm always right," he said with a wink.

Joe Moore pushed away from his rolltop desk and took out his pocket watch. "I can't believe it! You're on time. But wait, if you keep bantering with my assistant, you'll wind up late for our meeting."

George glanced toward the window and muttered, "Well, Joe, I was just being friendly. I thought I was early, but I'm always willing to hurry for my attorney. You charge by the minute, don't you?"

"Very funny, George. No need to hurry and no need to say *adieu* to Vinnie. She's been helping me with my research. I've been looking for precedents to strengthen my argument for Sam Harlowe's hearing."

"I'm not surprised," said George approaching the windows. "I know Vinnie has strong feelings about prison reform and some history with Mr. Harlowe. What can I do to help?"

Nodding toward the table and chairs near his desk, Joe said, "Have a seat. I'll show you my list."

Joe shuffled some papers, put on his glasses, and beckoned Vinnie to join them.

"If you don't mind, I'd like Vinnie to join our meeting."

"I think that's a wonderful idea."

"Let's get down to business then. You know a few members on the pardoning board, right?"

"Yes, I do, and they're good men."

"What are they looking for? I mean, what is the key to winning their approval?"

"That's easy," said George leaning forward. "They want proof that the prisoner being considered for a pardon will have a steady job and a place to stay on the outside. If you can show that Sam Harlowe has those two things, they may give him a second chance."

While Vinnie took notes, Joe muttered, "Sam needs a job and a room." Then peering over his glasses, he smiled. "I knew you'd have an answer, George. Thank you!"

"Happy to be of service. Now that we've shed some light on the matter of redemption, may we resume our friendly conversation?"

Vinnie tilted her head, and Joe tapped his lips with his index finger.

"I'll take those befuddled looks as a yes," said George with a playful wink. "Shortly before taking command of the *Phineas W. Sprague*, Arthur told me Corinne wanted to apprentice as a midwife. Is that true?"

"Yes," sighed Vinnie, splaying her fingers on the table. "That seems to be her heart's desire, though it's a hard road."

"It's a noble one, and I'd like to help. There's an excellent midwife in Warren named Mrs. Martha Slocum, and she's a friend of the family. Since she's getting on in years, I thought she'd be willing to share her skills and wisdom with someone younger. I took the liberty of speaking with her about Corinne and she'd like to meet her. If they get along, she may offer to take her on as an apprentice."

Vinnie's eyes widened. "I've heard of Mrs. Slocum, and I think Corinne would welcome a chance to meet her."

"Then she will. I'll arrange it."

"I don't know what to say except thank you. Thank you twice, once for Sam and once for my Corinne."

"No need to thank me. The Rowleys are family to me." He pointed at Joe and chuckled, "Now Mr. Moore is another story. He's my attorney, a thorn in my side!"

George stood up to leave but paused when he spied Thomas Carr through the glass door. The postmaster burst in like a stiff breeze. "Have you heard?" he shouted.

"Heard what?" asked Joe.

"The *Edward O'Brien* was wrecked off the coast of Honolulu. Just came off the wire."

"When?" boomed George.

"Twenty-seventh of February."

"And the crew?" asked Joe.

"They listed John McNeil as dead. That's all I know."

Vinnie gasped, "My God—Peggy!" Then she jumped up, grabbed her coat, and rushed out the door.

"Where is she going?" asked Thomas.

"She's going to Peggy McNeil, John's mother," said George, bowing his head.

Wedding Bells

At the end of June 1902, Amelia Sutton sat in the front parlor of her beautifully decorated home on Pine Street and started to fidget. Even though she was wearing a lapis-blue gown and her silver-streaked hair was coiffed to perfection, she looked as anxious as a schoolgirl moments before a test.

Vinnie noticed and whispered, "Every flower is in its place. Red roses in the hall, white daisies in the library, and blue lilies in the dining room. And there's Owen standing under an arch of oak leaves and orange blossoms. He sure looks handsome in his black tailcoat and white tie. Now focus on that paper wedding bell, the one that took you hours to make, and smile."

"Yes," Amelia laughed, "I almost gave up on that bell, but there it is, silver and white."

"And here we are at our children's wedding. Your son is about to marry my daughter. Who could've imagined?"

"No one," whispered Amelia, taking her friend's hand.

They waited for Helen Carr to touch the ivory keys and play Mendelssohn's "Wedding March." As soon as they heard the music, they stood and looked back to see the bridal party enter the room. First, Maria and Galen walked arm in arm to take their places up front with Owen and his best man, Emery. Corinne, the maid of honor, walked up the aisle wearing organdy over pink silk with a garniture of ribbon and lace. Finally, the bride appeared on her father's arm, sparkling in a gown of white liberty gauze over white silk and holding soft pink roses. When she reached Owen, her father kissed her and let her go. Amelia, sitting in the first row, shed a tear and wiped it away with her handkerchief bearing the monogram *JSR*.

The clock in the hall chimed nine o'clock, and the reverend pronounced the radiant couple man and wife. They kissed. Then Owen took Olivia's hand and they turned to face the assembly of guests. Everyone stood and applauded, including Arthur in the fifth and last row.

After the newlyweds dashed down the aisle and slipped out the door at the back of the parlor, Arthur took his wife's hand and kissed it. "They're the picture of bliss, aren't they?"

Standing on tiptoes, Lilla kissed her husband's cheek. "My dear, I hope they're as happy as we are."

He chuckled, "I'm not sure that's possible." Then he kissed her so everyone could see.

Lilla giggled. "Though I'd love to linger, I suppose we must venture into the library and congratulate our friends."

"Yes, let's wish them every wonderful thing."

Taking Arthur's hand, Lilla smiled. "I think this house is a lovely blessing. Your mother told me Amelia Sutton signed the deed over to her son."

"Really? That surprises me. I wonder where Amelia and Maria are planning to live."

"Well, according to your mother, who hears everything, Amelia wants to move to her childhood home on Main Street. The Harvey Counce House is a pretty Italianate just down the hill from Pine Street, but sadly it's been empty since Madeleine passed away. The timing is perfect. Amelia is ready for a change, and I bet she's hoping Olivia and Owen fill the James R. Sutton House with lots of children."

Placing his hand on the small of her back, Arthur replied softly, "Ah, yes, grandchildren are always wished for. I suspect my parents are praying for a little George and a little Mary Ella, too."

Stepping into the library, Lilla grinned, "Though we can't promise those names, we can try to make them happy—"

"Happy? Who's happy?" asked Galen, coming up behind them.

Glancing over her shoulder, Lilla blushed. "Everyone. A wedding is a happy occasion, and the Suttons' home is glowing."

"I agree! I've never seen so many candles, and the two of you look like a pair of turtle doves."

"And we're not the newlyweds."

"But you're still in love," winked Galen.

"So how does it feel to be the newest attorney in town?" asked Lilla. "I hear you've joined Mr. Moore's practice. Will he be putting your name on the door?"

"Frankly, I don't know the answer to that question. The names Gould and Moore have been on that door for as long as I can remember, and I could never replace Mr. Gould. His boots are too big to fill."

Shaking her head, Lilla murmured, "But Galen, Mr. Gould is not coming back from the dead."

He cocked an eyebrow. "I know that, but he's legendary. He fought for justice and won more than he lost. If I could achieve half as much, I'd consider myself lucky."

"And you will," said Arthur slapping his back. "Now let's congratulate Mr. and Mrs. Sutton. The reception line is shorter, and I can smell that delicious spread waiting for us in the dining room."

"So can I," laughed Galen. "But first I have to find the lady I came with."

Lilla's hazel eyes opened wide. "Who would that be?"

"I could tell you," grinned Galen, "but I prefer to show you."

"Touché," said Lilla with a smile. "We'd love to meet her."

When Owen saw that Arthur was next in line, he endeavored to hurry Mr. and Mrs. Thomas Carr and their daughter, Helen, along.

"Thank you for coming," he said shaking Thomas's hand and kissing Elizabeth on the cheek. "Thank you again, Helen, for playing the piano so beautifully tonight."

"It's my wedding gift," she blushed. She turned toward Olivia, gave her a hug, and murmured, "You're as beautiful as the golden-haired princesses we used to read about. I wish you every happiness."

Olivia squeezed her tight. "Thank you a hundred times over. Rest assured: I'll sing at your wedding!"

Helen stepped back and laughed then exited the library, making room for Arthur and Lilla.

"Why, if it isn't Captain and Mrs. Elliot!" teased Olivia, kissing Arthur on the cheek as Owen hugged Lilla. "Did tonight's ceremony stir up sweet memories of your own?"

"Yes, indeed, though it feels like we're still on our honeymoon."

"But you're not," Owen chimed in. "You're getting ready for another voyage on the *Phineas W. Sprague* while your father and his partners draw up plans for a three-master to be launched next year, followed by a pair of four-masters. And the last of the trio will be yours to command in aught four."

Arthur's back straightened. "Well, how is it a man who gave up the sea to become a cooper, and now spends his days making barrels for the lime companies, knows so much about the future plans of the Dunn and Elliot shipyard?"

As Owen's smile disappeared, Lilla took his hand and smiled. "You have a beautiful home here. I'm so happy you and Olivia will be enjoying it together."

"Yes," said Olivia, fixing her gaze on Arthur's crimson face. "I prefer dry, steady floors to the rolling deck of a schooner."

"You've always made that crystal clear," said Arthur matter-of-factly. He swallowed hard, shook Owen's hand, and leaned close to whisper, "You're the best man for Liv. I hope you can make her happy."

"You know I'll try," said Owen.

Later that evening, as guests began to leave, Emery approached his sister. Draping his arm around her, he smiled. "You make a beautiful bride, Liv. Owen is a lucky man. Tell me, what's a recent Colby graduate going to do in this big old house while her husband makes barrels for J.A. Creighton and Company?"

"Well, Doctor Rowley, I'll be working at the library five days a week. Anne Gerry asked me to apply a few months ago, and the Board approved my application last week. Apparently, the library is growing, and they need more help."

"Does mother know? I seem to remember Peggy McNeil trying to convince her to join the library staff."

Olivia took a deep breath and exhaled slowly. "I haven't told her yet, but I think she'll be pleased. She's keen on Colby women using their minds to build a strong community. I don't think she's fully recovered from the fact that her alma mater decided to create separate divisions for men and women, thereby ending coeducation on campus."

"But are you sure Mother doesn't want to work at the library?"

"Yes, I'm sure. Ma always wants to please Peggy, but when Peggy retired and then lost her son on the *Edward O'Brien*, Ma avoided the library. She told me she could still see little John hiding between the stacks. Though she spends every Saturday knitting with Peggy, she's content working for Mr. Moore during the week. In fact, she's even more of an activist for prison reform."

"Funny, it seems like every industry, including the prison, is doing well in Thomaston, except the ship-building business."

Olivia shook her head. "Don't be gloomy, Em. We have a lot to celebrate. The weather is warming, the songbirds are back, and I'm about to depart on my honeymoon."

She paused and scanned the room. "Why, my husband is standing by the door right now! He has the biggest grin on his face, and he's giving me that come-hither look."

"I see him," said Emery cupping his chin. "Galen is standing next to him with Honor Gibbons on his arm. He looks happy, too."

"Yes, he does. What do you think? Is he serious about her?"

"He's crazy if he isn't. She was at the top of her class at Harvard, and now she's a third-year at Harvard's medical school."

"Hmm. Do I detect a bit of jealousy?"

"No, I just wonder how a Boston-trained doctor feels about practicing in or around Thomaston, because our brother has no intention of leaving our hometown."

"Well, Em, that's a discussion for another day because Owen is now over there in the corner talking with Mrs. Carr and giving me that come-save-me look."

"Yes," said Emery, "that's a definite cry for help, but before you go, I have some news—"

"What?"

"Thomas Dunn is retiring."

"I don't believe it!"

He put his hand on her arm and gave it a quick squeeze, "Oh, sweet Olivia, believe it. Time and tides change, and so do we."

To Forgive or Not

On the Ides of March, 1903, heavy gales threatened every vessel on the ways. Along Water Street, shipbuilders scurried to tighten ropes, cover tools, and secure sails. Teamsters shouted "Giddy-up," attempting to get their wagonloads of coal to the lime kilns before the sky opened. It was midmorning, but darker than dusk. Gray was also urging his team to go faster, hoping to arrive at the Upper Corner on time. Pummeled by sleeting rain and worried about the meeting they were racing to attend, Vinnie fixed her eyes on his dripping nose and chin. Rain or shine, he gave her strength.

"I'm glad I wore my mackintosh. It's raining pitchforks and shovels!" she shouted into the wind. "And I'm glad we stopped to talk with George. He knows the warden and the chaplain. I wanted to hear what he thought about Sam's chances for a pardon, but I wish we'd left the loft before the storm broke."

Without turning his head, he shouted back, "Broke? That's one way to describe this fury. If Sam Harlowe hadn't broken out of prison nearly thirty years ago, we wouldn't be headed to a hearing right now."

She shook her head and water flew from the upturned

brim of her soggy boat-shaped hat. "Keep going. Remember what Aunt Susan used to say?"

"No," he boomed, "but I'm sure you're going to remind me."

"When it's dark, stay the course. There's light up ahead."

He laughed out loud. "Hold on! I think we're headed for the mouth of Jonah's whale." He hollered, "Giddy-up!"

As they approached the prison, Gray slowed the team and waved to the guard on duty. The guard, aware of the day's event, recognized Mr. and Mrs. Rowley and let them pass. After tying up the horses, Gray escorted his wife through puddles and mud onto the boards leading to the main building. When they walked into the hearing room next to the warden's office, Vinnie took off her mackintosh and shivered.

"Let me take that," said Gray, glancing at a row of pegs on the back wall. "I'll hang it with mine."

"Thank you, darling. I wish I had a dry blanket, though. I'm chilled to the bone."

Stepping closer, he murmured, "I suspect it's not the weather making you shiver."

"Don't worry," she whispered. "I'll stay the course. There's light up ahead."

Gray gave her a wink and walked off to hang up their coats.

Pausing to collect her thoughts, Vinnie focused on the five men seated behind the long oak table at the front of the room. The fate of Sam Harlowe was in their hands, and they all looked rather old. Every man at the table had a mustache hiding his lips, and four out of five had wire-rimmed glasses. Vinnie struggled to read them. Would they be merciful or damning? As she studied their poker faces, another chill traveled down her spine.

The pardoning board faced four rows of chairs divided by a broad center aisle. Warden Hillman Smith was sitting to the right of the aisle, Joe Moore was sitting to the left, and Sam Harlowe was sitting beside him. Vinnie also noticed Elizabeth Elliot Carr in the second row. Mrs. Carr, dressed to perfection, was sitting next to a silver-haired woman who Vinnie presumed was Lucy Harlowe Morgan. About a month ago, Mr. Moore had told her that Sam's sister had never given up hope that someday Sam would be granted a pardon. As one of Henry Ford's most trusted secretaries, she had managed to convince her boss to offer her brother a job at his new automobile factory in Detroit. That job might prove to be Sam's saving grace. Though no one expected a sixty-year-old woman to travel alone from Michigan to Maine, Vinnie wasn't surprised to see her sitting next to Arthur's Aunt Lizzie.

When the inspector from Augusta rapped his gavel on the oak table, Vinnie and Gray quickly took their seats behind Lizzie Carr and Lucy Morgan. Leveling her gaze on the five gentlemen at the table, Vinnie took a deep breath.

Glancing back, Lizzie whispered, "Don't worry, my dears, we have a few friends on the board."

"Yes," whispered Vinnie, "the doctor is on our side."

Lucy chimed in, "And the chaplain."

Taking her hand, Lizzie smiled, "Yes, he's also a friend."

"Don't forget Mr. Blunt, the overseer," added Gray. "He's become a strong advocate for Sam's release."

"But I'm worried about Mr. Rice," said Vinnie. "He was the warden back in seventy-four when Sam tried to escape."

"Yes, and he threw Sam in the dog-hole for fourteen months, the cruelest punishment on record—"

The presiding inspector rapped his gavel again. "Come to order!"

A hush fell over the hall, and the inspector nodded at the secretary sitting at a desk in the corner. He addressed the assembly in a stern voice. "For the record, we're here today, the twenty-eighth of February, 1903, to decide whether or not the prisoner, Sam Harlowe, convicted of murder in 1865, should be granted a pardon on the grounds of sustained good behavior for the past twenty-eight years and four months. Warden Smith, you may address the board."

"Thank you, Inspector. I'll be brief because I believe you are all familiar with Sam Harlowe's case. He has been incarcerated at the Maine State Prison for thirty-eight years. From 1865 to 1874, he attempted to escape three times; during his last failed attempt in 1874, he broke into Emery and Susan Payson's home on Wadsworth Street and held their niece at knifepoint, forcing her to supply him with clothes and money..." Removing his eyeglasses, the warden looked directly at Vinnie, sitting in the third row.

He cleared his throat and continued. "However, in 1887, while working in the woodshop under the supervision of Mr. Blunt, Prisoner Harlowe tried to save Mrs. Emery Payson from a fatal blow to the head. After teaching a rug-making class on the women's floor of the prison, Mrs. Payson and her niece were passing through the woodshop when a fight broke out. The fight was a distraction to allow some of the prisoners to escape. Though the ruse was unsuccessful, one of the inmates pushed Mrs. Payson and she struck her head on the corner of a workbench. Without a moment's hesitation, Sam Harlowe carried her to the infirmary. Lavinia Rowley witnessed Harlowe's act of kindness. She is here this morning to speak on his behalf. Though Mrs. Payson did not survive her injury, Sam Harlowe's actions that day suggest a change of heart."

Pausing again, the warden took a handkerchief from his pants pocket and wiped his brow. "I believe that since his failed attempt to escape in 1874 almost thirty years ago, Sam Harlowe has been reformed. Unfortunately, some members of the prison board do not agree with me. In fact, several retired wardens, including one here today, have written dissenting letters, and I must submit their opinions, as well."

Warden Smith bowed his head as he stepped up to the center of the long table and handed the inspector two letters. He returned to his chair and tapped his lips with his forefinger as if he wished he could say more.

The inspector examined the letters, then passed them to his left and fixed his gaze on Mr. Rice, the unhappy retired warden.

"Mr. Moore," boomed the inspector. "I believe it's your turn."

"Thank you, sir," said Joe, approaching the table with a handful of papers. "I have a dozen letters here that support the pardoning of Prisoner Harlowe. Ten of these letters were written by townspeople who've had ongoing contact with Sam Harlowe during the thirty-eight years he's been incarcerated at the state prison. The penultimate testimony is from his sister, who is present today, and the last is written in the prisoner's own hand. I submit them for the board's perusal. With your permission, I'll summarize the argument for Sam Harlowe's pardoning."

The inspector nodded. "Permission granted, Mr. Moore."

"For the past twenty-nine years, Sam has had an exemplary record of good behavior. As evidence of that good behavior, I have a letter from Mr. Blunt, who for many years served as an overseer at the prison's woodshop. Today, he is a member of the pardoning board, but in the years following Sam's attempted escape and subsequent punishment—fourteen months of solitary confinement in the dog-hole on a diet of hardtack and water, except for a good meal on Christmas—Mr. Blunt encouraged and witnessed Sam's transformation from a violent criminal to a model prisoner seeking redemption."

Handing the letter to the inspector, Mr. Moore cleared his throat. He glanced back at Vinnie and continued, "In 1874, the extreme length of time Harlowe was forced to spend in the dog-hole was deemed appropriate by the warden and the Board of Directors of the Maine State Prison. However, many upstanding members of the community pleaded for more humane treatment. Mrs. Lavinia Rowley and her late aunt were among them. I have in my hand one of many letters Mrs. Rowley has written on behalf of Sam Harlowe. Her letter is especially significant because when Harlowe breached the prison wall in 1874, he broke into Susan and Emery Payson's home and forced their niece, Lavinia, to hand over money and clothes to assist in his escape."

Once again, Mr. Moore approached the long oak table. He handed a letter to the inspector, then glanced at Mr. Rice, the former warden. "Mrs. Rowley is seated in the hall today to support the pardoning of Prisoner Harlowe, and she has asked to speak."

The inspector looked up and down the table. Seeing no objection, he nodded. "I'll allow Mrs. Rowley to address the board and all here present, but in the interest of time, do you intend to present all twelve letters?"

"No, sir, there's only one other I wish to focus on today."

"And what letter would that be?"

"The letter from the prisoner's sister, Mrs. Lucy Harlowe Morgan."

The inspector leaned forward and splayed his hands on the table. "Well played, Mr. Moore. It appears you've saved the strongest testimony for last. However, I wish to hear from Mrs. Morgan first, and then Mrs. Rowley."

"As you wish," replied the attorney.

Turning on his heels, he strode back to his seat. Before sitting down, he leaned over and whispered some last-minute instructions to his character witness.

"All right, Mrs. Morgan, this is the moment you've been waiting for. Make it worth the trip *and* the wait."

Lucy stood up, smoothed her dark-blue skirt, patted her neatly coiffed hair, and walked to the front of the room to face the five men who had the power to set her brother free.

"Good morning, gentlemen," she said in a light, airy voice.

All the men acknowledged her greeting with a nod, but only the inspector replied. "Good morning. Please state your full name and address."

"My name is Lucy Harlowe Morgan. I reside at 560 Mack Avenue in Detroit, Michigan."

"Thank you, Mrs. Morgan. Please tell us in your own words why the State of Maine should pardon Sam Harlowe, who was convicted of killing a guard at the Wiscasset Jailhouse in November 1865."

Folding her hands, she looked into the inspector's eyes and found her voice. "Sam was barely eighteen years old when he was arrested for petty theft. Our father had answered the call and joined the Union Army in sixty-one. I was seventeen years old when he left, and Sam was fourteen. Our little sisters were eleven, nine, and five. We were always hungry, and my mother and I couldn't find enough work to feed us, so Sam dropped out of school to work odd jobs that paid next to nothing. He wasn't fully grown, but he was the man of the house. I was lucky. I married an older man who worked for the railroad. I followed him to Chicago and then Detroit. Sam wasn't so lucky. He started to steal. At first, it was just apples and bread, but then he lifted a gentleman's pocket watch, and that was—"

"Mrs. Morgan," said the inspector curtly, "the board is fully aware of your brother's path to perdition. What we need to know is whether or not he's been reformed. Murder, not theft, is the crime that has put him in prison for thirty-eight years. Can you offer any assurance that he will not fall back into a pattern of violence?"

"Respectfully, I know my brother is not a murderer. He never intended to kill that jailer. Yes, he was angry, and he shoved him. He shoved him hard because that man spit in his food, pushed his face into a concrete wall, and treated him like a dog for thirty days while he waited for trial. He was a boy, not a man, when he made that mistake, but he was tried as a man six months later and he's been in prison ever since."

Mr. Moore stood up and a hush fell over the hall. "Inspector, may I speak with Mrs. Morgan for a moment?"

"Of course."

Joe walked over to Lucy and whispered in her ear. When he returned to his seat, Lucy studied the five men in front of her. She lifted her chin and squared her shoulders.

"Under the supervision of Mr. Blunt, my brother has become one of the best carpenters at the prison. Even as a boy, he was good with his hands. Over the years, Mr. Blunt has written to me periodically, telling me that Sam can repair almost anything. If it's broken, Sam can fix it. Well, I'm Henry Ford's private secretary, and Mr. Ford builds automobiles, so I asked him if he'd be willing to give my brother a second chance, a job at his new factory in Detroit—" Lucy paused to take a breath. Then she looked up with watery eyes and murmured, "He said yes."

Everyone in the hall sighed and everyone on the board smiled except for Mr. Rice.

"Thank you, Mrs. Morgan," said the inspector softly, "that will do."

As Lucy sat down, Joe Moore stood up. "With your

permission, Inspector, Mrs. Rowley would like to say a few words."

"Yes, but let's be sensitive to the hour. It's well past noon, and my stomach isn't the only one growling... Mrs. Rowley, seize the moment."

Vinnie stood up, but rather than approach the board, she turned to face the nearly thirty townspeople who, despite the red sky that morning, had pushed through the storm to attend Sam's hearing.

"You all know me, and you knew my Aunt Susan and Uncle Emery, too. I'm the college girl who was held at knifepoint by an escaped convict. I'm the young mother who accompanied her aunt to the prison to help the female inmates learn how to hook a rug and make something beautiful out of scraps of red and black prison garb. I'm the woman who has worked at Gould and Moore's law office for decades, trying to reform our prison system while helping the incarcerated find redemption and a second chance. I am wholeheartedly in favor of pardoning Sam Harlowe. He has spent almost twice as many years inside this prison as he lived outside, and I believe he deserves a second chance. If Sam Harlowe can live the remainder of his life as a free and peaceful man, we have not failed."

The hall erupted in applause, and the inspector was forced to rap his gavel repeatedly before order was restored.

"Mrs. Rowley, thank you for that moving testimony. We, the pardoning board, understand that you have strong feelings about this case. We've heard your voice loud and clear. Now we must deliberate."

Rubbing his chin, the inspector looked out at the towns-people filling the hall. "Before we adjourn, I want to remind you all that the law can pardon, but only the heart can forgive. You all have that power." He picked up his gavel and hit the table one more time. "This hearing is adjourned."

1903 Wrapped in Blue

As Corinne folded clean white sheets at her kitchen table, she gazed at the blanket of snow covering the hill outside her window and relished the quiet. Like the fabric in her hand, her house sparkled with morning light. Gazing through the glass, she stared at a grove of frosted evergreens and wondered what the morning would bring. Eight days until Christmas, and she wasn't ready. She hadn't even hung a wreath on the door yet. Closing her hazel eyes, she took a deep breath and let it go, feeling oddly content. Tomorrow she'd cut some boughs and decorate.

In November, Martha Slocum, a widow for twenty years and a midwife for more than half a century, had been forced to retire because her eyesight was failing. To avoid making costly mistakes, she decided to pass her practice on to Corinne, her capable apprentice, and move to Massachusetts to live with her sister. Before leaving, though, she gave her neat little cape to the only midwife in a three-town radius. Yesterday, December 16th, had been Corinne's trial by fire. From one sunrise to the next, she had helped to bring three babies into the world. Over the hill in Warren, the first baby, a girl, slipped out at dawn without a hiccup; in Cushing, the second sweet girl was pushed into the world with great distress at half past four; at dusk, the promise of a third little miracle brought the new midwife galloping back to Thomaston, though the babe didn't arrive till after midnight. And when she caught that baby boy, Corinne murmured, "Thank you, God," then silently thanked Mrs. Slocum for teaching her how to manipulate an infant who appears to be stuck and needs a little encouragement.

Vinnie knocked. Without waiting, she opened the door and called her daughter's name, "Corinne…Corinne, honey…are you home?"

Her mother's mellifluous voice drifted into the kitchen and pulled Corinne out of her morning reverie. "Ma?" she called back.

Stepping into the kitchen, her mother smiled. "Yes, it's me. I've come to check on you. Rumors are flying around town. Is it true?"

Corinne blinked as if waking from a winter's dream. "What's true?"

"Did Lilla have a baby boy last night?"

"News really does travel fast around here," replied Corinne, placing the folded sheet on top of the stack in front of her.

"Yes," said Vinnie. "Everyone knows it was a difficult delivery. I can't believe you've been on your own for just a month or two and you helped Lilla through her first travail."

"I wasn't alone, Mama. Lilla showed great resolve, and her mother-in-law was there, too. I was lucky to have Mary Ella in the room. After all, she did birth eight children. Arthur's number four, right?"

"Yes, he's the fourth child, third son. Now the captain has a son of his own. He must be overjoyed this morning. Have they decided on a name?"

"Oh yes, they were ready. His name is John Edward."

Tapping her lips with the tip of her finger, Vinnie's eyes twinkled. "That's a good, strong name, though I bet they call him Edward."

"How did you guess?"

"I know Captain Arthur. He's devoted to his family and Thomaston. His great-grandfather was named John, so that's a family name."

"But it was Arthur who told me they would call the baby Edward."

"I'm not surprised," said Vinnie, taking her daughter's hand. "Follow me into your front room and I'll show you."

Standing at one of the north-facing windows on the east side of the house, Vinnie pulled back the lace curtain and touched the glass. "Honey, your house sits up here on Browns' Hill, also known as Brooklyn Heights. It has a clear view of the Burgess O'Brien shipyard, which has borne the name O'Brien in several forms, O'Brien and Watts, Edward O'Brien, and Burgess O'Brien. Arthur always admired Edward O'Brien, and so did his father. Edward is a good name for a boy from Thomaston."

Corinne looked out at the snow-covered bank leading to the river and sighed. "I hope there are always shipyards along the Georges, and that there are always plenty of men to build strong vessels and sail them up and down the coast, around the Horn and up to Puget Sound, or across the Pacific to the China Sea."

"I do, too," said Vinnie, putting her arm around her daughter. "I do, too."

As the sun disappeared behind her, Corinne spurred Lincoln to a canter. She passed the sail loft heading up Elliot Street to George and Mary Ella's gleaming Italianate with its black ironwork and fancy brackets. Corinne hurried to get there because she was hoping to check on Lilla and the baby before the family sat down for dinner. She was expecting a crowd.

Imagining John Edward asleep in his cradle with his mother, father, and extended family cooing around him, she smiled behind her plaid scarf. She wondered how long it would take for everyone to call the little one Teddy. Eventually he would grow into his given name, but for now he was definitely a Teddy.

When she arrived at the back of the house, the barn doors were open, so she dismounted, led Lincoln into an empty stall, grabbed her medicine bag, and walked around to the front door. After just two knocks, Mary Ella answered.

"Oh, Corinne, we've been expecting you. And by *we*, I mean a bunch of Elliots! Come in. Let me take your coat."

"Thank you, Mrs. Elliot. I hope I'm not interrupting dinner, but I do need to examine Lilla and Edward. It was a difficult delivery."

"Indeed, though we've been celebrating the happy ending all day. And Teddy is perfect!"

"I've been calling him Teddy, too."

Mary Ella laughed. "We all are. He's such a little bag of sugar. The nickname suits him. He's our Teddy to love. We're all so grateful you were here to help with his special delivery."

Stamping her feet on the rug braided with scraps of blue, rose, and black fabric, Corinne shook her head. "No need to thank me. Lilla did all the work. How is she this evening?"

"She's still hurting from her travail, but she's been sleeping when Teddy sleeps, and that's brought some color to her cheeks."

"Sleep is good," said Corinne, glancing right into the parlor then left into the sitting room. Seeing both empty, she cocked an eyebrow. "Where's Arthur and the rest of the family?"

1903 Wrapped in Blue

"Follow me. I'm the old hoot who knows everything, especially the whereabouts of my children and newest grandchild."

Placing her hand on the beautifully carved newel post, Corinne smiled. "Lead the way *Nana*. I'm here to see Teddy, his mama, papa, bumpa, aunts, uncles, and cousins so I can report you all well!"

Without glancing back, Mary Ella replied, "Of all the signals *Bumpa* and I know, that's the one we love the most."

"What signal is that?"

"Report me all well," said Mary Ella.

Upstairs, Arthur greeted Corinne with a quick hug and ushered her down the hall to the rooms that he and Lilla were planning to occupy until they found a suitable place of their own. As soon as they stepped into the sitting room, which opened up to a large south-facing bedroom, Ida, Aunt Lizzie, and Cousin Helen swarmed around them, buzzing like honeybees.

"Whoa!" said Corinne as if she were reining in her Morgan after a wild ride. "One at a time, please."

Ida asked, "Have you seen Teddy? He's so sweet! He smells like a buttercup, except when he—"

"Yes, yes I know, Ida. I was here last night, remember?"

"Of course," replied Ida in a whisper. "How could anyone forget? I was sitting downstairs in the front parlor the whole time, and—"

Resting his hand on his sister's shoulder, Arthur spoke up. "Corinne is here to visit with Lilla and Teddy, not us. Let's give them a little peace and quiet, shall we?"

Instantly, the honeybees stopped buzzing and swiftly cleared a path, allowing the midwife to see the mother and baby entrusted in her care. With a gentle smile, Corinne walked over to Lilla, who was sitting up in a four-poster bed, looking like a queen holding her prince, wrapped in blue.

While peeking at the baby, she took Lilla's hand and softly asked, "How's sweet Teddy's mother feeling today?"

Lilla smiled, "I'm feeling better than yesterday."

"I can see that," said Corinne, placing her left hand on Lilla's forehead. "You don't have a temperature and your cheeks are nice and pink. There's no sign of an infection."

"That's good news, right?" murmured Lilla.

"Yes, and the best news is that Teddy looks content, as well."

Leaning back into her downy pillows, Lilla's eyes sparkled.

"Now, if you'll let Papa hold Teddy for just a moment, I'll check your bleeding then quickly examine your baby boy and return him swaddled tight and ready to latch, encouraging your milk to flow."

"Oh dear, that sounds like a tall order," sighed the young mother.

"But I'm here and ready to help," said Arthur, standing at her bedside.

"Thank God," replied Lilla as she handed Teddy to his father. "I can't imagine not having you close."

With those words, Arthur's face paled. He knew that in one year's time, he'd be at the helm of Dunn & Elliot's newest schooner sailing to faraway ports, leaving his wife and son behind for months on end, maybe longer.

Less than an hour later, as the extended Elliot family prepared to sit down for a quick supper, Aunt Lizzie walked Corinne to the door.

"I wish you'd stay and dine with us. You know Mary Ella has prepared enough food for an army."

"Oh, thank you, Mrs. Carr, but I have reports to fill out, and there's another expectant mother getting ready to deliver in Cushing. Probably tonight."

"What a godsend you are, my dear. Some say doctors, like your brother Emery, will be delivering babies soon, but I don't believe it. When it comes to giving birth, most women prefer midwives over doctors."

Slipping on her coat, Corinne laughed. "I'm not sure about that. Sometimes I wish I had gone to medical school. Doctors can use forceps, and when necessary, they can perform surgery to save the mother, the baby, or both. Honestly, I wish Em had decided to practice in Thomaston instead of joining that group in Rockland. I mean, it's wonderful that they converted that big house on Maple Street into a hospital, but we could use Dr. Rowley's help here in Thomaston."

"Your brother is a surgeon and a dreamer. No one can alter his path."

Turning to leave, Corinne grinned. "You're right. He's our Don Quixote."

"Who?" queried Lizzie, cocking her head.

"My mother used to read to us about the adventures of Don Quixote. He's the crazy hero in Miguel de Cervantes's novel."

"A crazy hero? Isn't that unusual?"

"Yes, and that's why he's so endearing. He's a poor old nobleman who has lost his fortune, lives a dull life, and dreams of righting all the wrongs. In his mind he's a knight, and he tilts at windmills."

"Oh, I see," nodded Lizzie. "He's a crazy dreamer, like you, Emery, and your mother, too....Did I tell you I received a letter from Sam Harlowe's sister?"

"No," said Corinne, stopping at the door. "What did Mrs. Morgan say?"

"That Sam was working at her boss's automobile factory in Detroit and doing well. She also asked me to thank your mother—in the beginning and at the end. I gave the letter to Vinnie last week. I'm surprised she hasn't mentioned it."

"So am I," said Corinne. "I have one more call to make, but I'll stop by the house on my way home and ask her about it."

"Knowing how busy you are, she probably didn't want to distract you. My word, ever since Martha Slocum retired, you've been a phantom—the only people who see you are having babies. Be careful, dear. Don't neglect your own life. Someday you may want to have a baby of your own."

"That may be true, but for that I'll need a husband. Do you have one in mind?"

"No," said Lizzie with a chuckle, "but I'll keep my eyes open and let you know when I spy a possibility."

"Please do," Corinne giggled. "I'll be turning twenty-one soon, and the only men I meet are already fathers."

"Don't worry. I have a talent for tying young hearts together."

Walking out the door, Corinne called back, "Thank you, Mrs. Carr. I'd be happy if you tied a love knot for me!"

"You mean a sailor's knot?" called Lizzie.

Corinne didn't answer. She mounted Lincoln, waved goodbye, and rode toward the crescent moon.

The *E. Starr Jones*

Standing in the entryway of his newly established home a few doors down from his parents' house, Arthur tried to hurry his wife, who was carefully bundling up their one-year-old. Soon, the *E. Starr Jones* would be launched at the shipyard just down the hill and he was anxious. The captain couldn't be late. As they rushed to their carriage, Lilla glanced back, checking that the door was closed, and smiled at the sight of the wreath trimmed with pinecones and bright-red berries. Her smile disappeared, though, when she looked toward the river and saw the crowd gathering by the water's edge.

Arthur noticed a hint of sadness creep over his wife's face and instantly understood the bittersweet feeling. Today's launch was the beginning of a long farewell. On this new day with no mistakes in it, the twenty-eight-year-old captain with coffee-brown eyes and thick, dark hair was grateful his growing family had a place of their own. Though he knew he would be gone for almost a year, he was content because Lilla had feathered a nest on Elliot Street. Shaking his head, he marveled at his father's fore-sight. Ten years ago, George Elliot had had the where-withal to purchase a vacant house from the estate of a neighbor with no heirs. That decision had turned out to be a wise investment, enabling a steady stream of sea captains to rent a safe place for their families while they were at sea.

Now, *he* was the captain renting that cozy house, and when he set sail on D&E's new four-masted schooner, their ninth since 1891, his burden would be lighter because Nana and Bumpa would be watching over Lilla and Teddy. He'd be taking command of the *E. Starr Jones*, as fine a vessel as any Chapman & Flint Down Easter, with a clear head and a full heart.

In November 1904, the Elliot family was enjoying fair winds, but like all families who depend on the sea, they knew the winds were fickle and the tides were ever-changing. Less than a year ago, on the twenty-sixth of January, Thomas Dunn, a founding partner of Dunn & Elliot and George's cousin, had passed away. At the time of his death, Mr. Dunn was one of the most successful men in Thomaston and the oldest shipbuilder in Maine, having launched his first schooner, *Seventy-Six*, in 1864. While some attributed his longevity to luck, his surviving partners believed their family's love and devotion had played a key role. In January 1905, the pride of the D&E fleet, *E. Starr Jones*, would set sail for the Gulf of Mexico, and Captain Arthur J. Elliot would be at the helm, continuing his family's seafaring tradition.

On the twenty-ninth of December, after spending Christmas in Thomaston, Arthur would take a train down to New York and prepare to embark, leaving a wife and son at home. Though the captain wasn't looking forward to saying goodbye, he was grateful Lilla and Teddy would be safe on Elliot Street, close to his parents, extended family, and dear friends. The twenty-eight-year-old captain wasn't abandoning his family; he was leaving them with loved ones he trusted with his life and treasure. The *E. Starr*

Jones would sail to Baltimore to load coal for Galveston and Vera Cruz. On the return passage, she'd drop anchor at Port Tampa to load phosphate rock, then sail around the Florida peninsula and return to Baltimore. Arthur had decided to sail without Lilla and Teddy because he knew that those combustible cargoes would pose a threat to the safety of his vessel. It was a painful decision.

Since their wedding day in January 1900, he and Lilla had enjoyed sailing together on the *Phineas W. Sprague*, especially on their honeymoon when they sailed from New York to South Amboy, Providence, Philadelphia, and New Orleans before returning to New York for a reunion with family, including their mothers. After enjoying a month of luxury in the city, they continued their voyage. In June they sailed to Suriname, Trinidad, Washington, Baltimore, and Portland. Then they rested for three weeks in Thomaston before returning to Portland to sail again. Finally, on New Year's Day 1901, they set sail for New York, the last passage of their extended honeymoon. While under way, their schooner's boom broke, they ran short on provisions, and were almost marooned on Fire Island when the schooner froze off the coast. Those were the extraordinary days of fire and ice, and he would never forget them. Now he was resolved to keep his family safe at home.

By the time Arthur and Lilla arrived at the shipyard, George was already standing on the quarterdeck of the *E. Starr Jones* with his partners Richard O. Elliot, his first-born son, and Richard E. Dunn, the son of his late partner. As they hurried toward the gangplank, their friends and hundreds of spectators greeted them with warm salutations: *Congratulations! Good morning! What a day!* But it was Vinnie's voice that stopped them.

"Lilla! Arthur!"

With Teddy in her arms, Lilla turned toward the call. When she spied Mrs. Rowley standing beside her husband, surrounded by Emery, Galen, Olivia, Owen, and Corinne, she reached for her husband's hand.

"Arthur, Mrs. Rowley is trying to get our attention. Do you see her? She's standing by the stern with her whole family."

The handsome young captain, wearing his black peacoat and mariner's cap, looked toward the water and spotted the Rowley family standing by the river with Brooklyn Heights in the background. At that moment, Emery ran toward them.

Shifting Teddy in her arms, Lilla waved, and Olivia, Owen, and the others waved back. Seconds later, Emery appeared beside them, slightly out of breath.

"My mother wanted you to have this before the christening and the launch," said Emery, handing Arthur a wrapped package and a sealed letter. "She said you should open the package right away but save the letter until after you sail."

Taken off guard, Arthur looked at the flowing script on the envelope and choked with emotion.

Emery filled the quiet pause. "You know my mother. She wants to keep everyone warm and safe. I could be wrong, but I bet that package contains one of her softest wool scarves."

Through misty eyes, the captain looked at his friend and smiled. "I bet you're...right," he stammered. "Please thank her and all the Rowleys and Suttons for standing on the water's edge this cold day. Your presence means the world to me."

"Godspeed," said Emery. "You deserve your dream."

Arthur's set jaw broke into a boyish grin. "We both do, and I think we're almost there." He reached out and gave his friend's hand a hearty shake.

Shortly after Arthur, Lilla, and Teddy arrived at the gangplank, George and Mary Ella walked down. Glancing at his watch, George muttered, "For a minute there, I thought the captain was going to be late for the launch of his new command."

"As it turns out, I'm right on time," smiled the captain.

"I knew you wouldn't miss the christening," chimed in Ida as she walked down the plank. "This is my first time, you know."

"Yes," laughed Arthur. "I'm aware, and I see you're dressed for the occasion."

"Is that a compliment?" teased his sister.

"Indeed, it's a *high* compliment. You look all of twenty-one in your flowered hat and tight-fitting coat."

Ida laughed. "Oh, Arthur, I look twenty-one because I *am* twenty-one."

"You see, I'm exactly right. You're a woman fully grown." He coughed and Ida blushed.

George cleared his throat. "Well, since my children are all adults, including Ida, my youngest, I think we should head over to the bow so Ida can break that bottle of sea water she's carrying."

Lilla raised an eyebrow. "Sea water?"

"Yes, my dear," said George. "The Dunn and Elliot Company doesn't believe in spilling champagne. We christen our vessels with a splash of sea water before we slip them over the ways."

"I see," she said, tilting her head. "It makes sense, but I never would have guessed there was *sea water* in the bottle."

Ida chuckled, "You mean it makes *Elliot* sense."

Stepping closer, Arthur reached for Teddy. "Let me hold him so you can have your hands free when Ida cracks that glass."

"He's right," murmured Ida. "Has he told you about the tradition of the one-dollar gold coin?"

"No," she said, shaking her head.

George winked. "Don't worry, Lilla. It's an old Dunn and Elliot tradition. It's a blessing, not a curse.

Minutes later, Ida broke the bottle over the bow of the beautiful new four-masted schooner, and the crowd roared as the *E. Starr Jones* broke her earthly bonds and slipped into the river. Amid the euphoria, Ida turned and pressed a gold Indian-Head-Princess coin, minted in 1861, into her brother's hand and wished him good luck.

After a spectacular day, a group of family, friends, and investors gathered at 10 Elliot Street. Once again, George and Mary Ella welcomed everyone with Yankee hospitality. The dining room table overflowed with turkey, cranberry sauce, mashed potatoes, roasted carrots, squash, biscuits, butter, and, of course, a punch bowl filled with intoxicating eggnog. In less than an hour, most of the guests were noisy and merry, especially Aunt Lizzie.

"Well, sweet Corinne, you look *unusually* ravishing tonight," said Lizzie, coming to Corinne's side with two glasses of the magical holiday drink.

"Why thank you, Mrs. Carr, and you look as lovely as ever."

"Oh, my goodness, you really are an angel, though I wish you'd call me Lizzie or at least Aunt Lizzie. Almost everyone does."

"All right, Aunt Lizzie, I can do that."

"Wonderful! Now I can tell you why I've brought you this love potion," said Lizzie, handing her a glass. "See that young man over there, the one standing with my brother George?"

"Yes," said Corinne, "though I've never seen him before."

"No need to whisper, dear. In a few minutes, I'm going to introduce you. He's handsome, isn't he? I mean, look at that thick, curly hair and those chocolate-brown eyes."

Blushing, she whispered back, "Indeed...he's a tall, good-looking man, though I can't really see his eyes from here."

"Trust me, dear, those eyes will melt your heart—"

"Aunt Lizzie," she said boldly, "my heart's not frozen."

"Of course not; I was speaking metaphorically. I know how you love to read. What was that young hero's name in Dumas's novel?"

"D'Artagnan?" she asked.

"Yes, that's the one. Now drink your eggnog and allow me to work my magic. Believe me, that handsome young man is not a poor nobleman. He's a live Yankee. In fact, he reminds me of Charlie Flint."

"Charlie Flint? I haven't heard that name in a long time."

"No sense looking back, but everyone in town knows Charlie Flint and your mother were the closest of friends, until she met your father, of course."

"What happened to him? I've never seen him in Thomaston."

"You're young, and he left a long time ago, seeking adventure."

"Did he find it?"

"He certainly did. He was always rich, but now he's powerful and famous, too."

"How so?" asked Corinne, sipping her drink.

"Well, he has an uncanny talent for bringing small, profitable businesses together to form highly lucrative companies like U.S. Rubber in 1892, and American Chicle and American Woolen in 1899. Some say he's becoming the 'Father of Trusts.' Maybe he is, but he doesn't have any children."

"Does he have a wife?"

Lizzie nodded. "Yes, he does. He married Kate Simmons from Troy, New York, over twenty years ago. I met her once and thought she was beautiful. From what I hear, she's a talented musician and exceedingly generous. They're in the papers quite a bit. I'm surprised you haven't noticed."

"Why would I? Mother never mentions either of them."

"I'm sure that's true, but ten years ago Charles Ranlett Flint fitted out a fleet of naval ships for the government of Brazil and every shipbuilder in Maine was talking about that."

"Well, ten years ago I was eleven and not a bit interested in naval ships, Brazil, or rich, powerful men."

Lizzie threw back her head and laughed. "Oh, sweet angel, I think you're enjoying that drink. It's time to meet Mr. Jeremy Brown from the South Street Seaport."

"In New York City?" gasped Corinne.

"Yes! To be more precise, he works for Mr. Flint on the island of Manhattan. Are you ready?"

Corinne fixed her gaze on the tall, quiet man with a chinstrap beard tracing a chiseled jaw and smiled behind her crystal glass. She touched the rim to her cherry-red lips and drained her eggnog laced with whiskey.

"I'm ready, Aunt Lizzie. He looks—"

"Don't say another word. Just follow me."

Two months later, it was Vinnie and Gray's turn to host a celebration. On the first of February, under the guise of Valentine's Day, fifty formal invitations—white paper hearts trimmed with delicate red dots—were sent to family, friends, neighbors, and business acquaintances:

Please join Mr. & Mrs. Gray Rowley
For a Valentine's Day Celebration
Sunday, February 14, 1905

Three to five o'clock
20 Hyler Street, Thomaston
Hors d'oeuvres and libations will be served
R.S.V.P. regrets only

Since only ten invitees responded with regrets, Vinnie, Olivia, and Corinne, along with Amelia and Maria, spent two full days cooking, baking, cleaning, and decorating for forty guests. They flew around the house like a flock of noisy magpies. Amid their rolling pins and feather dusters stood Lavinia, the lady of the house. With a blue cotton scarf covering her hair and a red apron tied around her waist, she looked like a waif, but the minute she lifted her chin and spoke, she was completely in charge.

"Stop!" called Vinnie from the bottom of the stairs. "The sun went down hours ago and we all need to get some rest. The ham is baked, the bread is out of the oven, the cheese is ready for slicing, and the cake has been iced—"

"And the upstairs bathroom has been scrubbed," laughed Olivia, walking down the stairs with a bucket in her hand.

"Thank the angels and Olivia!" called Amelia from the kitchen doorway.

"Indeed," said Vinnie, touching the smooth maple handrail. "Thank you, Liv!"

Corinne chimed in, "Thank you, everyone. I didn't think we could prepare for a party so quickly."

"Really? How could you doubt us?" asked Amelia with laughter in her eyes. "I have to agree with your mother, though. If we want to look our best tomorrow, we have to get some sleep tonight." Then she took off her apron, handed it to Vinnie, and stepped into the hall to retrieve her coat.

Maria followed her. "We'll be back tomorrow before noon," she said with a grin. "We'll take care of the last-minute details, like making the tea sandwiches, so you can make yourselves beautiful. That won't take any time at all."

"You're too kind," said Vinnie. "You know it will take me twice as long as my girls to get ready. After all, I'm twice their age."

Smiling in agreement, Amelia put on her hat and coat. Waiting for her daughter to button up as well, she scanned the softly lit parlor and sighed. "I hate to leave the warmth of your fire to face the expanse of ice outside, but I'll urge the horses to carry us home and we'll all fall asleep in our own beds dreaming about the pretty dresses we'll be wearing on Valentine's Day."

Corinne ran to the door and gave them both a hug. "I'll see you tomorrow, then."

The next day, Gray Rowley opened the front door of his graceful home and welcomed his first guest, Jeremy Brown, followed by Mr. and Mrs. Flint.

"Good afternoon, Mr. Rowley," said Jeremy.

"Come in, come in," replied Gray, shaking the young man's hand. "Corinne will be down in a minute."

As Jeremy slipped off his coat, Charlie stepped forward.

"Mr. Rowley, it's been a long time. Do you remember me?"

"Of course I remember you! Whenever I start to forget, your face appears on the front page of a newspaper."

Charlie laughed. "I'm sorry about that. This mug of mine could stop a stampede of buffalo any day of the week."

"I don't know much about buffalo, but the pictures I like the best are the ones that have your lovely lady at your side."

"You mean my wife, Kate," said Charlie, taking his wife's hand. "And now I know why Vinnie was so drawn to you. You're charming, Mr. Rowley."

It was Gray who laughed. "I'll take that as a compliment if you call me Gray." He offered his hand to Kate. "It's a pleasure to finally meet you, Mrs. Flint. I've read a lot about you, and every word was glowing."

"That's hard to believe, considering how critical the New York papers are, though I appreciate your kindness. Please call me Kate."

"Well, Kate, I would hope big-city reporters would recognize a heart of gold when they see one, though they're probably rare."

"But they're not rare in Thomaston," said Charlie, spying Corinne. "Look at that sparkling angel at the top of the stairs."

Following his boss's gaze, Jeremy looked up and smiled like he was about to be kissed by the woman he loved. Corinne rushed down the stairs with her hand gliding on the smooth bannister and the hem of her burgundy gown dusting every step. As soon as her black silk pumps touched the carpet at the bottom of the stairs, Jeremy was there, and she hugged him.

"Oh, my darling, you've been gone three weeks, and—"

"I've missed you, too," he whispered before kissing her softly on the ear and the cheek.

Gray cleared his throat to intervene. "Corinne, this is Mr. Charles Flint and his wife, Kate. They've come to meet you...at Jeremy's request."

Blushing, Corinne dropped her arms. "Oh, Mr. and Mrs. Flint, I'm so glad you could come." She took a breath and focused on Kate. "Jeremy tells me you're a talented composer." She offered her hand to Charlie, "And Mr. Flint, if I remember correctly, you delivered a Chilean ship to Japan when it was at war with China and then became the U.S. consul at New York for Chile."

"Yes, and Nicaragua and Costa Rica, too," said Charlie with a twinkle in his eye. "Don't believe everything

Jeremy tells you, though. He's prone to exaggerate. In truth, I've been lucky. I was quite young when I became a partner in W.R. Grace and Company, then I joined Flint and Company, and later Flint, Dearborn and Company. You could say I'm deep into merchant banking and international trade, and so is Jeremy."

As soon as Jeremy's name was spoken, Corinne's black lashes fluttered like butterflies—and Charlie was rendered speechless, as if her hazel eyes had cast a spell. He cleared his throat.

"I'm afraid I'm to blame for Jeremy's absence. I needed him on Broad Street in New York. He's become indispensable to the firm. I find it hard to believe he's been with us ten years." Then the consummate integrator, Charles Ranlett Flint, swallowed hard. "Jeremy was about your age when he started, just twenty-one years old."

When Kate glimpsed emotion creeping onto her husband's face, she looped her arm in his. "Jeremy's father used to work for Flint and Company. In fact, Jeremy's parents were good friends of ours. I'm sure Jeremy has told you that his parents died in a train accident when he was a senior at Columbia. Since their passing, he's become part of our family, more like a son than an employee."

Bowing his head, Jeremy pinched the bridge of his nose and murmured, "I'm lucky, and I know it."

"So am I," said Corinne, reaching for Kate's hand. "Now come meet my mother and brothers and my sister and brother-in-law. We're a noisy bunch, but you'll love us!"

"I know I will," Kate smiled.

At that moment, Vinnie and Olivia stepped out of the kitchen, Emery and Galen entered the hallway from the dining room, and Owen opened the door and walked into the house.

Surrounded by family, Charlie looked from mothers to daughters to sons and sons-in-law, and in that circle he saw the most beautiful shades of smiling eyes—deep blue, warm hazel, light green, and chocolate brown—and he thought to himself, *Wouldn't Aunt Susan and Uncle Emery be proud of how their family has flourished.*

Part Five

1908–1924

From Sea to Shore

As the *E. Starr Jones* dropped anchor at the South Street Seaport in New York, Captain Arthur Elliot looked up at the D&E flag blowing in the wind and murmured, "Thank you." Keeping his eyes on the blue sky, he took a breath and imagined his future away from the sea. In a few days, after the lumber from Norfolk had been unloaded and the crew had gone ashore, he would make his last entry in the logbook, pack his personal belongings in a duffel bag and sea chest, and allow the first mate to take command. In January 1908, Arthur was choosing his family over the sea, and he was resolute in his decision.

Thirty days ago, he had missed Teddy's fourth birthday, and eighteen months before that, he had missed hearing his son say "I love you" for the first time. Lilla was due to deliver their second child at the end of February and he was anxious to get home. He wanted to hold their newborn and stay ashore so he could see the first smile, hear the first word, and witness the first step. More than anything else, he wanted to teach his children how to row, fish, and sail on the Georges River; he wanted to enjoy all the golden moments of their lives. If all went well, he'd be in Thomaston for the birth of the new baby, and ready for a new role in the Dunn & Elliot Company.

A loud voice interrupted his reverie. "Captain, the sails have been stowed. The vessel is secure, and the winds are beginning to ease."

"Excellent, Mr. Falk. Tell the Dane to put on a stew and bake plenty of biscuits. The crew has earned a hot supper. We'll begin unloading tomorrow."

"Aye, sir. The gales were heavy up from Cape Hatteras. We were lucky to have such a strong crew."

"Indeed, salt water runs in their veins."

The young man returned the praise with a nod and a smile.

"Mr. Falk, I'd like you to join me for dinner at five o'clock sharp to discuss an important matter. Tell the second mate to take the watch."

"Yes, sir. I'll be there at five. Thank you, Captain."

Three days later, on January 19, 1908, Arthur heaved a duffel onto his shoulder, shook the hand of his first mate, and stated, "It's time. She's yours until the company decides on a new captain. Like I said the other night, I'm going to recommend you. As of today, I'm officially a partner, but I don't know how much influence I'll have on my father, brother, and cousin. They may think you're too young, but I was younger than you when I took command, so I'll argue that twenty-two is old enough."

Lifting his chin, the mate met his captain's gaze. "I think I speak for the whole crew when I say we'll miss you on the quarterdeck."

"I wish you fair winds and following seas, Mr. Falk. The next time we speak, I hope it's captain to captain." He shifted his duffel and chuckled, "Don't forget to send my sea chest to Thomaston before you fly light to Baltimore."

When the mate exhaled, his breath was visible, but he couldn't speak. He swallowed hard and tried again. "I don't know what to say. I couldn't have asked for a better master. You've been firm, but fair, and you've taught me everything I know about navigating and forecasting the weather. I hope I can measure up..." He swallowed again and pushed his dark, unruly hair away from his face. "I'll do my best to keep the *E. Starr Jones* out of harm's way."

"I know you will," said Arthur. "You're from Cushing, right?"

"Yes, sir."

"I'll rest easy, then. She's in good hands."

From South Street, Arthur took a yellow taxi, one of the New York Taxicab Company's finest, over the Brooklyn Bridge to Montague Terrace. When he gave the driver the address of Jeremy and Corinne's brownstone in Brooklyn Heights, he chuckled.

"What are you laughing at?" asked the driver with the lilt of an Irish brogue.

"Oh, nothing really. It's just that I come from the mid-coast of Maine, and there's a hill in my town called *Brooklyn Heights*, just like the place you're taking me to right now."

"You don't say! How'd that happen?"

Settling into the dusty, cold backseat, Arthur replied, "It's a long story, but here's the gist of it. Two wealthy brothers from Maine set up a shipping business in Manhattan after establishing a successful shipyard in Thomaston. As partners, they always kept things equal, including the size and value of their homes. In New York City, the only way they could maintain that balance was to buy a whole street in Brooklyn Heights and build matching houses on opposite ends—two corners of Montague Terrace, overlooking the Promenade. They convinced Edward O'Brien, a millionaire from Thomaston, to build a house on the same street."

"My gosh, that's a tall tale!"

"Ah, but it's true," he murmured. "I know lots of stories like that." Then he peered out the window and almost shouted, "Look! We're driving over the East River in an automobile with an engine, not a sail or a team of horses; and we're on the Brooklyn Bridge, which is anchored with granite from Vinalhaven, an island off the coast of Maine."

"Where do you come from again?" asked the driver, shaking his head.

"From Thomaston, Maine, where they make tall sailing ships."

"Ah, like me, you're from a faraway place. I'm from Carrickmacross, where they make lace and break hearts. I couldn't make enough money in Ireland to feed my family, so I had to cross the sea to find work. I've never known such sickness as I felt on that ship. No, I'm not a sailor, but I can drive this car seven days a week. In a year, I'll have enough money to bring my wife and son to America."

For a moment, Arthur fell silent. Looking through the window, he could see the *E. Starr Jones* tied up at the dock on the Manhattan side and he could hear the hum of the tires on the pavement. Riding across the Brooklyn Bridge in the falling snow, his senses were awakened and he longed to be home.

"When did you arrive?"

"Ten months ago, though it seems longer," said the cab driver.

"Eh," he sighed, "I know that feeling…to be across the sea from those you love."

When the Irishman parked the cab at the curb in front of a handsome brownstone with a granite stoop and tall glass windows, he jumped out to open Arthur's door and grab the duffel bag from the back. Without hesitating, he carried the bag up the steps and set it down in front of the three-quarter glass door with the word *Four* etched across it. He looked up and down the street and whistled. "Holy cow! I've never seen a block as pretty as this."

Still on the sidewalk, Arthur spun around to take in the view. "It is magnificent!"

"'Tis that. And I'm going to show this place to my Franny and little Martin when they come. Brooklyn Heights is a dream."

"I agree," smiled Arthur as he walked up the steps. "How much do I owe you?"

"Two bits."

Pulling a money clip out of his inside pocket, Arthur handed the driver a five-dollar bill. "Thanks for the ride and the conversation."

"I did say two bits, didn't I?"

"Yes, you did. I added a little extra to help speed up Franny and Martin's arrival."

Rubbing his chin, the Irishman closed his pale-blue eyes and whispered, "God bless you. Thank you."

"You're welcome," said Arthur as he turned to ring the doorbell. He glanced back and added, "Good luck and good day, sir."

The driver tipped his cap before sliding back behind the wheel of his taxi. As he drove away, he tooted the horn.

When Corinne opened the door, she squealed, "You're here! We've been expecting you for days."

"I may be the captain of a schooner, but I have no control over the wind."

Coming to his wife's side, Jeremy laughed. "But Arthur, when you're flying the flag of D and E, you control almost everything else!"

He flashed a smile. "Don't believe everything you hear on the docks. Besides, I've charted my last voyage. As soon as I take care of some business on Broad Street, I'll be on my way home."

By the tone of his voice and the set of his jaw, Corinne knew her friend was serious. When he was thirteen and she was six, he was her hero. More than once, he had saved her from the perils of living near a shipyard filled with sharp tools, hard pine, and rough men. Gazing up at his weathered face shielded by the brim of his mariner's cap, she couldn't imagine him away from the helm of a schooner for more than a few months. Reaching for his hand, she took a breath. Change was in the air, and no one could stop it, not even Arthur.

"Well, that's a shock," said Corinne with the twitch of a smile. "Come in, please. Let me take your hat and coat. Jeremy can bring your bag upstairs, and we can have a little something to eat by the fire. I know you have a meeting with Flint, Dearborn and Company, so you're not hopping on a train for a couple of days. When you're not at their office, I want you smoking your pipe and reading the paper in my front parlor."

His eyes crinkled at the corners. "I'd like that. We have a lot of catching up to do. I'm here for three whole days, though I'm anxious to get home."

"I bet you are!" called Jeremy from halfway up the stairs with Arthur's ditty bag resting on his shoulder. "Try not to worry. You'll be with Lilla before that new baby arrives."

Arthur called back, "I hope you're right." Then he followed Corinne into the kitchen and paid her the ultimate compliment. "Your home is beautiful, and you look radiant."

"Oh, Captain, you sure know how to make a woman smile!"

"I suppose I do," he said, admiring the room and the pretty lady pouring a glass of whiskey at the sideboard. "On this occasion, I'm being truthful, not just charming."

Cocking an eyebrow, Corinne handed him the glass. "Let's sit by the fire. I can tell you have a lot on your mind."

"I could never hide anything from the Rowley family. You're all a bit clairvoyant."

"I'm not sure *that's* true," said Corinne, "but your face is easy to read."

Arthur tossed back the whiskey and grinned. "Like a chart of Penobscot or Muscongus Bay, right?"

She refilled his glass then poured two more and deftly filled a tray with cheese, nuts, and shortbread. As she lifted the tray, Arthur intervened to take it from her.

"You and Jeremy are so welcoming. The least I can do is carry the refreshments into the parlor. Besides, I think you're the one who should sit in the parlor and relax."

"Why do you say that?"

Arthur grinned. "I recognize the glow."

"What glow is that?" asked Jeremy stepping into the kitchen.

Before he could answer, the back door opened and a red-headed woman blew in with a burst of cold air. "I'm sorry I'm late, ma'am. It started raining when I left Queens, and it's turned to sleet."

"You're not late, Molly. You're just in time to meet our guest, Captain Arthur Elliot from Thomaston, my home-town."

"Pleased to meet you, Captain," said Molly, unwrapping her scarf. "I hope you like shepherd's pie."

"Home cooking sounds wonderful to me."

"Ahh, Mrs. Brown said you were a charmer, and so you are," said Molly as she quickly hung her coat on a peg by the door and tied on a clean white apron.

"We'll be chatting in the parlor, Molly. We'd like to sit down for dinner at six."

"Don't you worry, Mrs. Brown. I'll be quick and it'll be ready by five of." She turned on her heels and headed for the pantry, but not before giving Arthur a big smile.

The captain smiled back and followed Jeremy and

Corinne into the parlor, carrying the silver tray and trying hard not to spill the glasses of whiskey.

Corinne tilted her head toward the low table between the matching settees. "You can set that heavy tray over there."

"It's not heavy. I just don't want to waste any of this delicious whiskey."

"Your senses are sharp," said Corinne sitting down next to her husband. "There's no mystery here. I'm sure Lilla has mentioned I've lost two babies in three years. This time feels different...this one is holding on."

Quiet filled the room and Jeremy cleared his throat. "We decided to wait till Corinne was showing. The pain and disappointment of losing a babe—"

"I know. You were right to wait, but now you're show-ing." Lifting his glass, he took a big gulp. He fixed his eyes on Corinne. "I'm guessing five months along."

"That would be a good guess. I haven't told the hospi-tal yet because they'll make me stop working."

"That's truly a loss for Brooklyn Hospital! I'm sure they'll miss you, and you'll miss being a midwife, but I have to agree with your bosses. Isn't the hospital on Dekalb Avenue in the center of the borough?"

"Yes, it borders the west side of Fort Greene Park."

"Well, that's too far to walk from here, and not an easy drive, especially in winter."

Reaching for his glass, Jeremy added, "There's the risk of contracting some dreaded disease, like tuberculo-sis. Corinne and I have talked about this ad nauseam. The hospital's policy is clear, and I concur. I'm not sure my wife wholeheartedly agrees, though."

Corinne sat up straight. "Since moving here, I've worked solely on the maternity ward. I haven't made a house call in years. On the ward, we follow all the best practices for minimizing the spread of germs. I believe

I'm just as safe helping mothers deliver in the hospital as I am on the Promenade of Brooklyn Heights."

"You may be right, but now is not the time to prove a point," said Arthur gently. "It's time to keep your baby safe."

She pouted but then gave her friend a slight smile. "When did you get to be so wise?"

"The day Teddy was born. In less than a month, Lilla will give birth to another little one, and I'm determined to be there on that day and as many days after that as I possibly can."

"You will," said Jeremy, tossing back his whiskey. "Everyone at Flint, Dearborn as well as Flint, Eddy Company are talking about Dunn and Elliot's newest partner. We're excited such an old salt—"

"Who's an old salt? I'm only thirty-two, and unless I'm mistaken, you're older than I am."

"You're right," laughed Jeremy as he stepped over to the side table where Molly had quietly placed the bottle of whiskey. "You were sailing before the mast when you were still in your teens, and your insight into the American merchant fleet is invaluable. Let's face the fact: In aught eight, the company is better served with you in the office than on the deck of a schooner."

"Sadly, that's true," said Arthur, raising his glass so his friend could fill it. "The *E. Starr Jones* was built before the investors disappeared. We haven't launched a vessel in four years. It's our sail loft that keeps us afloat. We have contracts to replace the suit of sails of every vessel we built at our shipyard and other yards as well, including the ones that John McDonald built for Chapman and Flint. If those ships and schooners are still under sail, it's because of a Dunn and Elliot sailmaker."

"The finest suit of sails money can buy," smiled Jeremy, sitting back down and taking his wife's hand. "Your father had something to do with that, my dear."

"Yes, he did. For me, that's a silver lining in my family's history, but I want to talk about the present. How is Lilla, and who's going to deliver her precious baby?"

Arthur leaned back and grinned, "I've been waiting for that question since the moment I arrived."

"Well then, tell us!"

"Lilla would like to deliver tomorrow, but the little one isn't due until the end of February, so I'm hoping for a Valentine's Day birthday."

"Who will be there to assist?" Corinne asked.

"Dr. Honor Gibbons."

Jeremy fired back, "Is that the lady doctor Galen wrote me about?"

"Galen wrote you about Honor?" asked Corinne, knitting her brows.

"Yes, he wrote about a month ago—"

"Please take your seats in the dining room," said Molly, ringing a little bell. "Dinner is ready."

"Hold that thought, my darling," teased Corinne. "I want to hear all the details."

"So do I," said Arthur with a wink. "Montague Terrace is certainly intriguing—full of life and mystery."

A Midnight Delivery

As shadows of twilight fell over Thomaston, the Maine Central slowed to a stop at the station, nestling into the dooryard of General Knox's old farmhouse. Galen was waiting on the platform. Wearing a top hat and a bright-red scarf, he looked more like a snowman than an attorney-at-law. The frigid cold weather and the fact that the train was a half hour late didn't seem to bother him, though. As soon as Arthur disembarked, he reached for his hand and shook it hard.

"Welcome home! It's been too long!"

"Aren't you a sight for sore eyes! Thanks for meeting me in the middle of a snowstorm."

Laughing, Galen threw up his hands. "Eh, this isn't a storm. This is Maine on the eve of February."

Arthur looked up at the dark sky, then dropped his eyes to admire the fresh white powder sliding toward the Georges. He took a deep breath and let it out. "Gosh, it feels good."

"It's going to feel even better when I drop you into the arms of Lilla, who's expecting you *and* your newest offspring!"

"I can hardly wait. Where's your sleigh?"

"Here. Let me take your bag," Galen replied with a smile spreading across his clean-shaven face. "My car is across the street."

"Your *car*!" exclaimed Arthur. "Since when do you drive a car?"

"Since I bought a Model T—or a Tin Lizzie, as some like to call her."

Despite the falling flakes of heavy snow, Arthur took off his cap and ran his fingers through his thick brown hair. "I don't know what to say. From horses to a Model T, that's a big change. I guess eight months is a long time to be away."

"Not for you. Your voyages usually take you away for a year or more."

"Not this time," said Arthur, shaking his head as he walked toward the black automobile with a touch of brass and the name *Ford* written in cursive across the front. "I suppose you've heard the news."

"Yes, we all have," said Galen as he tossed the heavy bag into the back of his shiny new automobile. "It's the right decision. Commercial trade is changing faster than anyone expected. The firm needs you at home, not coasting from here to the West Indies and beyond. In truth, Lilla needs you, too."

Sliding into his seat, the travel-weary captain nodded and swallowed hard. "Since Teddy arrived, I've been sailing without Lilla, and the days and nights at sea have gotten longer. Now, with our second little one on the way, I can't imagine leaving again."

"Arthur, you're one of the hardiest captains I know. You deserve this time with your family. It's all right to stay ashore. Let the men without young children sail to Trinidad, Suriname, and Montevideo. You've already been there over and over again."

Glancing sideways, Arthur chuckled, "Your great-aunt Susan must be dancing in heaven, and your mother must be pleased as well."

"What makes you say that?" asked Galen without taking his eyes off the icy road.

"You're driving a Ford, and Sam Harlowe, the prisoner they saved from damnation, works at the Ford Motor Company. Heck, maybe he built the seat or the hood of this fancy automobile... Imagine that!" said Arthur, slapping his knee.

"Why Captain, I think you're beginning to relax."

"Just a bit...until Lilla begins her travails. I must say I was glad to hear that Dr. Gibbons plans to be there when the time comes."

Just hearing her name, Galen smiled. "Don't worry. Honor will take good care of her. She's an excellent doctor with a heart of gold."

"Yes," said Arthur, nodding, "and I suspect you know her better than most since you've been spending so much time together. At least that's what your last letter implied."

"You cut right to the core, don't you?"

"I do. No time to waste. Besides, you're not fixing up Mrs. Slocum's cape just for yourself. What are your plans?"

Galen stopped the car in front of Arthur and Lilla's modest home, directly across from the beautiful Italianate on the corner. He turned off the motor, put his lips together, and whistled.

"Have I struck a chord?"

Galen quietly replied, "I'm in love with Honor."

"So I'm right then!"

Galen nodded but didn't smile. "See that big white house over there?"

"Of course," shrugged Arthur, "that's Captain William Willey's house. His father built it in 1843, but Captain

Willey only lived there for six years with his wife and children before he drowned along with his entire crew off the coast of Ireland."

"I know the story well."

"Aye, every old salt likes to tell the tragic story of William Willey. His ship *Alfred D. Snow* earned a reputation for surviving heavy gales while rounding Cape Horn, like the one in eighty-three when she was blown so far off course she had to drop anchor at Pitcairn for repairs, and the islanders presented Captain Willey with pieces of the HMS *Bounty* as a souvenir."

"I believe it was that voyage that convinced Mrs. Willey to never go to sea with her husband again."

"Cordelia was a wise woman. The triangular voyage from New York to San Francisco to Liverpool, then back to New York required not one but two passages around the Horn. Captain Willey made that voyage repeatedly and was a fearless Cape-Horner. But in January of eighty-eight, his storied Down Easter was driven onto the rocks at Broomhill Point near the entrance to Waterford Harbor. She called for the succor of the Irish Coast Guard, but their closest tug arrived too late. The crew of the *Dauntless*, along with some volunteer fishermen—"

"Fishermen?"

"Yes, *fishermen*. The crew of a fishing boat saw the ship was in distress and convinced their captain to let them take out a lifeboat during the fiercest moments of the storm. They couldn't reach the sinking ship, though. Like the Coast Guard, the fishermen had to watch from afar as the only lifeboat launched from the Down Easter was swamped, drowning all aboard, and the remaining sailors hanging from the mainmast were washed away."

Shaking his head, Galen murmured, "Thank God Captain Willey's wife and children were at home. The wreck of the *Alfred D. Snow* has become part of Irish and

American lore. I'm not sure what's true and what's not, but I'm certain the sum of her loss was greater than twenty-nine men and a cargo of wheat bound for Liverpool. Every sailor who drowned that day left someone behind."

He paused, staring at the house across the street, then turned to face his friend. "The captain had a son and two daughters, and his widow raised them in that big house without him. Now they're grown and his widow lives there alone."

Arthur felt a chill but didn't move. "Thank you for confirming my decision to retire from the sea. I've been luckier than most. I remember hearing that after the wreck of the *Alfred D. Snow*, only the bodies of Captain Willey and the ship's carpenter, John Lermond, were returned to Maine for burial. The captain was identified by his cameo ring, and the carpenter was identified by the measuring stick they found in his pocket. The Irish embalmed them in whiskey and sent them home."

"Let's not be too gloomy. When the *Alfred D. Snow* rolled on her side, there was one survivor."

"No, the whole crew perished that day."

Tapping his lips with his finger, Galen smiled. "Every *man* aboard died, but not the ship's dog. Many of the townsfolk in County Wexford reported that the crew's dog, Dash, was saved. He was adopted by a good family and lived out his days in County Waterford, a good place for a sheepdog."

"If that doesn't beat all. Is it true?"

"I'm not sure, but I think it may be. A few weeks ago, when I was drawing up a will for a client of mine, I read some accounts from Irishmen who witnessed the wreck. True or not, your safe return is a reason to celebrate—a second child for you and a bride for me! I'm going to ask Honor to marry me. I've added an ell onto Mrs. Slocum's house, which, for the record, is mine because I'm making the payments, and I'm going to carry my bride over the threshold this June."

"That's if she says yes," said Arthur as he opened the car door.

Galen hopped out, grabbed Arthur's bag from the backseat, and walked around the hood to stand by his friend. "Oh, she'll say yes."

Reaching for his duffel, Arthur grinned. "I know she'll say yes because she'd be a fool to say no, and I wouldn't let a fool take care of my pregnant wife."

For once, the attorney was rendered speechless.

Three weeks later, close to midnight on February 21, 1908, Lilla Burbank Elliot gave birth to her second son at home overlooking the D&E Shipyard. Dr. Gibbons caught the baby boy and minutes later swaddled him and placed him gently in his mother's arms. Arthur was pacing downstairs, but his sister Ida quickly called him to the birthing room. When he arrived at Lilla's bedside, he dropped to his knees, touched his newborn son, nestled in his mama's arms, and let the tears flow.

"Captain, what's the matter?" asked the doctor. "You have a healthy baby boy."

"I know," said Arthur. "That's why I'm weeping. He's a miracle."

"Aye, Captain," she murmured while shifting the newborn so his mouth could touch his mother's breast. "What will you call this amazing grace?"

Lilla's eyes met Arthur's and they smiled at each other. Arthur looked at the tall, slender doctor with a mass of auburn hair piled on her head. "His name is Albert Burbank Elliot."

"I think that fits like a fine suit of sails."

"Thank you...thank you for everything, and please call me Arthur. Galen is one of my closest friends, and I know he's enormously fond of you, so I hope we'll be friends, too."

Fixing her eyes on mother and child, Dr. Honor Gibbons whispered back, "I think we're off to a good start." She turned and quietly left the room, giving mother, father, and little Albert time to get acquainted before the family waiting downstairs rushed in and interrupted their moment of joy.

The clock in the hall struck midnight, signaling a new day and a new beginning.

At the End of the Lane

Driving south on Wadsworth Street, Emery glanced at his mother sitting on the passenger side of his new Model T and shouted over the motor. "You're unusually quiet."

With her eyes fixed on the lane, Lavinia smiled. "I was just remembering how I used to run down this hill." She stretched her arm out the window and pointed west. "Right about here, I'd be heading over to the Chapman and Flint shipyard to see my uncle Emery, your name-sake. So much has changed since then."

"That's true, but a part of me believes everything changes and everything remains the same. It's 1913, and though science has advanced the way we practice medicine, the way we care for people is still guided by our humanity. What we fear, love, dread, and desire doesn't change much."

Cocking her head, Vinnie studied her son's profile, noting his straight nose, chiseled jaw, and stylish black derby. "You're a smart man, Doctor Rowley. Have I told you I like the cut of your jib and that black derby you're wearing?"

"No, but I'm not surprised. You're my mother, after all."

"Yes, I am," she said with a lilt in her voice. Then she caught a glimpse of the Georges River and grinned.

At that moment, the lines on her face etched by sixty-one years of struggle, heartache, and love faded slightly, and Vinnie sparkled like that girl who had arrived an orphan and found a home on the lane that ran from the prison to the river. When Emery parked his fancy new automobile as close as possible to the Burgess and O'Brien Store, Vinnie jumped out.

Honor and Galen were waiting in the shade of an old chestnut tree with their eight-month-old daughter, Susie, asleep in her carriage and their three-year-old son, Liam, playing with his toy bunny. They had left their house at half past nine to walk across the toll bridge, enjoy the sunshine, and exhaust their toddler before the grand opening. Rocking the carriage, Honor hoped their plan would work. Today was a big day for Thomaston. An old, beloved store was about to change hands. As soon as the red ribbon was cut, the Dunn & Elliott Store would open where the Burgess and O'Brien Store had operated for more than fifty years. A Thomaston tradition was about to rise again. Honor was excited because she knew how hard her husband, father-in-law, and some of their dearest friends had worked to complete this achievement.

As soon as Galen spotted his mother and brother approaching the store, he waved and called out, "Ma, Emery, over here!"

Hearing his voice, Vinnie looked toward the river and waved back. Glancing at Emery, she smiled wryly. "I guess we're not the first ones here. Now, where do you suppose your father and his bosses are? I expected to see Arthur standing at the door with scissors in hand."

"That's funny. I expected Pop to be the one holding the scissors while George made a speech with Arthur and the other partners at his side clapping at all the appropriate moments."

"Don't be smug, Em," said Vinnie, lifting her skirt so she could walk faster. "Today is a milestone. The Dunn and Elliot Company is stepping into the future and so are we. We haven't built a sailing vessel since the *E. Starr Jones*, and we can't rely on making replacement sails if the ship-yards are closing and the merchant fleets are dwindling."

Emery stopped, took off his derby, and ran his fingers through his short, sandy-colored hair. "Maybe I'm just feeling the heat, but isn't that Charlie Flint standing next to Pop, Olivia, Owen, and my darling mischievous neph-ews over there?"

"Where?" asked Vinnie, scanning the crowd.

Emery pointed at the weathered building twenty yards away. "There! Under that big sign. You know, the one that says 'Dunn and Elliott Company Store.'"

"Oh, my Lord! What's he doing here?"

"I bet he came with Corinne and the kids. Owen was supposed to pick them up at the train station. Jeremy couldn't come because he had to go to Nicaragua on Flint business, so Charlie is here in his place to keep an eye on Reuben and Julia."

"That sounds like something Charlie would do," said Vinnie, shaking her head. "Why don't you tell Galen and Honor to come up to the store? They'll be cutting the ribbon soon, so try to hurry them a bit. I'll say hello to Charlie and wait with your father and the rest of the family by the door."

"Okay, but that baby carriage is apt to slow us down. Don't let them start without us!"

When George stepped up to the ribbon stretched across the open door of the newly scrubbed, painted, and fully stocked grain, coal, and supply store, the crowd roared and George beamed, but it was the captain who spoke.

"On behalf of the Dunn and Elliot families, I'm honored to recognize the grand opening of a Thomaston tradition, the store at the foot of the lane, and to formally announce the new owners of the Burgess-O'Brien wharf and coal business. Though the Dunn and Elliot sign mounted on the storefront behind me is new, the store's service to this community will remain the same. Thank you for coming out to support us today, and we hope you'll keep coming."

As soon as Arthur tipped his cap, his father cut the ribbon and the crowd cheered as Thomaston Academy's Fife and Drum Corps played "Yankee Doodle."

"This song is appropriate," shouted Charlie over the music.

Gray nodded. "They play it better than any other."

"What's that?" asked Charlie, cupping his ear.

"I think he said it's the only one they know, but he's being facetious," said Vinnie, stepping closer.

Charlie laughed. "Facetious? You must have gone to Colby."

"'Tis true, and I've been working for lawyers for thirty some—"

"And now you're working for Galen," chimed in Gray, "but today we're celebrating, so let's step inside and have some punch, shall we?"

Charlie pulled a flask from the pocket of his well-tailored suit and winked. "Yes, that sun is strong, and I'm parched."

"Oh no you don't, Charles Ranlett Flint," chided Vinnie, folding her arms. "In New York, you may be the Father of Trusts, the businessman with a talent for growing companies, but in Thomaston, you're the boy who spent his summers at the Chapman and Flint yard, learning how to build ships from John McDonald. Now, in spirit if not name, you're the grandfather of Reuben and Julia Brown."

As Charlie slipped the flask back into his pocket, his rugged face, shielded by a thick handlebar mustache, turned red. Dropping his gaze, he cleared his throat and said sheepishly, "Of course, you're right. I'm here to help care for Reuben and Julia, so I need all my wits about me. Besides, I'm the one responsible for their father's absence. Jeremy is in Central America because of me. He's my right hand at Flint and Dearborn."

"Oh, Lavinia, give the man a break," pleaded Gray. "This is the first time since Corinne and Jeremy's wedding that he's been home. He's earned a shot of whiskey in his punch. It *is* almost noon."

Vinnie linked arms with both of them. "Maybe half a shot. We do have a lot to celebrate." She tilted her head and fixed her eyes on Charlie. "Tell me again how you formed the Computing-Tabulating-Recording Company."

"That's a mouthful," Charlie acknowledged, patting her arm. "Two years ago, I merged the International Time Recording Company, Computing Scale Company, and Tabulating Machine Company to form CTR, based in Endicott, New York, and that deal may define me."

"Why is it so important?"

"Because if America is going to compete with cheap labor abroad, we're going to have to develop technically, and CTR is all about automation and efficiency."

As they headed over to the refreshments on a table near a window with an amazing view of the Georges River, Corinne rushed over and placed her two-year-old's hand in Charlie's. "Reuben needs to find a privy. Can you keep an eye on Julia for a minute? I just changed her nappy and fed her so she should be good."

Charlie grinned and lifted the towheaded toddler into his arms. "I'm always happy to watch this little angel.

And if I remember correctly, there's a privy by the lilac bush out back."

"Thank you," mouthed Corinne as she placed her hands on her five-year-old's shoulders and pushed him gently toward the door, circumventing the townsfolk crowding the expanse of D&E's gleaming pine floor.

An hour later, Gray, Charlie, and Galen excused themselves from the festivities at Dunn & Elliot's newly acquired property and strolled down Water Street to visit Gray's office at the sail loft. In the middle of the day under the warmth of a summer sun, they walked quietly, enjoying the peaceful beauty of a soft breeze, a topaz sky, and shimmering water.

"It feels like home, though the changes are disconcerting," Charlie murmured.

Glancing at his friend, Gray paused to puff on his pipe and think. In the shadow of Dunn & Elliot's loft, the heart of Thomaston's waterfront since 1874, the three men stood and pondered their past and future.

Galen mumbled, "It's too quiet."

"The shipyards are closed or closing," said Gray.

"It's a stark difference from my youth," added Charlie. "Back then every yard was bustling six or seven days a week, and at times the noise was deafening. Now we can whisper and be heard."

"I remember," said Gray, "when Washburn Brothers and Company purchased Sam Watts's yard at the foot of Knox Street. The Washburn yard closed two years ago."

"Wasn't the Sam Watts yard one of the oldest in town?" asked Galen.

"Yes," nodded Charlie. "Watts built the *Alfred D. Snow* in seventy-seven. He retired in eighty-one. Before he took down his sign, he had built over fifty barks, schooners,

and square rigs. At the height of his career, he was building in more than one yard."

Gray cupped his chin, weighed his words, and quietly
said, "When you talk about Thomaston's history, I can't
believe you left."

Dropping his gaze, Charlie swallowed hard. "My feet
may have left, but my heart never did."

Gray fell silent, and Galen filled the pause by kicking
a stone. He hurled another into the river and followed up
with a question. "Did you hear that Mrs. Willey died?"

"Yes, I read about her passing in the *Courier-Gazette*—I
have it sent to me in New York. It's hard to believe her
husband drowned twenty-five years ago and she stayed
in that big house. I spoke with Corinne about it. She told
me Arthur would like to buy that mansion overlooking
the river."

Galen smiled. "Well, he's renting one of his father's
smaller properties on the other side of the street. His family is growing, though. I suspect he'd love to live in the
Captain Willey House on top of the hill."

Patting Galen on the back, Charlie looked at Gray.
"Your son is sharp, and his eyes are wide open."

"He's like his mother."

"Then he's truly blessed," said Charlie, glancing back
at the lane and the bridge spanning the Georges.

A Rallying Cry

Cordelia Willey's son, Walter, sold his mother's coveted home on the corner of Dunn and Elliot Streets to Captain and Mrs. Arthur Elliot on a blustery day in March 1917. Shortly after they signed the documents, Lilla and Arthur brought their children over to their dream house. As soon as Arthur opened the front door, Edward and Albert ran up the stairs while their mother, holding Barbara's hand, trailed behind. Arthur looked up and flashed a smile. He touched the newel post and said a quick silent prayer that D&E would find some new investors so they could keep building ships. Over the past few months, their fleet had dwindled to just four schooners, putting the yard in jeopardy. Arthur knew he was taking a chance buying a house when the future of shipbuilding was so uncertain, but he was still a live Yankee, and he was banking on a rising tide.

"Pa!" shouted Edward. "Come and see my room. It's huge!"

"I can see the Georges from my window," added Albert.

"I'm coming," called Arthur, climbing two steps at a time.

"Please hurry," laughed Lilla. "Barbara has discovered the flush toilet."

A month later, Arthur's prayer was answered, but the reply was bittersweet. On April 2, 1917, the United States officially entered World War One, and the demand for ships skyrocketed. Though Richard F. Dunn had left D&E by then, George Elliot and two of his sons were ready to answer the call. They moved quickly to resume construction of four-masted vessels—schooners and barkentines. With workers returning to the Thomaston shipyards, the Dunn & Elliot Store was happy to hire two more clerks to stock the shelves with groceries and fill the bins with coal.

By July, the horror of war had intensified overseas, but at home the keel of the *Margaret Throop* was laid down with optimism and a new spirit of patriotism. She was the first new schooner in over a decade to be on the ways at the Dunn & Elliot shipyard. The shipbuilders were humming. Encouraged by their shanties, the townsfolk were spending money again. They were eager to meet and greet each other on the lane, at Mill Creek, on Main Street, or in their neighbor's dooryard. Olivia Rowley Sutton shared their enthusiasm.

After clearing the breakfast dishes, Olivia wiped her hands on her apron and turned to face her boys, Robert, Francis, and Luke. "Dad is waiting in the barn with your fishing poles and bait, so grab those lunch pails on the sideboard and hurry up." Nodding toward the kitchen door, she added, "Only the early bird catches a fish."

"But Ma, I'm not a bird," said Luke, the six-year-old, revealing his missing front teeth.

"Oh yes, you are. You're my little wren. Don't worry. Your brothers will make sure you catch a fish, won't you, boys?"

"Sure," said Robert, rushing to the kitchen door. "We'll all catch fish. We've never been skunked at the Crick."

As soon as they were gone, she stepped up to the telephone mounted on the wall, gave it a crank, held the receiver to her ear, and asked the operator to connect her to Lilla Elliot. Fortunately, the line was clear, and Lilla answered her assigned ring, a special cadence of four rings, two long rings followed by two short rings.

"Hello."

"Good morning, Lilla. It's Olivia."

"Who else would it be? I'm surprised the line was clear, though. You better talk fast. Others will be hopping on soon."

"Okay, I'm calling because I have an idea."

"Oh, Liv, you always have an idea. What's the latest?"

"A surprise. Let's throw a party for Arthur's forty-first birthday."

"You know he hates surprises. Besides, his birthday is less than two weeks away. We don't have enough time."

"That's plenty of time to plan a small garden party. You have the garden and I'll invite the guests!"

"I'm curious," said a mellifluous voice. "Will I be invited?"

"Who's speaking?" asked Olivia.

"Maria, your sister-in-law."

"Of course, we share a party line, don't we?"

"And I'm coming, too," said another sweet voice.

"May I ask who's speaking?"

"Arthur's favorite cousin."

"Helen! I'm so glad you joined the line!" laughed Lilla.

Eleven days later, on a hot Wednesday afternoon, Gray found Arthur by the ways, inspecting the day's work. The hull of the *Margaret Throop* was taking shape on schedule, and the mood in the yard was almost festive.

"Arthur, your wife just called," shouted Gray. "She said you promised to come home early to take the boys fishing at the Crick. They're waiting for you."

"What?" asked Arthur cupping his ear. "Can't hear you."

Striding up to his boss, who was only a few years older than his sons, Gray cleared his throat. "Sorry to shout into the wind like that, but Lilla just called to remind you that you're due home. You promised to take your boys fishing."

"It's only a quarter past four," replied Arthur.

"I'm just the messenger, but Lilla said you promised to be home at four o'clock. I'm guessing she thinks you're late."

Arthur shook his head. "Well, I better hurry then. Tell the clerk to call her back. I'll be there in fifteen minutes, twenty at most."

"Don't worry. I'll call her myself."

"Thanks, Gray. Where would I be without you?"

Walking away, the sixty-nine-year-old called back, "Stranded, without a suit of sails."

"True," shouted Arthur. "Thank God you're with me."

But Gray didn't catch the praise—he was engulfed in the music of the joiners, the symphony of buzzing saws, pounding hammers, and a stiff breeze.

At half past four, Arthur drove up Elliot Street, rounded the corner at Dunn Street, and parked his Model T near his side door, not realizing that the barn behind the ell of his rambling house was packed with friends and family. As soon as he stepped out of the car, the barn doors opened and thirty people jumped out hooting and hollering, "Surprise!"

Dumbfounded, the captain scanned the crowd for Lilla. When he found her, he opened his arms, and she ran to him.

Hugging him tight, she exclaimed, "Happy Birthday, my love! We wanted to surprise you."

"You have," laughed Arthur. "You have definitely surprised me."

Taking his hand, Lilla led him to the barn, which had been cleared, swept, and decorated from the floor to the rafters. There were lanterns, colored streamers, and long tables covered with white linen cloths. Every table was filled with pitchers of ale and fruit punch, and huge platters of fruit, fried chicken, and cornbread. Best of all, there was a band and a dance floor. The old barn had never looked so good. Arthur noticed every glimmer of light, including the love in his wife's eyes. Within seconds, the pair was enveloped by their children. George and Mary Ella stepped up to hug their son and congratulate Lilla for pulling off one of the biggest surprises in Thomaston history. Arthur's siblings formed a ring around him, and Galen placed two fingers in his mouth and whistled.

"Listen! Everyone!"

He paused as a hush fell over the barn. He resumed. "We all want to wish Arthur a happy day and many more. There's food to eat, ale to drink, and a dance floor waiting, so on a count of three let's shout, 'Happy Birthday, Arthur!' and start the party. Lilla, will you count?"

She nodded. "One...two...*three!*"

The crowd roared, "Happy Birthday, Arthur!"

Olivia seized the moment to tap the double bass player on the shoulder. "A two-step, please."

The dance floor filled, and Vinnie came to her daughter's side. "What makes me think this party was your idea?"

"Oh, Ma, we all needed it."

"Indeed we did. First there was no work, then there was no *end* to work. There's still a lot to worry about."

Olivia wrung her hands. "I'm so grateful Rockland-Rockport Lime was able to buy so many of the struggling lime companies before they closed. Maybe it's true that lime is being replaced by more efficient building materials, but the lime kilns of Maine are still valuable."

"Yes, they have value, but we can't deny that the newer materials are cheaper and easier to produce and deliver. I think that's called progress."

"I suppose," sighed Olivia. "I'm just glad the Lime Rock Railroad has made it easier to move limestone from the quarries to the kilns. They offered Owen a job when he needed one."

"Oh, my dear, they're lucky he said yes. They desperately needed someone to manage their scheduling and payroll, and Owen was the best man for the job. Besides, his position at Lime Rock hasn't stopped him from making casks. He's still a cooper, and the lime industry needs him."

Olivia met her mother's eyes and matched them with intensity. "If it wasn't for Lime Rock, we would've been forced to leave Thomaston and look for work elsewhere."

"But you didn't. Sometimes God answers our prayers the way we hope," said Vinnie, gazing at the dance floor. "Oh my!" she exclaimed, spying a pretty young woman resting her head on her son's shoulder. "Is that Jane Fenn dancing with Emery?"

Olivia followed her mother's stare and whispered, "That can't be Jane. She wasn't on the guest list."

"Well, I don't know another woman with curly raven-colored hair who would wear a designer dress and black patent leather slippers to a barnyard dance. Do you?"

"No," said Olivia, pursing her lips and twirling a strand of her straight blond hair.

"Isn't Jane's father one of the owners of the Lime Rock Railroad?"

"Yes, maybe that's the connection. Owen works for him."

"I'm not sure I follow," said Vinnie cocking an eyebrow.

"I bet Owen introduced Emery to Jane, and that's why she's here."

Watching her son spin the tall, slender brunette at the center of the barn's dusty floor, Vinnie murmured, "It's about time that man fell in love."

"What did you say, Ma?"

"I said your brother looks spellbound."

"Yes," grinned Olivia. "He's in love at last."

A U-Boat off the Coast

The church bells started tolling at a quarter past five, slowing traffic on Main, Knox, Pine, Green, Wadsworth, Hyler, Water, and every other street in Thomaston. As soon as Vinnie heard them, she put on her red hat, her dark-blue coat, and her fur-lined boots and rushed out the door.

"Gray, the bells...we have to go," she called over the wind and snow.

He put down his shovel, strode to her side, and wrapped his arms around her. "There's no need to hurry, my love. We're already too late. We knew this was coming—"

"We didn't say goodbye," she said, choking back tears.

"No, but George knew how we felt, and Mary Ella and his children were with him."

"His grandchildren, too," cried Vinnie, burying her face in his chest.

"They need some time to grieve privately before they have to face the whole town."

"You're right," she said, stepping back. "I'll make a lemon cake and drop it off in the morning. But first I have to telephone Emery and Corinne. They can't hear the bells in Rockland and New York."

He reached for her hand and pulled her back. "Tell them gently, Liv. They loved him, too."

She kissed him and whispered, "I know."

Early the next day, a line started forming outside Ten Elliot Street. Shopkeepers, bankers, schoolteachers, block makers, shipwrights, spar makers, sailmakers, coopers, doctors, lawyers, and prison guards all wanted to pay their respects to the senior partner of Dunn & Elliot Company. The line snaked around the elegant Italianate from the front door facing east to the barn door facing north and continued west to Captain Arthur's house on the corner of Dunn and Elliot Streets. Scores of people bundled in coats, hats, and scarves stood in drifting snow, waiting to say farewell to a seventy-eight-year-old giant who had died before seeing his newest schooner slide over the ways. If construction continued on schedule, the *Margaret Throop* would launch in May.

Captain Arthur Elliot stood at his father's gravesite along with his mother and his sister, Ida, his five brothers and their wives, his niece Madeline, Aunt Lizzie, Cousin Helen, his three children, and his closest friends. The Dunns, Rowleys, Counces, and Suttons were all there, including Corinne and Jeremy Brown from New York. Though it was a frigid day, the sun was shining, and all the granite tombstones glistened in the February light.

When the Congregational minister stepped to the head of the mahogany coffin covered with a blanket of white lilies, everyone bowed their heads and recited the Lord's Prayer. Then Helen stepped forward and sang "Amazing Grace," and the tears began to flow. The Elliot men pulled out their handkerchiefs and offered them to their wives.

Richard placed his arm around his mother's shoulder and Arthur held her hand. Vinnie softly cried on Gray's shoulder, and Olivia crumpled in Owen's arms. Every face was veiled with sorrow. The hole before them seemed deeper than any other. George Elliot was following Thomas Dunn, Sam Watts, Edward O'Brien, and so many other great shipbuilders. It was the end of February, but it was also the beginning of the end of an era. The tall sailing ships were passing out of sight.

By the middle of May, the lilacs were in bloom, the azaleas were budding, and the grass was greening. The launch of the *Margaret Throop* had lifted everyone's spirits, especially at the foot of Green Street. Though he was buried in paperwork, Gray was humming when Emery entered his office at the northeast corner of the sail loft.

"Hi, Pop, can you spare a minute?"

"For you?" he asked, peering over his spectacles.

"Yeah, for me."

"Well, I hate to stop reading this fascinating letter from the captain of Dunn and Elliot's newest four-master—"

"Lockland Heyliger?"

Nodding, Gray answered with a question. "Do you remember him?"

"Of course. He took command of the *E. Starr Jones* after Arthur."

"That was ten years ago. Now the *E. Starr Jones* has a new captain and Lockland is in command of the *Margaret Throop*."

Emery smiled wryly. "The seafaring life is ever-changing."

"Lockland is a good man. He's from Saba, the Caribbean Netherlands, and he owns a good share of the schooner, so he doesn't waste time in port. He trades one cargo for another and keeps sailing. But enough about our interest in the West Indies. What brings you to Thomaston on a Tuesday afternoon? Shouldn't you be taking out an appendix or something in Rockland right now?"

"Probably, but my partner can handle it. I have something important to tell you."

Gray took off his glasses and pointed to the oak chair in front of his desk. "Have a seat. I'm all ears, son."

Sitting down, Emery cleared his throat, focused on his father's weathered face, and paused.

"What's on your mind, son? Spit it out."

"I'm going to ask Jane to marry me."

Gray slapped his knee. "I knew it!" he cried, jumping up and rushing to the front of his desk. Pulling his oldest son out of his chair, he slapped him on the back. "That's wonderful news! Have you told your mother?"

"Not yet. I wanted to mention it to you first."

"Well, I'm honored, but now let's head over to the house. I want to be there when you tell her. I want to see her face light up!"

Stepping out of the office, Emery nodded to the men working on the gleaming expanse of floor covered with rows of sailmakers' benches and heavy white duck. He looked up at the ship's knees—solid hackmatack supporting the loft's upper floor like the deck of a ship—and whistled. As sunlight streamed through the tall windows, he bowed his head, humbled by such craftsmanship.

Moments later, as they exited through the Water Street door, Emery queried his father, "Hey, Pop, didn't you take Ma to dances on the loft's top floor?"

"As a matter of fact, I did. Why?"

"I don't know… I guess I'm thinking about the wedding. I don't mean to get ahead of myself, but if Jane says yes—"

"There's no *if* about it. She's going to say yes. You're the best catch in Knox County."

"Thanks, Pop, but—"

"No buts," said Gray, climbing into his son's shiny Model-T.

"Yeah, I'm confident there'll be a wedding. It's just…"

"Spit it out, Em."

"Jane is twenty-eight. She's almost ten years younger than I am, and she's anxious to start a family. Our world is in such a mess, though. There's a war going on across the Atlantic and it's affecting everyone and everything…"

Glancing at his son, Gray murmured, "All that's true, so what's your point?"

Starting the engine, Emery looked straight ahead and said, "I don't want to wait a year or even six months. I want to marry Jane as soon as possible."

Driving up Green Street, Emery shifted, and Gray fell silent until they pulled into the drive at 20 Hyler Street.

"Would you like to be married at the loft?"

"Yes," said Emery, turning off the motor. "Jane's mother was stricken with consumption three years ago and went to the sanatorium in Hebron. Within a year, she died, and Jane's father remarried three months ago. In truth, Jane doesn't want a big wedding. She attends the Congregational Church in Camden, and the minister is a friend. I think he'd be willing to marry us at the loft if we ask him."

With smiling eyes, Gray replied, "Well, Doc, it sounds like a solid plan, but how soon is soon?"

Still sitting in the driver's seat, he leaned back and took a deep breath. Glancing at his father, he grinned. "July."

A few weeks later, Vinnie watched from her kitchen window as her towheaded granddaughter picked a bunch of anemones and irises and placed them in a basket.

"It looks like Susie has an eye for pretty flowers."

Peering over her mother-in-law's shoulder, Honor smiled. "Just like her nana."

"I'm not so sure about that."

"Well, Galen always says—"

"What do I always say?" asked Galen, letting the screen door slam behind him.

His wife jumped and turned around. "Oh, Galen, you're early. I was just telling your mother how much Susie reminds you of her."

Vinnie touched her crown of white hair and laughed. "How's that possible? She's only six."

"Some things are set at birth, Ma. You can't deny them, and you can't change them."

Pausing, Vinnie studied her son's face. "Why so serious, Galen? It's the end of May and the birds are singing."

Galen sat down on the nearest Windsor chair and murmured, "I got some bad news at the office this morning... That's why I'm early for our Saturday lunch. Where's Pop?"

"He's out back with Liam," she murmured. "I'll get him."

"No, Ma. I'll get him."

"Galen, what is it?"

Standing up, he reached for his mother's hand. "A German U-boat sank the *Hattie Dunn* off the Virginia coast near the entrance to Chesapeake Bay."

Honor gasped and Vinnie went pale.

"Are there survivors?" whispered Vinnie. "Have we heard from Captain Holbrook?"

"According to this morning's report, Captain Charles Holbrook of Tenants Harbor and his crew of six were taken prisoner before the Germans lit the charges. Our Dunn and Elliot schooner is the first American vessel to be sunk in this blasted war. The schooners *Edna* and *Hauppauge* were also blown up, but they didn't sink. We believe all three crews are being held captive on the

U-boat. For obvious reasons, the German captain is keeping their location a secret."

"Oh, dear God," whispered Vinnie, pressing her hands together and raising them to her lips in prayer. "Get your dad and take him to the yard."

"I will. I talked to Arthur before I came over. He and his brothers are headed over to Tenants Harbor to tell Mrs. Holbrook and her children what's happened. After that visit, they'll start calling the families of the crew. They're going to need some help, though."

Honor followed him out the door, calling back to Vinnie, "I'll bring the children in for lunch then take a drive over to St. George and pay Mrs. Holbrook a visit. She and her children are patients of mine."

Vinnie nodded. "Of course, you should go. I'll take care of Susie and Liam."

On the first of July, Corinne arrived at the Thomaston train depot with her ten-year-old son, seven-year-old daughter, and a trunk-load of luggage, ready to plan a small but charming wedding for her brother and his bride-to-be. The timing was perfect. Flint, Dearborn & Company had sent her husband to Central America on the thirtieth of June, and he wasn't due back in New York until the twentieth of July. Since Emery and Jane's wedding was set for the twenty-seventh, she'd reserved a seat on a northbound train departing Grand Central on the twenty-second. If he made all his connections, Jeremy would be able to join his wife and children for the special family event. In the meantime, Reuben and Julia would be able to escape the stifling heat of New York City and explore the wonders of Maine. Corinne would be able to help plan the first wedding at the Dunn & Elliot sail loft.

Catching a whiff of her mother's strawberry-rhu-
barb pie, Corinne smiled. For a moment, she almost forgot her husband was far away. The newspaper headlines
were alarming and the stories coming out of Europe were
terrifying. She closed her eyes, took a deep breath, and
savored the scent.

Opening her eyes, she looked at her mother and sighed
wistfully. "It feels good to be home."

Vinnie wrapped her arms around her, pressed her
face into her wavy auburn hair, and murmured, "Oh,
Corinne, I've missed you. It's been too long, and so much
has happened."

"I know," said Corinne. "I've been thinking about
Captain Holbrook and his crew. Are they all right?"

"Yes, they're okay. It's a miracle they weren't killed."

Corinne poured two glasses of lemonade, placed them
on the kitchen table, and pulled out a chair. "Let's sit
down and talk."

"That sounds lovely," said Vinnie as they both sat down.

"Pa took the kids straight to the barn. They've been
begging to see the horses since we stepped off the train."

"Your father's a smart man. He knows how to keep
children busy and happy."

Lifting her glass, Corinne chuckled, "I may have suggested it. I wanted us to catch up quietly before all the
excitement begins."

Vinnie sighed. "So much excitement...some good and
some not."

"Oh Ma, I'm sorry the war has come so close to home.
Tell me about the *Hattie Dunn*."

"It's hard to talk about," she said softly, reaching for
a month-old newspaper stacked on the chair beside her.
Setting the paper on the table, she shook her head. "I've
been saving the articles. On the twenty-fifth of May, a
German U-Boat stopped three American schooners off

Virginia, took their crews captive, and bombed all three. The *Hattie Dunn* was the only one that sank. The other two were severely damaged but remained afloat. As soon as D and E was notified, Arthur and his brothers drove over to Tenants Harbor to be with Captain Holbrook's family. The waiting was the worst part, but there were no casualties. All three crews were released and made it home."

"Oh my God! That's too close."

"Ah, but the story continues. On the second of June, off the coast of New Jersey, the same U-Boat destroyed the *Isabel B. Wiley*, a Bath-built schooner, and kept hunting. Before dusk, they attacked five more vessels, two schooners, two freighters, and a passenger liner. On that horrible day, there were thirteen casualties, but the German captain wasn't to blame. Thirteen passengers aboard the *Carolina* drowned when their lifeboat capsized. The captain's mission was to destroy American merchant vessels, and he did."

Corinne dropped her gaze and swallowed hard. "How many vessels were lost in all?"

"In a month, twenty-three. Someone in Washington called Arthur yesterday. They need more schooners."

"How dreadful! And what a change for Dunn and Elliot."

At that moment the door burst open, and Julia ran in followed by her big brother and Grandpa.

"Hello, Nana! We're here for a whole month! And guess what?"

"What, my darling?" asked Vinnie, cupping Julia's sweet round face in her hand.

"Grandpa's going to teach me to ride!"

Looking up at Gray, she smiled. "You're going to start her on Trixie, right?"

"Yes, dear, the sweetest little mare in the stable."

"Good. What's Grandpa going to teach you, Reuben?"

"He's going to teach me how to sail," grinned the ten-year-old. "I already know how to ride."

Corinne spoke up, saying, "Well, you're very lucky because Grandpa is a master of both! He can ride and he can sail."

"Ah, you're too kind," said Gray with a wink. "I'm just a sailmaker who happens to love boats and horses equally."

"He loves dogs, too," said Reuben. "We're going over to Uncle Galen's house after supper. Grandpa wants us to meet Dudley, the newest puppy in the family."

Julia turned toward her mother with woeful eyes. "I wish we could have a dog."

"I do, too," said Corinne, patting her daughter's curly red hair, "but you and Reuben go to school, and I work at the hospital whenever they need me. Who would take care of a puppy at our house?"

"Daddy?"

Reuben laughed. "He works for Flint and Dearborn, and you know he travels a lot."

Pouting, Julia looked at her nana. "Why don't you and Grandpa have a dog?"

"We did. We had two dogs."

"What happened to them?"

"They died, honey."

Gray sat down, put Julia on his knee and whispered, "We loved Whit and Twain so much we couldn't replace them."

"But love doesn't die. Right, Mommy?"

"Yes, dear, that's right."

Julia looped her arms around her grandfather's neck. "Someday you'll find another dog and bring him home. And just like Whit and Twain, you'll love him too much."

Burnt to Bitterness or Spun to Gold

Vinnie's heart sank as she read the banner headline of the *Courier-Gazette*: **Spanish Flu Ravages New York City**.

"What's wrong?" asked Gray. "It's a beautiful September morning, and you look like you just saw a ghost."

"Not a ghost, but a dark shadow."

"Nonsense," boomed Gray. "Dunn and Elliot just announced we're to build two barkentines, the *Cecil P. Stewart* and the *Reine Marie Stewart*, and we've already laid the keel for the first. The yard hasn't been this busy in years."

"I'm glad the shipyard is doing well, but the world is not," she said, lifting and folding the newspaper so the headline stood out. "Look at this."

He looked at the bold print and shook his head.

Vinnie dropped the paper and stared at her husband of forty-one years. "I'm worried about Corinne. In July, she told me that Brooklyn Hospital had asked her to work full-time. I told her to think about it before saying yes. She explained why she couldn't say no—hundreds of doctors and nurses have joined the Army Medical Corps to support the war effort, and the city's hospitals are grossly understaffed."

"I remember talking to Jeremy after Jane and Emery's wedding. He said Corinne had made up her mind and they were going to ask their nanny to move in with them."

Sighing, Vinnie stood up. "Why do I fear that beautiful summer wedding was the last happy celebration our family will have for a long time?"

He looped his arm around her small waist and pulled her close. "Don't say that. We'll be all right. The Rowley family is strong and resolute. We can't stop Corinne from doing what her heart wants. She was born to help others, like your mother, Cora."

"You're right," she said, resting her head on his shoulder. "You're always right."

"Not always," he whispered, "but I've been praying a lot, and it seems to help."

She kissed his cheek and gently pushed him away. "I pray best when I'm riding a horse. Maybe we should saddle Rocky and Trixie and ride over to Brooklyn Heights, the one that's in Maine, not New York."

"Now that's something we can do," chuckled Gray. "But first I have to kiss you."

On Monday morning, Gray stepped into the light, airy law office of Moore and Rowley on the second floor of the Stimpson Block and cleared his throat. Instantly, Joe, Galen, and the new assistant, Maria Sutton, lifted their heads and dropped their jaws.

Galen stood up. "Pop...what brings you uptown?"

"Ayuh, need to talk with you," he said, taking off his hat. Glancing at Joe, he nodded. "Good morning, Mr. Moore, or is it afternoon?"

Putting down his pen, Joe chuckled, "It's almost noon. Maria and I were just heading out for lunch."

"Well, don't hurry on my account. Galen and I can step outside."

"That won't be necessary," said Joe as he slipped on his suit jacket. "This is Maria's second week on the job, and I promised to take her to lunch and give her a chance to ask lots of questions. It's hard to fill Lavinia's shoes, you know."

Standing near the door, Maria smiled. "It's true, Mr. Rowley. Last Friday I wanted to call her and tell her she was too young to retire."

Gray gave her a wink and a smile. "I'll tell her you said so, but the job is yours and you'll do just fine."

"Thank you, Mr. Rowley. I appreciate your kindness."

When Maria and Joe had left, Gray dropped his head and Galen sat down to listen.

"Jeremy called me long distance," said Gray in a low but steady voice. "It was a good connection, but bad news…"

"You're scaring me, Pop. Just say it."

"Your sister is spiking a high fever," said Gray in a single breath.

"Corinne is sick?"

"The Spanish flu is hitting New York City with a vengeance. She's been working nonstop on the maternity ward. About a week ago, the hospital ran out of beds on every floor—"

"Is she going to make it?"

Shaking his head, Gray looked into his son's slate-blue eyes.

When the tears subsided, Galen pulled out a handkerchief, wiped his nose, and picked up the phone.

"Who are you calling?"

"I'm calling Emery. I assume Mother knows."

"Yes, Jeremy called her first."

"So, I should call Emery, right?"

Shaking his head, Gray murmured, "No, I called him. He's on his way."

"What about Olivia?" he asked, still holding the receiver.

"I thought we could walk over to Pine Street and tell her together. The boys don't get out of school until three."

Galen hung up the receiver and spun his chair around to face the window. Then he asked the hardest question. "What about Reuben and Julia?"

"A few weeks ago, when Brooklyn Hospital started to fill up, Corinne and Jeremy sent them to the Flints' summer home with their nanny. It's only an hour outside the city, but the estate functions like an island. They're all right, and Charlie has promised to do everything he can to keep them that way."

"I'm sure he will," said Galen, swallowing hard and standing up. "Not even Charlie can fix this."

Olivia was toiling in her garden, clearing the flower beds of zinnias and snapdragons, and making room for hardy chrysanthemums crowned with burgundy and gold when she heard footsteps. Turning, she lifted her hand to shield her eyes and gasped.

"My gosh, you look paler than ghosts. Why are you here?"

Galen reached for her hand and pulled her up. He tossed his head toward the house and said, "We could use a drink. Do you have any hard cider?"

"Sure," she said, looking from her tall sandy-haired brother to her even taller, but balding, father. "I'll pour us all a glass. Follow me."

Inside, Galen sat at the big round table at the heart of the sun-filled kitchen while Gray stood at his daughter's elbow, watching her pour three tall glasses of cold cider. No one said a word.

When Olivia sat down, Gray sat next to her and took her hand. "Honey, your sister was struck with the Spanish flu. She has a bad fever."

Bolting up, Olivia said, "How bad?"

"Bad enough," whispered her father.

"We have to go!" she cried. "We have to go right now!"

"No," said her father. "We have to wait."

"Pop's right, Liv."

"Not this time," she shouted. "Corinne needs us—"

"No, Olivia, Pop's right," said Emery from the doorway. "All we can do is wait and hope."

Falling back into her chair, Olivia sighed, "So we wait, then."

Galen took a swig of cider and set his glass on the table. "But not here, right Pop?"

"That's right," nodded Gray. "We're going home to sit with your Ma till we know for certain."

Olivia leaned forward, placed her hands on the arms of her Windsor chair, and pushed herself up. "I'll call Owen and tell him to pick up the boys."

"I'll call Honor and tell her to meet us on Hyler Street with Liam and Susie."

"Who wants to drive with me?" asked Emery.

"You drive like you're driving an ambulance," chided Galen. "I'll walk."

"Me, too," said Olivia.

Gray disagreed, though. In a huff, he put on his cap and looked his oldest son in the eye. "I'll ride with you, Doc. Let's go."

Ten days later, on the thirtieth of September, Jeremy arrived at the train depot with his two children and Charlie and Kate Flint. Lavinia and Gray were waiting on the platform along with Emery and Jane, Galen and Honor, Olivia and

Owen, and their children. Captain Arthur, Lilla, and their children were also present. The men hoisted Corinne's casket to their shoulders and carried her body to the black carriage standing ready. Her prize Morgan horses, Lincoln and Dusty, would take her to her final resting place at the village cemetery. Her family and friends would follow in a long, winding funeral procession. The sky was the bluest blue, but no one noticed.

At the gravesite, not far from the tombstone of Aunt Susan and Uncle Emery, Lavinia was the second to last to say goodbye. She laid her red rose on top of the blanket of flowers and dropped to her knees. As her tears became sobs, Gray bent down to comfort her. He put his arm around her and rocked from side to side, whispering, "Oh, my love, oh, my love, I'm with you."

Choking back tears, Jeremy placed his rose on top of the others and joined his children and the rest of the family as they walked toward the cars waiting to take them home. No one looked back, but the wailing stayed with them.

After the funeral, friends and family gathered at 20 Hyler Street. Amelia and her daughter Maria took care of every detail. There were pitchers of lemonade and hard cider lined up on the sideboard. The dining room table was covered with platters of roast beef, baked ham, biscuits, sliced fruit, and a wide assortment of cakes and pies. In every nook and cranny, there were clusters of people dressed in black, holding a plate or a glass and speaking softly, creating a hum that permeated the house.

Trying to escape, Olivia slipped outside and found Jeremy standing alone on the side porch, his back to the door. He didn't turn around, so she stepped to his side.

"Can I get you something to eat?"

"No, I'm not hungry."

"How 'bout a drink?"

"I'm not thirsty, either."

She nudged him with an elbow. "Corinne always loved sliced ham, applesauce, and buttered biscuits. We have two out of three, and she'd want you to have some."

Bowing his head, he squeezed the bridge of his nose, holding back his emotions.

"We're here for you. We're all here for you, but your kids need you to stay strong—"

"Why? They hardly know me. I've spent so much time away, focusing more on business than family. Now my wife, my love, is gone." He turned to face her and the dam broke.

"Oh Liv," he sobbed, "what will I do without her?"

"You'll live, and you'll love Reuben, Julia, and all of us. We're a family, Jeremy...we're *your* family. Now, come inside."

Moments of Epiphany

By the end of January, the hull of the *Cecil P. Stewart*, the first barkentine on the ways at D&E since 1880, was taking shape and the yard was alive with caulkers, shipwrights, and demanding bosses, like Captain Arthur. On the morning of January 26, 1919, Gray was there, too. He stood next to the captain checking on the progress of the ship he planned to fit with the best suit of sails on the east coast. Everyone was glad to see him, especially Arthur.

"She's going to be a beauty, right?"

Gray rubbed his beard and nodded. "Aye, she even looks good without a deck."

Arthur laughed, "Imagine that! A hull of a ship!"

The two Yankee shipbuilders, one middle-aged and the other seventy years old, looked up at the bow of their newest bark and filled their lungs with the scent of salt and pine.

"It feels good to be building again," said Arthur, glancing sideways. "Soon we'll be starting on her twin sister, *Reine Marie Stewart*. I know it's been hard—"

"I'm better at work than at home."

"I think about her, too."

"Of course, you do," he said, patting his boss's shoulder. "She's impossible to forget."

"How's Jeremy?"

"Surviving. Vinnie wants him to move up here with Reuben and Julia."

"What does he want?"

"He wants Corinne."

Looking over the river to Brooklyn Heights, Arthur cleared his throat. "I was visiting with Olivia and Owen last Sunday and Maria was there. She said there was a sweet cape for sale in Tenants Harbor. She thought it would make a perfect summer home for Jeremy and his children."

"I've heard," said Gray, grinning.

The captain shook his head. "Let me guess: Olivia told Vinnie all about it."

"Yeah, she did. And on Monday morning, bright and early, Vinnie made a long-distance call to Jeremy in New York."

Both men laughed, and for a moment, Gray felt the weight on his heart lift. Then he saw Frank Elliot running down the hill and froze.

Frank was shouting, but the wind was catching his words. When he was ten feet away, he stopped to take a breath. He shouted, "Arthur! It's the *E. Starr Jones*. She's run aground." A few seconds later, he handed his brother a telegram.

Silently, Arthur read the message: *E. STARR JONES ran aground 25 January off Rio Grande do Sul, Brazil, en route to Buenos Aires. Expected to be total loss. Crew safe.*

"How bad?" asked Gray.

"She's gone," said the captain.

When the crocuses and daffodils started popping up in her dooryard, Vinnie knew it was time to convince Jeremy to buy the cape over in Tenants Harbor, the one Maria

Sutton had discovered. Vinnie and Olivia had deemed it perfect for a summer hideaway. Above all, she wanted to keep her family close, and New York wasn't close enough. Corinne had been gone since the end of September, and yesterday was the first time she had seen Jeremy, Reuben, and Julia in six long months. Like Olivia, she believed the little cape was a dream house, and today was the day to set that dream in motion if she could just get everybody into their automobiles.

"Jeremy, you can sit up front with Gray. Julia can sit with me in the back, and Reuben can drive with Aunt Olivia. How does that sound?"

Gray chuckled, "Just say 'yes, ma'am.' That's what I do, and it works."

"Yes, ma'am," repeated Jeremy. He turned toward his son and winked. "Behave yourself. I'll see you in Tenants Harbor."

"Don't worry, Pop. My cousins will be in the backseat. They're the ones who'll be raising a ruckus."

"He's right, Uncle Jeremy," chimed in Luke. "Ma says trouble follows us wherever we go, especially me. I have to be naughty, though. I'm the smallest." He tossed his head and grinned. "If I wasn't so skinny, we couldn't all fit in the backseat of that car."

"I'm counting on it," said Jeremy as he climbed into Gray's dusty Model T. "Now follow us and try not to get lost."

Luke nodded then looked over his shoulder and hurried his mother. "Come on, Ma! They're leaving, and we don't want to fall behind."

"Don't worry," laughed Olivia, herding the boys into her car. "I know the way."

Twenty minutes later, Gray parked his fancy automobile behind the house, which was nestled in a grove of pines and set back from the road. As soon as they piled

271

out of the car, they rushed around the house to the front door facing the harbor and stopped to admire the view. The light skimmed across the water and boats shimmered like pearls on a string.

Vinnie giggled, but Jeremy gasped, "Oh, sweet Lord! Look at that!"

And Gray, putting his hand on Jeremy's shoulder, said, "A slice of heaven."

"Is Mommy here?" asked Julia.

Jeremy bent down and whispered in her ear, "I'd like to think so."

At that moment, Olivia arrived with her sons in tow. The boys were excited and making lots of noise. Luke, the youngest, shouted, "Uncle Jeremy, this place is *beautiful*!"

"Yes, yes it is," laughed Jeremy.

As soon as Vinnie heard that happy sound, she smiled. "Let's go inside, shall we?"

On the morning of June 18, 1919, Galen arrived at his office at half past eight to get ready for the close of Jeremy's first real estate transaction in Maine, an event celebrated by many in Thomaston, Rockland, and Saint George, but especially by Vinnie and Gray. Anticipating a crowd, Maria arrived at nine o'clock sharp, holding a tray of doughnuts. When Galen spotted her through the glass, he hurried to open the door.

"Thank you," she said, taking a breath. "I have a jar of sweet cider in the car. I thought the children might come, so we should have some refreshments."

"Good thinking. I'm not sure if the kids are coming, but I know my parents are. They want to celebrate the event."

Maria shook her head and smiled from ear to ear. "I can hardly believe it myself, but sometimes God winks at us. The moment I saw that house, I thought of Jeremy and his children. I wasn't surprised when Olivia told me later that as soon as they saw it they knew it was the right place."

"Yeah, that's what my mother said, too. Of course, now she hopes Jeremy will love it so much he won't want to leave."

"It's possible."

Galen looked at Maria and sighed. "That may be true, but last night after dinner, Jeremy reminded me that he makes a very good living at Flint and Dearborn, and that's how he can afford to buy a second home. He also told me his children are doing well in school, and that their nanny is conscientious and dependable."

"Conscientious and dependable. Is that enough?"

"Hardly, but that's not for us to decide. Our job is to make sure that by the end of business today, Jeremy Brown is the owner of the sweetest cape in Saint George, and his children can spend their summers a stone's throw away from Tenants Harbor."

Three days after the Browns moved into their summer place, the candlestick phone sitting on the sideboard rang and Jeremy answered.

"Hello. Yes, operator, please put him through."

"It's a girl! I'm a father!" boomed a voice so loud that Reuben and Julia, unpacking boxes in the front of the house, scrambled to the kitchen to listen.

"Congratulations! How's Jane?"

The voice was softer, so Julia stepped closer.

"Twelve hours. Were you in the room?"

Reuben noticed the change in his dad's face.

"Wise decision. In this case, you're the father, not the doctor. I'm glad Honor was there. When it comes to labor and delivery, she's a blessing."

"What's the baby's name?" piped up Julia.

With his lips near the mouthpiece, Jeremy asked that key question.

He bowed his head and listened.

"What is it?" whispered Reuben.

Keeping the receiver on his ear, Jeremy winked.

"Oh, that's a beautiful name. It's perfect—"

He cleared his throat. "I can't wait to meet her. Tell Jane to get some rest. She's earned it. Tell her we'll be in Rockland tomorrow."

Turning to face his children, he said goodbye and smiled. He hung up the phone, pulled Reuben close and reached for Julia.

"What's her name?" they asked in unison.

"Corinne Marie."

The Last Sail

From the launching of the *Cecil P. Stewart* and the *Reine Marie Stewart* in 1919 to the launching of the *Edna Hoyt* on December 11, 1920, the Dunn & Elliot shipyard was humming. There was music in the air, but it wasn't Christmas music. The riggers preferred the old shanties, bold and unholy, the kind of songs you could sing while hauling yards or hanging on the ropes, not standing in church.

The *Edna Hoyt* was gleaming on the ways and everyone in Thomaston was ready to see their five-masted schooner, built at a cost of 280,000 dollars, slip into the Georges River and sail into history. Gray was standing next to Arthur, Richard, and Frank, the senior partners of the Dunn & Elliot Company.

Though Frank was unmarried, the other men were accompanied by their wives and children, all dressed to perfection. The wives and daughters wore cloche hats and long fur coats. Underneath were flapper dresses with dropped waists and short hemlines. Amidst the crowd were a half dozen photographers from local and national newspapers capturing their exuberance with glass negatives. The *Edna Hoyt* was the star of the show. For the mariners, she was the prettiest lady on the waterfront, and they bathed in her beauty.

"She has the finest suit of sails I've ever seen," said Arthur, nudging Gray.

"Aye, I'm glad the sky is blue and the winds are fair so we can fully appreciate those glorious sails."

"I'm going to miss this when I'm working at a bank someday," Richard lamented.

"Don't even say that!" added Frank. "You're never going to work at a bank, and these days will never end."

"Oh, they'll end all right," sighed Gray.

That's when Vinnie took her husband's arm. "But not today, dear. Not today."

She waved at Galen and Honor, who were arriving just in the nick of time.

"Have we missed anything?" asked Honor, slightly out of breath.

"No, but the fireworks are about to start!" exclaimed Frank.

Holding his daughter's hand, Galen laughed. "If the *Edna Hoyt* is as good as she looks, she'll float like a dream."

Looking up at the sky, Gray beamed. "She'll fly like an angel."

The next day, Vinnie climbed the back staircase to check on her husband. It was already half past eight and Gray was usually up and dressed by six. Last night they had celebrated until the wee hours of the morning, falling into bed exhausted but happy. Now, stepping into their bedroom, she wondered if they were too old to have so much fun. After all, she was sixty-eight and Gray was seventy-two.

As she opened the drapes, she murmured, "Never too old for love," then turned to say, good morning to the love of her life—and froze.

Gray stared at the ceiling and was as white as can be. Vinnie knew instantly that his heart had stopped beating, but she touched his wrist, hoping to find a pulse. She didn't find one, so she kissed his lips and sat beside him bathed in the morning light, waiting for grief to strike. She started to cry. Her tears flowed and her nose ran. She shivered and heaved until she ran dry. Then she lay down beside her husband and closed her eyes. It was Sunday, the Lord's day, and she prayed God would take her, too.

When she opened her eyes, nothing had changed except the light in the room. Rays of sunshine were illuminating Gray's pipe, which he had left on his bureau. Vinnie got up and put it in her pocket. Then she went downstairs and called her son Emery. He answered on the second ring.

"Hello, Doctor Rowley speaking."

"Emery," said Vinnie quietly.

"Ma? Are you all right?

"Yes, I'm all right, but your father died this morning."

"What? That's not possible. I saw him yesterday. He was fine."

"I know, but he's gone. It's a terrible shock. Oh, Em!"

The line went silent.

"I'll be there as soon as I can. Stay with Pop," said Gray, his voice cracking. "I'll call Galen and Olivia. They'll probably get there before me."

"Okay. Don't forget to call Jeremy. He's family, too."

"Of course, and Corinne was the first to know."

The line went silent again.

"I believe that. Your father and sister are together again."

"All in God's time," said Emery. Then he murmured, "I love you, Ma," and hung up the phone.

After the funeral, a telegram arrived from Charlie Flint. Emery, Galen, Olivia, and Jeremy were sitting in the front parlor when the delivery boy knocked.

"Telegram for Mrs. Gray Rowley," said the bundled youngster, shivering in the cold.

"Thank you," said Emery, reaching in his pocket for some coins. "Be careful riding that bike on these icy roads, you hear?"

"Yes, sir," replied the boy. He took the two silver coins, said "Thank you," and ran back to his bicycle.

With the telegram in hand, Emery closed the door and headed upstairs.

At the end of the hall, he tapped twice before entering the master bedroom. The drapes were closed, but a sliver of light slipped through the window and cast a soft light on his mother's face. She was lying on her side with her hands tucked under her cheek, her knees slightly bent. As a doctor, he was used to seeing the sick, injured, or grieving in this fetal position, but as a son, he had only seen his mother this vulnerable once before.

"Are you sleeping or just resting, Ma?" he whispered.

"Just resting."

"I have a telegram for you. It just came a minute ago."

"I don't have my glasses."

"Would you like me to read it to you?"

"All right," she said, sitting up.

"May I open the drapes?"

"Of course, dear. You can't read without light."

He pulled the drapes open. Then he stood directly in front of her, unfolded the slip of paper, and read.

IN SOUTH AMERICA. RECEIVED WORD OF GRAY'S DEATH. MY HEART ACHES. HE WAS THE BEST MAN. BE HOME NEXT MONTH. SEE YOU THEN. SO SORRY VINNIE. ALWAYS. CHARLIE.

Vinnie pressed her hands together then raised them to her lips. "I'm all alone," she said as if she were praying.

"For the first time in forty-three years, I'm alone."

Emery sat down beside her. "You're not alone. We're all here."

"It's not the same," she said, crumbling into tears.

Emery put his arm around her and whispered, "Let it out, Ma. I can take it."

The world keeps spinning. Everything changes and everything remains the same. But in 1924, the Rowley house on Hyler Street became unbearable. In a crazy, paradoxical way, it was both too empty and too crowded. Sitting in her cozy kitchen, Vinnie felt a chill. Tucked into her maple four-poster under Aunt Susan's patchwork quilt, she couldn't sleep. Every nook and cranny of her storied home was stuffed with memories that haunted her. In typical Lavinia style, she seized the sixth of April to place an ad in the classified section of the *Courier-Gazette*: *Cherished Family Home for sale in Thomaston. Call Lavinia Rowley at TH3-6472 for more details.*

After washing the breakfast dishes, Amelia dried her hands and waved goodbye to Maria as she headed out the door.

"Have a good day at the office, dear. Try to keep the peace at Moore and Rowley."

"I'll try, Mother, but peace and justice don't always go hand in hand."

Amelia chuckled. "They're lucky to have such a clever assistant."

Glancing back, Maria just smiled.

Amelia watched from the window as her petite forty-year-old daughter slid behind the wheel of her Model T. She sighed. In truth, she was grateful that Maria had said no to her many suitors. Without her, she would have had to sell her family's homestead, the graceful Italianate that kept her close to family and friends. If Maria were to leave, it would be difficult to live alone. James had been gone for thirty-one years and she still longed for him. He had been in his early forties, a captain in his prime, when he drowned.

She shook her head, wishing to forget, then thought of Gray, her husband's best friend, who had lived to see his daughter die when she was only thirty-four years old, the greatest sorrow a parent could bear. She couldn't help but wonder if Corinne's untimely death had hastened Gray's passing. Without a doubt, Corinne had been the apple of her father's eye. At least they were together again. Stepping outside to pick up the paper, she spied a pair of cardinals in the dooryard and smiled.

Amelia sat in her rocker in the morning light and opened the *Courier-Gazette*. After scanning the headlines, she turned to the classifieds. Her eyes widened. Vinnie's ad was at the top of the page. She rocked forward, stood up, and rushed to the telephone to call her dearest friend. After six rings, she put the receiver down. No one was home.

Vinnie walked up to her son's office and knocked politely at the door. Maria waved her in with a smile.

"How are you, Mrs. Rowley?" asked Maria.

"Oh, Maria, when are you going to stop calling me Mrs. Rowley? Just call me Vinnie like your mother does."

She pressed her lips together then broke into a grin. "Today's the day, Vinnie!"

"It has a ring to it, don't you think?"

"Yes it—"

"Good morning, Ma. Were you hoping to talk with me or Maria?"

Rolling her eyes like the child, not the mother, Vinnie murmured, "With you."

"All right, then. Let's take a stroll up to the café."

Glancing at Maria, Galen tipped his hat. "When Joe gets here, tell him I'll be back in half an hour. On some days, we're more like ships passing in the night than partners sharing an office."

"I guess today is one of those days," Maria smiled.

As they headed down the stairs, Galen asked his mother what was on her mind, but she dodged the question. "Maria is a wonderful woman. It's a shame she's never married."

Galen shook his head. "So, you don't want to talk *with* Maria, but you want to talk *about* her?"

"No, silly. I want to talk about selling my house, but I do wish Maria would find someone."

"Wait a minute," said Galen stopping on the boards in front of the post office. "You're selling the house?"

"Yes."

"All right, I understand that impulse, but let's sit down and discuss this further over lunch. As for Maria, *never* is not the right word."

"What do you mean?"

"How old is Maria? Forty-four or forty-five? There's still time."

Vinnie looked up at her son's knitted brow. "Galen, you're a good man."

"Aw, thanks," he chuckled. "Now, if I could only talk you out of selling the house…"

"I'm not sure that's possible. It's too big for me. Honestly, I find myself roaming around the rooms, dreaming of the past and dreading tomorrow. I need a change."

"Ma, you don't have to sell your house to change the way you feel."

She threw back her head and laughed. "Oh, my dear boy, you truly are the best talker in the family. If anyone can change my mind, it's you." She took his arm, and they strolled to the corner café.

Bittersweet

Charlie and Kate Flint arrived at the Thomaston train depot on the twentieth of June, and Jeremy was waiting. As they stepped off the train, he reached for their bags and set them down so he could give them each a big hug.

"I'm so glad you're here," he said with a husky voice. "The kids are excited to see you, too."

"Where are those funny faces I love so much?" asked Charlie, scanning the platform.

"They're at the house, rolling out the red carpet."

Kate laughed. "No need for fanfare. We're not royals. We're just a couple of people who love you all."

"Ah, Kate, we don't deserve you."

"Oh, yes you do."

"You certainly deserve me," added Charlie. "You've helped Flint and Dearborn reach for the stars, and you've given me and Kate a family to adore."

Jeremy picked up the two suitcases and grinned. "Is this all?"

Kate laughed. "No, there's one more. The porter said he'd carry the heaviest off the train for us if we could wait a few minutes."

"All right," said Jeremy, nodding toward the foot of Knox Street. "My Chrysler is parked over there. I'll come back for that last bag and we'll be on our way to the cape by the sea. You're going to love it."

"We already do," said Charlie.

Twenty minutes later, they pulled into the gravel parking space behind the house and the children ran out to greet them. In a blink, Reuben wrapped his arms around Kate, and Julia hugged Charlie—then they switched. Standing at the back door, Maria was moved to tears. On that sun-drenched day close to the lapis-blue water of Tenants Harbor, she glimpsed abiding love and wanted to dive in.

A few days later, Maria and Jeremy wanted to spread some happiness, so they decided to throw a Fourth of July party and invite the whole family. Knowing that Maria's handwriting was simply elegant, Jeremy offered to bring the invitations to the post office if she would write them. She agreed, and he sat beside her while her pen glided over the paper.

> *Celebrate the Fourth of July*
> *At the Browns' Home in Tenants Harbor*
> *Six o'clock till way past dark*
> *R.S.V.P. TH3-6455*

Over the course of the next two weeks, the phone kept ringing as everyone who called said yes to their kind invitation.

On the Fourth, the Rowleys and the Suttons came in carloads. When the families appeared in the dooryard, Jeremy and Maria were outside setting up three long tables with help from Reuben, Julia, Charlie, Kate, and a three-month-old puppy. No one was surprised to see the red-and-white tablecloths, or the baskets filled with flowers and flags, but a few were surprised to find the puppy. Emery was stunned to see Maria standing next to Jeremy. Before he could say a word, though, the puppy greeted him.

"Who is this?"

"Her name is Lu," giggled Julia, "and she likes to jump."

"I can see that," said Emery, rubbing Lu's ears. "Where does she come from?"

"Aunt Olivia and Uncle Owen gave her to us. Their Bella had a litter, and Lu was the cutest by far."

"Let me guess: Lu's short for Louisa."

"Why, yes! How'd you know?"

"Louisa May Alcott was your mother's favorite author," said Emery. "She always said if she had a dog she'd name it after an author. That's what our Pop used to do. Growing up, we had a dog named Whit after Walt Whitman."

Scooping Lu up in her arms, Julia smiled. "Well, that explains it. My dad chose her name."

Emery bit his lip then strode to the water's edge to take in the salty air and let out the choking sorrow.

After dessert, Emery took Galen aside. "What's going on with Jeremy and Maria? Is there something I should know?"

"If there is, I'm not the person to ask."

"Oh, the hell you're not," quipped Emery.

"Look, they're adults. They're also lonely. Jeremy has the kids, but that's not enough. And Maria...she's a gentle soul. Just like everyone else, she needs love in her life."

Emery dropped his head and kicked the dirt.

"You used to do that when you were a kid," said Galen, raising his brows.

"Do what?"

"Kick the dirt when you were upset, angry, worried... feeling something you can't describe."

The six-foot-two big brother looked up and swallowed hard. "I miss her. I miss her every day. I miss Pop, too."

Putting his hand on his brother's shoulder, Galen murmured, "We all do, but Corinne would want Jeremy to be happy. Pop would want that, too."

"My brain agrees. My heart, not so much."

"Maria loves Reuben and Julia as much as she loves Jeremy. Can't you see that?"

"I don't want to interrupt," called Jeremy, approaching the brothers from behind, "but we're going to light some fireworks in a minute."

Emery spun around, ready to tell Jeremy exactly how he felt about Maria's new supporting role. Instead, he saw the cousins, all eight of them, including little Corinne in her Cousin Robert's arms, and he paused. His family was all around him, and he wanted to keep them close.

While Kate could vacation in Maine till August, Charlie had to return to New York by July 15th to negotiate the most important merger of his career. Before leaving Tenants Harbor, he arranged to visit his oldest, dearest friend. So, on a beautiful Sunday afternoon, he stepped onto the side porch of 20 Hyler Street with a bunch of daisies in his hand and knocked. Vinnie opened the door and greeted him with a bright smile.

"You're right on time."

"Am I?" he asked, handing her the flowers. "When it comes to you, my timing always seems to be off."

"Not today," she said, standing on tiptoe to kiss his cheek. "Come in and sit in the parlor while I put these blooms in a vase."

Taking off his hat, he stepped inside and sat in the Eastlake chair next to the fireplace. Waiting, his eyes fixed on the row of family photographs decorating the mantel, then he stood to study them. When Vinnie entered the room holding a turquoise vase filled with the daisies, he didn't notice.

"They're wonderful memories," she whispered, "but sometimes haunting at night."

He turned quickly. "I couldn't resist these snapshots of happy days. You and Gray were blessed with a beautiful family. How could any of these portraits haunt you?"

"Corinne and Gray are gone forever. You know that and so do I."

"Oh, Vinnie, I'm so sorry I wasn't here for you when Gray passed, and I'm sorry Corinne died in Brooklyn far away from you. But Vinnie, love endures. Your life is proof of that, and so are your children and grandchildren. The pictures on the mantel are a testament to undying love. They're not ghosts to be feared. They're a part of you and they're forever."

Vinnie put the delicate McCoy vase on the table in front of the settee, next to the tray of refreshments, then stepped close enough to Charlie to whisper, "Thank you. You're the only brother I ever had, and I want to believe *our* family's love will survive."

"Believe it," he said, hugging her tight. "Now let me pour you a glass of brandy and tell you about the deal I'm closing on this week that will help Reuben and Julia and all their cousins for years to come."

"Pray tell," she said with a twinkle in her eye.

Filling her glass, he shared his hope for the future. "On Thursday, the company I formed in 1911 will become the International Business Machines Company, or IBM. Its potential to create technology will transform the way we communicate and manage information."

"Oh, Charlie, the newspapers are right, you're the 'Father of Trusts.'"

His face lit up, and she glimpsed the boy she had met fifty-nine years ago on the hill. They sat and sipped their brandy. Then he broke the silence with a question.

"If you could have one more big adventure, what would it be?"

"That's easy," she giggled. "I'd like to go up in an airplane like the one I saw on the front page of *The New York Times* in August 1908. You were standing next to Wilbur Wright and his Wright Flyer in Le Mains, France."

"Gosh, you have a great memory. That seems like a lifetime ago. Hart O. Berg and I managed the Wright brothers' interests in Europe for years. I met them in 1906, shortly after the government took a pass on buying their invention, the 'heavier than air' flying machine."

"I remember reading about your tour. You were pictured with royals and heads of state."

"Indeed, I was. The European royals and the rich came out in droves to see Wilbur's demonstrations. They were thick as thieves. The Wright brothers, though, were raised with principles. First, they offered the United States their Flyer, then the Brits before taking it to Europe. We offered airplanes to every minister of war in the world, and they all had reservations. The Germans showed the most interest. In fact, the emperor told Wilbur his invention had changed modern warfare."

"He was right, wasn't he?"

"He certainly was. In 1908, Hart Berg and I helped the Wright brothers sell their invention to a German company. A year later, the United States Army bought an airplane from the Wrights for thirty-thousand dollars, five years after their first flight at Kitty Hawk."

"If only our leaders had looked in the right crystal ball, so many lives would have been saved in the war."

"They didn't," sighed Charlie. "Wilbur died twelve years ago, knowing his patent would have been a state secret if the government had bought his Wright Flyer in aught four."

"That's not your fault. You're a broker, not a fortune teller."

He emptied his glass and murmured, "You're too kind."

"Do you keep in touch with Orville? Do you think he would take me up in one of his airplanes?"

Standing up, he smiled. "Lavinia, my dear, your wish is my command. If I ask him, he'll say yes, and I'll take you to the airfield myself."

"Thank you, Charlie. Thank you for everything." She walked him to the door and kissed him goodbye.

In the fading light of a long summer day, Arthur, Richard, and Frank stood on the clean expanse of the sail loft's floor, looking out on the Georges. Turning his eyes toward the east, the captain noticed the shipyard was quiet and the ways were bare.

"It's time," he said. "Let's face it. Our schooner fleet made a small fortune during the war, but since then there have been too many vessels with too little cargo coasting too slowly. We built the *Edna Hoyt* at a cost of two-hundred-eighty thousand dollars. Today we're going to sign off on an offer of twenty-five thousand. She cost too much."

"But it's not all about the dollars," said Frank quietly.

"I'm sorry, Frank. I have to agree with Arthur. We can't be blinded by the beauty of our first and only five-master. She's two-hundred-eighty-four feet of elegance, but she can't compete with steam and steel."

Arthur put his hand on Frank's shoulder. "The truth is we're in a shipping depression and it's getting deeper. We need to make a decision."

"All right," said Frank, "I'm with you."

The partners of Dunn & Elliot Company walked into their corner office. Captain Arthur sat down at Gray Rowley's old desk, picked up the phone, and dialed their attorney's number.

"Hello. This is Captain Arthur Elliot. Draw up the papers for the sale of the schooner *Edna Hoyt*. My brothers and I will be in to sign them as soon as they're ready."

As he placed the receiver back on the hook, he saw his brothers' chagrin. "Our shipbuilding days may be over, but we're still sailmakers, and the Dunn and Elliot store is still thriving."

"Yes," said Richard with the hint of a smile. "We built a fleet of fifty-six sailing ships, and thank God some are still afloat, and coal and groceries from our store are still in demand."

Looking up, Arthur caught a glimpse of the ship's knees bracing the ceiling and shot back, "And thank Thomas Dunn, George Elliot, and Gray Rowley for dreaming."

They sat for a while to reminisce about the *D.H. Rivers*, *E. Starr Jones*, *Margaret Throop*, *Cecil P. Stewart*, *Reine Marie Stewart*, and, of course, the *Edna Hoyt*. Then the three partners filed out the door, and Captain Arthur turned off the lights.

Author's Note

In the afterglow of launching my first novel, I received an invitation to speak at the Cushing Public Library. When I spoke with the director, she told me someone on their board had enjoyed reading *Daughters of Long Reach* and thought my maritime fiction would appeal to their patrons. She was right. In the spring of 2018, a group of enthusiastic ship-savvy readers welcomed me with open hearts. The winds of fate are fickle, though. On the day that I was supposed to inform and inspire, I met a soft-spoken woman who stirred my soul. She arrived early, handed me a dozen pages stapled together, and told me her name was Ida Clarke. I felt an instant connection—Ida and Irene are old-fashioned names, and they suggest a namesake.

Glancing at the cover photo, I was amazed. The image was black and white, but I could imagine the schooner's white sails against a lapis lazuli sky. I read the caption: "Four-masted schooner *D.H. Rivers*. Photo taken at sea by Captain Arthur J. Elliot." Then I noticed the handwritten note, "My grandfather," under the photographer's name. At that moment, Ida Elliot Clarke couldn't possibly foresee how hard I would fall for the sailmakers of Thomaston.

Even though I was 50,000 words into the sequel to *Daughters*, I found myself thinking about Ida's gift, so I sent her an email requesting a meeting to discuss the possibility of an Elliot-inspired novel. She said yes, but she also suggested we invite a local historian, Peggy McCrea, to join us.

A few weeks later, we met in Peggy's dooryard and talked about Thomaston's shipbuilding history. Ida brought old photographs, including a stunning photo of Thomas Dunn and George Elliot at their sail loft on Water Street surrounded by sailmakers and yards of white duck. The photos were incredible. I don't believe in coincidence, but I do believe there are forces that move us, and those forces brought Ida and me together.

Despite the onset of COVID-19, Ida and I met again in the spring of 2020. This time we sat in Ida's car with the windows open at the Upper Corner. We were there because Ida had a trove of photos and articles that she wanted to share, but I never expected to receive mementos from the christening of the USS *Elliot* (DD-967), named in honor of her cousin, Lieutenant Commander Arthur James Elliot II. The lieutenant commander, affectionately called Jack, was Captain Arthur J. Elliot's namesake. The young naval officer was killed by a B-40 rocket while leading a flotilla of Swift Boats (PBRs) in Vietnam on December 29, 1968. His grandfather, Arthur, had died seven months earlier, on the sixteenth of May, and his grandmother Lilla had passed only forty-one days before Arthur, on the fifth of April. Jack was 35 years old, his grandfather was 82, and his grandmother was 80. The three of them were lost in the same year, proving once again that truth is sometimes harder to believe than fiction.

I will always remember how I felt that day during the pandemic when Ida gave me a rubbing of her cousin's name taken from the wall in Washington, DC. Holding that piece of paper, I thought about the Vietnam Veterans Memorial, the stone that reflects the courage and sorrow of so many Americans, and I was moved to write *Lavinia Wren and the Sailmakers*, a story that reflects the resolute heart of a seafaring family.

Lt. Commander Arthur J. Elliot II was posthumously awarded the Bronze Star with Combat "V" for his heroic action in December 1968. While in command of River Squadron 57 on a mission to interdict the flow of arms from Cambodia to South Vietnam, Lt. Commandeer Elliot led a flotilla of twenty Swift Boats upstream on the Mekong River Delta. The jungle growth concealed the enemy, but the enemy could see the boats. When the flotilla returned, the Viet Cong were waiting. As soon as the PBRs entered one of the small lake areas, they were attacked by rockets and automatic weapons. Because the jungle was so thick, the boats couldn't see the exit, so Jack took his boat out, away from the protective armor of the flotilla, to search the lake's perimeter. As soon as he located an exit, he positioned his boat at the entrance and directed all the boats under his command out of the area. His PBR was the last to cut a circle and leave. Before she cleared the exit, Jack was hit by a rocket and killed instantly.

The keel of the USS *Elliot* (DD-967) was laid by Ingalls Shipbuilding in Pascagoula, Mississippi, on October 15, 1973. Two years later, on October 18, 1975, she was christened by her sponsor, Mrs. Albert B. Elliot. At our parking-lot rendezvous in 2020, Ida gave me the USS *Elliot*'s Cruisebook from 1985. Inside its cover I found a tribute to the destroyer's proud heritage, including Mrs. Elliot's words when she christened her son's namesake:

May she serve with distinction and pride and, as the years go by, forever reflect the courage and valor of the man whose name she bears. May God bless this ship, her officers and crew.

And beneath her words, the editor added a note, illuminating the role of the sponsor and a time-valued tradition:

According to tradition, the spirit of the sponsor enters the ship at the time of christening and remains there forever. The ship becomes a part of her, and she a part of it as it sails the seas.

The USS *Elliot* (DD-967) was the fifth Spruance-class destroyer launched by the U.S. Navy, but it was the first to bear the name of a hero of the Vietnam War. At her christening and throughout her service, the U.S. Navy emphasized her connection to the Elliot family and Maine's maritime history. Her coat of arms is a crest consisting of a mainmast and mainsail with a pine tree emblazoned on the sail, symbolizing the Elliot family's long association with the seafaring heritage of Maine. Following completion of her shakedown training and before joining the Pacific fleet, the Navy sent the USS *Elliot* to the harbor of Rockland near Thomaston, to honor her namesake's family and hometown. Jack Elliot was a fifth generation native of Thomaston, Maine. He left no children, but he did leave a legacy of courage for all who go to sea. In addition to the Bronze Star, Jack was awarded the Legion of Merit, the Purple Heart, the Vietnam Gallantry Cross with Palm, the National Order of Vietnam (Fifth Class), the Vietnam Campaign Ribbon, the American Forces Expeditionary Service Medal, and the U.S. Navy Expeditionary Medal.

Ironically, Lt. Commander Elliot was killed after his tour of duty had officially ended. Because his replacement had asked for a delay in assumption of command, Jack had agreed to extend his time on the Mekong Delta. In a tragic twist of war, Jack's replacement, Lieutenant Peterson, was also killed on 29 December 1968. He was killed in the same ambush, but on a different boat.

Of all the photos Ida shared with me in the spring of 2020, the one that gripped my heart the most was clipped from the *Courier-Gazette*, dated January 18, 1969, and I believe the caption is worth a thousand words:

MILITARY HONORS—The Flag which draped the casket of LCDR Arthur J. Elliot USN was presented to his parents Mr. and Mrs. Albert B. Elliot of Cushing at the Village Cemetery in Thomaston Friday afternoon by a member of the honor guard from Brunswick Naval Air Station. Funeral services with full military honors were held at the Thomaston Baptist Church...

At the forefront of the photo, Jack's parents are standing with their backs to the camera, receiving the Stars and Stripes that draped their son's casket. On the horizon, you see the replica of Major General Henry Knox's 1796 mansion, Montpelier. Those two images, brought together by the click of a shutter, took my breath away. What do Lt. Commander Arthur J. Elliot and Major General Henry Knox have in common? Thomaston, Maine.

Cast of Characters
(in order of their appearance)

Principal Characters:

Gray Rowley—Gray sails on the *Sunbeam* in 1865 and becomes a D&E sailmaker.

James Sutton—James is Gray's best friend. He sails on the *Sunbeam* and becomes a sea captain.

Lavinia Wren—Vinnie, an orphan, is raised by her Aunt Susan and Uncle Emery.

Charles Ranlett Flint—Charlie is the son of a prominent shipbuilder, Benjamin Flint.

Emery Payson—Uncle Emery is Vinnie's guardian, a well-known shipwright.

Susan Payson—Aunt Susan is Emery Payson's wife and Vinnie's guardian.

Madeleine Counce—Madeleine is the wife of Harvey Counce, a prominent ship carver.

Amelia Counce—Amelia is Madeleine's daughter and Vinnie's friend.

Thomas Dunn—Thomas started the D&E sailmaking business with his cousin George in 1865.

George Elliot—George is Thomas Dunn's partner at D&E and the father of Arthur Elliot.

Arthur Elliot—Captain Arthur is George and Mary Ella's son; he joins the partnership of D&E.

Emery Rowley—Emery (Em) is Vinnie and Gray's oldest son; he becomes a doctor.

Galen Rowley—Galen is Vinnie and Gray's second son; he becomes an attorney.

Olivia Rowley—Olivia (Liv) is Vinnie and Gray's oldest daughter.

Corinne Rowley—Corinne is Vinnie and Gray's fourth child.

Owen Sutton—Owen is Amelia and James's son.

Maria Sutton—Maria is Amelia and James's daughter.

Lilla Burbank Elliot—Lilla is Captain Arthur's wife.

Jeremy Brown—Jeremy works for Flint, Dearborn & Co.; Charlie Flint considers him a son.

Supporting Characters:

Captain Charles Ranlett—Charles Ranlett is the captain of the *Sunbeam* and Charles Ranlett Flint's namesake.

Jonathan Pease—Mr. Pease is the shopkeeper at the Upper Corner.

Peggy Catland McNeil—Peggy is Vinnie's teacher at the Bailey School; she becomes a librarian.

John McDonald—McDonald is the master shipbuilder for Chapman & Flint in Thomaston, then Bath.

Harvey Counce—Harvey is a prominent ship carver, Madeleine's husband, and Amelia's father.

Sam Harlowe—Harlowe is a prisoner at the Maine State Prison.

Edward O'Brien—The Honorable Edward O'Brien is a renowned shipbuilder and Thomaston's first millionaire.

Mary Low—Mary is the first woman to graduate from Colby College and Vinnie's sorority sister.

Louise Coburn—Louise is one of the first five women to attend Colby College and Vinnie's classmate.

André Beaumont—André is a professor at Colby College (University 1867–1899) and Vinnie's advisor.

Albert Gould—Albert is a Thomaston attorney.

Joseph Moore—Joe is an attorney and a partner in the law office of Gould & Moore.

E. Kate Simmons—Charlie Flint marries Kate Simmons, a composer.

Hugh McNeil—Hugh is a sea captain. He marries Peggy Catland.

Mary Ella Elliot—Mary Ella is George Elliot's wife and Captain Arthur's mother.

Ida Elliot—Ida is Captain Arthur's younger sister.

Elizabeth Carr—Lizzie is George Elliot's sister and Captain Arthur's aunt.

Helen Carr—Helen is Lizzie and Thomas Carr's daughter; she is Captain Arthur's cousin.

Richard O. Elliot—Richard is Captain Arthur's oldest brother, a partner in Dunn & Elliot.

Martha Slocum—Mrs. Slocum is Thomaston's midwife; Corinne becomes her apprentice.

Honor Gibbons—Honor is a young doctor. She marries Galen Rowley.

Lucy Harlowe Morgan—Lucy is Sam Harlowe's sister. She works for the Ford Motor Company.

Jane Fenn—Jane is the daughter of a prominent Camden family. She marries Dr. Emery Rowley.

Frank Elliot—Frank is one of Captain Arthur's younger brothers. He becomes a partner in D&E.

Sources

While researching the wondrous history of Thomaston, Maine, certain books, papers, and articles were invaluable, especially those that revealed the resolve, knowledge, and craftsmanship of the shipbuilders Dunn & Elliot, Edward O'Brien, and Chapman & Flint. I gratefully acknowledge the following sources for the information they offered me about sail lofts, shipyards, schooners, square rigs, U.S. Navy ships, and the Thomaston families who kept America sailing from sea to shining sea in the nineteenth and twentieth centuries:

Baker, William Avery. *A Maritime History of Bath, Maine, and the Kennebec River Region* (two volumes), Maine Research Society of Bath, 1973.

Hugill, Stan. *Shanties from the Seven Seas*, Routledge & Kegan Paul Ltd., London, and Henley, 1961.

Lagerbom, Charles. (2021, May 27). "The Wreck of the Alfred D. Snow"; https://waldo.villagesoup. com/2021/05/27the-wreck-of-the-alfred-d-snow-1890849/

Morse, Frank L.S. *Thomaston Scrapbook*, Vol. I, Courier-Gazette, Inc., Rockland, 1977.

Packard, Aubigne Lermond. *A Town That Went to Sea*, Falmouth Publications, Portland, 1950.

Parker, W.J. Lewis. "Sails, Ships & Cargoes." *Down East*, March 1971.

Stackpole, Renny A. *The Gillchrest Papers*, Indie Author Warehouse, Thomaston, 2017.

Stinson, John D. "Charles Ranlett Flint Papers, 1872–1930." November 1991. New York Public Library Manuscripts &Archives Division.

Thomaston Historical Society. *Tall Ships, White Houses, and Elms, 1870–1900*, Courier-Gazette, Inc., Rockland, Maine, 1976.

Thomaston Historical Society. *Tall Ships, White Houses, and Elms*, Vol. 2, 1868–1923, Courier-Gazette, Inc., Rockland, Maine, 1976.

Webb, Robert Lloyd. *Edward O'Brien, Shipbuilder of Thomaston, An Exhibition*, Maine Maritime Museum, Bath, 1990.

WESTPAC 85. *USS ELLIOT DD–967*, Walsworth Publishing Company, Missouri, 1985.

Acknowledgments

Even though *Lavinia Wren and the Sailmakers* is a work of fiction, it is inspired by real people—shipbuilders, sailmakers, sea captains, and their families. I have many people to thank for helping me discover their stories from the nineteenth and early twentieth centuries so I could weave them into a tale that rings true.

First and foremost, I am forever grateful to Ida Elliot Clarke for sharing her family's photos and stories with me. Without her kind and generous spirit, *Lavinia Wren and the Sailmakers* would not exist. She gave me a twelve-page article, "Sails, Ships & Cargoes," then introduced me to Peggy McCrea, a member of the Thomaston Historical Society who happens to live near the Dunn & Elliot sail loft. At Peggy's request, the owners gave us a tour of that historic building, and that's when Lavinia Wren and Gray Rowley took flight. Today, the D&E Sail Loft is a private residence, but once upon a time it was the place where some of the best sailmakers in the world produced the finest suits of sail that anyone ever saw.

Many dedicated historians and librarians contributed to the creation of Lavinia Wren's seafaring family love story. Thanks to Kirk Mohony, the director of the Maine Historic Preservation Commission, I was able to include an 1878 map of Thomaston, Maine. I am also indebted to H. James Merrick, the Reference and Collections Coordinator of Colby College's Special Collections & Archives, and Kelly Page, the manager of Collections and Library Services at the Maine Maritime Museum. I am deeply grateful to Tiffany Link, Research and Manuscript Librarian at the Maine Historical Society, and Mary Kate Kwasnik, the archivist at the Patten Free Library's Sagadahoc History & Genealogy Room. Tiffany and Mary Kate helped me discover the last details I needed to weave Charles Ranlett Flint into my fiction.

Every author hopes to find a talented editor, and I found two, Karen Schneider and Genie Dailey. They helped me fine-tune my narrative so *Lavinia Wren and the Sailmakers* would entertain readers and have them stay a while.

Applause, applause for the crew at Maine Authors Publishing! Without their talent and professionalism, Lavinia Wren's story would not be in print. *Merci beaucoup* to Laurie Burhoe, the amazing artist who painted the *E. Starr Jones* under sail and allowed me to put that glorious schooner on the cover.

Last but not least, *mil gracias* to everyone who encouraged me along the way, especially Joe, my husband and sailmaker.